TABLE OF CONTENTS

BUBBAS OF THE APOCALYPSE

Edited by
SELINA ROSEN

YARD DOG PRESS

Copyright information:
"Forward", "I Zing the Bubba Electric", and "Daddy Was A Big, Queer Bubba" © 2001 by Selina Rosen
"Cecil", "Erlene", and "Dog", © 2001 by Ajax
"Smart Fellers" © 2001 by Bill Allen
"Squash Anyone?" © 2001 by Garret Peck
"The Recipe" © 2001 by Robert D. Brown
"Easy Meat" © 2001 by Mark Shepherd
"Bubbas, Pickles, and the Yombies from Hell" © 2001 by Ed Cain
"Shop N' Save Zombies" © 2001 by Gary Jonas
"Candylight and the Three Bubbas" © 2001 by Laura J. Underwood
"Bubbas vs. Slime Devils" © 2001 by James S. Dorr
"The Wizard of Beer" © 2001 by Mark Fewell
"Quest For The Holy Grill" © 2001 by Everette Bell
"It *Is* Whether You Win or Lose" © 2001 by Rob Gates
"Doin' the Drive-In" © 2001 by Bradley H. Sinor and Lee Martindale
"The Fighting 77th" © 2001 by Keith Berdak

BUBBAS OF THE APOCALYPSE

Published by Yard Dog Press
710 W. Redbud Lane
Alma, AR 72921-7247

Editing & interior layout by Selina Rosen
Copy & technical editing by Lynn Stranathan Rosen
Cover art and interior art for "The Fighting 77th" by Keith Berdak, © Keith Berdak

ISBN-13: 978-1-945941-26-9

http://www.yarddogpress.com

First Edition: May, 2001
Second Edition: July, 2013
Third Edition, April, 2020
Printed in the United States of America
0 9 8 7 6 5 4 3

FOREWORD

In the year 2025 the worst happened. A deadly virus known only as Yuppie 25 escaped from a secret government lab, (it is believed that it was tracked out on a piece of toilet paper stuck to the bottom of a scientist's shoe). The airborne virus spread quickly through out the fifty states, and thanks to unusually low airfares that year within weeks the entire world was infected. Scientists worked day and night to try to find a cure, but most of them were already infected and succumbed to the Yuppie madness before they could find an antidote.

One scientist, Hector Von Trap, noticed that certain people of a certain class and life style seemed to be completely immune to the bug. Upon testing several of these subjects he found an unusual enzyme in their blood.

Further testing linked the strange enzyme to a cheap preservative used in generic barbecue sauce, which apparently mutated when it was grilled. He learned that individuals who had consumed large amounts of the barbecue sauce on grilled meats over their lifetimes had built up a natural immunity to Yuppie 25. Hector was well on his way to perfecting the cure when he succumbed to Yuppie madness and choked to death trying to eat his PC.

There was rioting on a global scale, as leaders died leaving countries with no leadership and no laws. The sick and dying filled with the Yuppie madness went on killing rampages. While those yet uninfected fought for their lives and searched for food. The cities and suburbs were the first to go up in smoke.

1

Within in a few months most of the population of the earth was dead. Only Bubbas and their families survived untouched.

In some business professionals who had spent their entire lives in front of PC's Yuppie 25 mutated and they live on as crazed deranged Yuppies. They have cocktail parties and still go into the office and try to maintain an upper middle class life style. They also eat human flesh.

While all of these Yuppie/zombies, sometimes called Yumbies, consume human flesh, mutations differ from one local to another. Some are groaning hardly moving imbeciles while other are fully mobile, you might even say upwardly mobile, and while they are completely out of their minds don't smell of rotting flesh and can even pass themselves off as normal for short periods of time. While the actual cause for the variations of zombie subculture is not completely known *(cause ah all them scientists dyin' off fore they could figger it out)* it is believed by most that the level of the severity of a Yuppies zombieness can be weighed in exact correlation to the amount of Brie he consumed in his life time.

Many Bubbas were out hunting or fishing when the virus hit, or were in trailer parks where no one was affected, so they had no idea that civilization was crumbling all around them. Since they never did pay any attention to that gol-danged CNN.

Bubbas are now our last best hope for humanity.
GOD HELP US ALL!!!

CECIL

by Ajax

Cecil was sleeping on the old plaid divan,
Snoring, not softly, while clutching a can
of Meister, Olympia, or Milwaukee's Best,
half empty and dribbling on his t-shirted chest.

His belly was peeping 'tween t-shirt and jeans,
still crusty with dinner, weiners and beans.
The ball cap he wore was still on his head,
"You sleep it off here" was what Erlene said.

With a short, pitched snort he jolted awake,
He scratched at his belly, and beans were un-caked.
The TV was loud, and through bloodshot eyes,
Maury was on, with some queer in disguise.

Erlene wasn't home, so he thought what the heck,
He cracked a fresh beer and went out on the deck.
His dog named "Dog" was asleep in the yard,
Cecil yanked out his willie, and let it drain hard.

The sun was well up, prob'ly past eleven
And Cecil admired his small slice of heaven.
A bass boat, a trailer, souped-up truck with a stick,
"My spread is a wonder," He said to his dick.

He jumped in his truck, "Dog" jumped in the back,
Cecil searched for some Skoal in a brown paper sack
He plugged his cheek full as he drove away,
"Yassir," Cecil said, "This'll be a good day."

SMART FELLERS

Bill Allen

"I tell you, I think they had somethin' to do with it!"

Jessup shook his head. "You're full of shit!"

"Listen," Aaron said, "they never messed with anyone but our kind anyhow. In the old days they never showed their faces 'cept to make us all look like a bunch of morons. You never heard nuthin' 'bout no saucer buzzing some New York Executive. They always came down and screwed with some dumbass's prize cow. You ever heard of a BMW mutilation? Yuppie 25 virus? More like UFO 25. Now that we's all that's left, they're coming out of the woodwork! I tell ya, them green bastards were behind it all."

Jessup hated to admit it, but there was some truth to what Aaron was saying. Which in itself was amazing due to the complete bullshit he usually spouted. "Okay, maybe so. But I still don't feel right about this."

"S'pose you'd rather have one of them probes up yer ass?"

"No, peckerhead, I know we gotta do it, but I don't have to enjoy it, do I?"

Aaron rolled his eyes. "Makes it a damn sight more fun."

They had been sitting in the tree stand for over four hours, ever since the sun went down behind the mountain. The crickets were chirping and all was peaceful now, but they knew it was just a matter of time till the ship returned.

They'd got Jimmy Joe last night. He'd been so shook up when they dumped him off this morning that he ran to the outhouse and wouldn't leave. He was too ashamed to let people see him walking like he had a corncob up his butt.

If only it had been so simple.

"Why do you think they do it?" Jessup asked. "I mean, what in the hell do they get out of it?"

Aaron grunted and shrugged. "Who knows? I don't really give a shit. I'm all about paybacks, Buddy." He patted the barrel of his shotgun. "I aim to plug me a little green man, stuff and mount him on the wall above the fireplace. I'll give him a double aught enema! Heh, heh."

They'd set up just outside of the trailer park near where Jimmy Joe had got caught. There was an old alfalfa field nearby that had all sorts of them crop circles. It was a regular ET airport. Aaron and Jessup had rigged up a deer stand in a tree at the edge of the clearing and were all camo'ed up and packing heat.

Aaron pulled out a bottle from his back pocket. "Have a little sour mash?" he said and swallowed a gulp.

Jessup nodded and took a nip for himself. This wasn't a job for a sober man. Hell, it wasn't a job for a man with a lick of sense when you came right down to it.

"You know what I miss most, Aaron? I miss cold beer. This home grown shit—no offense—rots my insides. I'd do damn near anything to have a nice, ice cold, foam brimming frosted mug of beer again."

Aaron chucked. "Yeah, whatever. I'd settle for a woman with all her teeth. That toothpaste stuff wasn't much when we had it, but now it's gone—damn!"

They both fell silent. They knew that it was an impossible dream. Nothing would ever be the same. But they could make a difference in their lives tonight. At least they wouldn't have to live in fear or sleep with their hind ends against the wall no more. Pretty soon, it would be all over.

Sure enough, they didn't have to wait long. A quiet hum built up to the east and there was a glow on the horizon. A ship rose and glided smoothly toward them. It was a saucer just like in one of them drive-in movies. Jessup could imagine seeing it hanging from a wire. But it was the real deal.

It touched down about 50 yards from the tree they were hiding in. Aaron and Jessup looked at each other and nodded silently. Both raised their weapons. Aaron with his shotgun and Jessup with his 30/30. Although Jessup could pick them off at a distance, both men had agreed to wait until the aliens were in shotgun range so that both men could do effective damage.

A door slid open on top of the craft and two green skinned, bubble headed, black eyed alien ass probers stepped out. A ramp grew from the side of the ship and they began walking down it. They each held a chrome colored space butt plug.

Jessup caught a sniff of something and realized that Aaron had shit his pants. Or else had let the juiciest fart he'd ever smelled. This was the moment that separated heroes from cowards. Jessup reckoned that he would have to sit there and live with Aaron's flatulence because he was there to protect his country from invaders. Freedom was never free; its cost always ran high.

The aliens walked their jerky walk until they were only 10 feet away. Then something startled them and they looked directly up at the men's hiding place. They must have smelled Aaron's fart.

It was their cue to fire. Aaron's shotgun blew the head off the first ET. Green slime and chunky bits of what looked like watermelon flew in all directions. The alien fell backwards. Jessup's shot had been a little off. He'd been going for the heart, but the alien had turned slightly and he had only shot it in the arm. Of course the alien now only had one arm. The other lay on the ground writhing around like a cut off lizard tail.

The little alien squealed, shot something at them from the butt probe and ran like crazy back toward the ship. Both men turned to fire on the fleeing back of the injured alien but there was something wrong with their weapons. The alien device must have somehow stopped them from working.

"Yeeee Haw!" Screamed Aaron, who jumped from the tree in pursuit. Jessup followed. Who knew what would happen if the little alien beat them back to the ship. He might get away and come back with a whole mess of reinforcements.

Aaron drew his knife from his belt as he began to catch up with the ET. The green man was at the top of the ramp just as Aaron and Jessup began to climb it. The door was sliding shut, the men dove.

They fell into the ship just as the door shut behind them.

The green man was holding the probe and pointing it at the men. He was backed up against some sort of control panel. There were only two chairs in the small one room ship. No reinforcements. The alien was on his own.

Aaron smiled and showed the critter his knife. "Just try to come on over here and shove that up my ass now, you bug eyed fucker."

Jessup saw that the alien was shaking. Slow drips of slime oozed from the stub of where his left arm had been. "He's scared, Aaron."

"He's got a right to be," Aaron said and laughed a low, cruel laugh.

The alien shook his head. Then lowered the probe.

Aaron began to move in for the kill.

"Wait," said Jessup.

The alien turned slightly and began to insert the probe into his own asshole!

"What in the hell is he doing?" Jessup said.

"Maybe it's Martian sign language for 'I know I'm screwed.'""

Suddenly the probe began to glow. Then an amazing thing happened. It began to talk!

"I mean you no harm." The voice spoke.

Aaron laughed. "Damn straight! I bet you'd be willing to lick my boots about now."

"We have only recently discovered that you do not share the universal language. We are sorry if we have harmed your people. We were merely trying to communicate."

"Communicate?" Jessup asked. "What do you mean? You were shoving probes up our asses!"

"Most species in the galaxy communicate by the sharing of chemical trace signatures generated by their bodies. We naturally assumed that your race shared this ability. After all, you are constantly producing such emissions. We were trying to perfect a translation device."

"What is the hell is he flappin his asshole about?" Aaron asked.

"I think he's saying that his people talk by farting."

"Yes!" The alien nodded. His colon generated voice sounded ecstatic. "That is correct. We were attempting to develop a 'fart translator' and of course we were unsuccessful. We now realize that your people use this 'farting' as a form of artistic expression. We only just made this breakthrough last night. Our mission tonight was to contact you and make arrangements to record your exquisite works or art for the entire galaxy to share and admire."

Aaron shook his head. "What a load of bull." He moved forward with the knife.

Jessup put a hand on his shoulder. "Hold up. ET, what's in it for us? "

"Payment?" He shrugged his frail green shoulders. "I'm sure something could be arranged."

"Pass me another brew, Aaron," Jessup said. He'd had about six already, but who was counting? Tonight he planned on swilling beer till he puked. He and Aaron sat in plush Lazyboys, surrounded by luxury. Cans of Spam were lined up against one wall while another sported an assortment of genuine black velvet paintings.

Aaron smiled. His new, perfect white teeth shined in the light of the lavalamp. He thew Jessup another beer. "This is the life! Them fellers were real understanding about getting shot."

"Yep, colony mind and all I reckon they're pretty much used to losing a few drones."

"Dumb shits. Say! How about we go to town and trade a can of Spam for a blowjob? Nova Dawn looked right hungry yesterday."

"Okay, right after we get off work."

"Is it that time?" Aaron asked.

Jessup looked at his shiny new gold wristwatch. "Well, Elvis's right hand is on the eleven and his left hand is on the two. I guess that means something. Close enough for me."

Together the men rose and walked over to a pair of silver toilets in the corner. They dropped their drawers and sat in unison. Lights flashed at the base of the stool, and their rears were encased by an airtight gasket seal.

Jessup sighed. "I remember when this used to be fun."

"Yeah, making it work really takes the joy out of it. But then again, it's a living,"

As if on cue, each man let go a loud, satisfying fart.

"Wow," said Jessup, pulling his britches back on. "I wish Momma would have lived to see me as a successful 'ar-teest'. She never thought I'd amount to nuthin'."

Bill Allen lives in Owasso, Oklahoma with his wife and two children. He is author of the novel SHADOW HEART and his short stories have appeared in various small press magazines. He is a former reviewer for Tangent magazine, former editor of The Iguana Informer and current boss hog of Ozark Triangle Press.

He is also a bubba.

Yes, sad to say, but he sucks down BBQ, beer and pork rinds behind closed doors. He also likes Spam and Velveeta (the cheese that will not die.) How does he survive this dichotomy of artist and hill ape? How does he maintain his sanity in the turmoil of this internal battle between intellect and ignorance...?

He Don't—he's plumb loco. He's crazier than a shithouse rat. Don't turn your back on him, I'm warning you. Especially when he gets that funny look in his eye.

SQUASH, ANYONE?
Garrett Peck

You've heard the old saying: "You can take the boy out of the country, but you can't take the country out of the boy." There is some truth to this statement, but it's no infallible maxim. I had been raised by rednecks, but didn't end up that way myself. It took quite a bit of work on my part, but I was successful in creating a better life for myself. Don't get me wrong; I love my family. I just wanted a different life than the one they led.

I was born to Ida Mae and James Robert—known to all and sundry as "Jim Bob"—Masters. We lived on a family farm in Hastings, Florida. Like most of our neighbors, we raised potatoes and cabbage. We also kept quite a few cattle. Most folks not involved in the meat business would never guess Florida is the second biggest beef producing state in the U. S., just behind Texas. When folks think of Florida, they think of oranges. That's one thing we didn't raise. Hastings is in Northeast Florida, where it still gets too cold for citrus. Our family was not one to hand over good money to a butcher when we had plenty of our own cows to eat. Pa would fire up the grill most every night and we'd eat steaks, ribs, hamburgers—always with a heaping helping of the cheapest barbecue sauce Ma could find. We used so much of it she would buy it by the gallon. It was a rare occasion when that gallon would last a full month.

All in all it was a simple, if hardworking life. On top of my schoolwork, there were always plenty of chores to do around the farm. Pa had me working in the fields and taking care of the animals from an early age. I might have even followed in their footsteps and taken over the family farm when the time came, if it weren't for one thing.

Television.

Due to all the work I was responsible for I never got to watch it a whole lot, but the times I sat in front of the tube were magical to me. It was like a window into another other world—a world where you didn't have to wade through piles of cow shit just to make a living. The advertisements intrigued me as much as the programs. They taught me that some people drove sleek, sexy sports cars instead of worn out pickup trucks. They taught me that some people work behind a desk, ensconced in modern glass towers. They could dress sharply without having to be concerned about getting shit all over them. These people also seemed to make much more money and to be able to afford all sorts of electronic gadgets that made life easier. Pa made it clear we couldn't afford and didn't need those things. "That's for city folks," he'd say.

I soon came to realize that if I wanted these things, I would have to become one of those "city folk" Pa was always decrying. The only way I could make that possible would be to go to college. I don't mean an agricultural college, either. Pa couldn't afford a real university, so the only way I'd be able to attend one would be to get good enough grades to earn a full scholarship. I redoubled my efforts at school and graduated at the top of my class. The University of Florida came through with the scholarship. I continued to work my butt off there and graduated in the top ten percent of my class, earning an MBA.

My folks were proud of my accomplishments almost despite themselves. Pa wanted me to come home and help him with the farm. He was getting on in years and it was getting harder and harder for him to keep up with all the work the farm required. I wasn't having any of it. I hadn't worked so long to get a business degree just to see it go to waste. I accepted a good paying job with Independent Life in Jacksonville instead. I think that hurt Pa, but to give him credit he never got angry about it. I was making good enough money that I was able to help him out financially. It might have hurt his pride a little bit, but he loved Ma too much to deny her anything.

Within two years I was making a cool 150 grand a year. I now owned a lot of those electronic devices I had coveted as a child. I drove a brand new BMW, wore a Rolex on my wrist and dressed almost exclusively in Armani suits. My satellite dish picked up over 1,000 channels. I was only 24 years old and upwardly mobile. Life was good and only promised to get better.

That's when Yuppie 25 hit and the whole country went down the tubes.

The virus, being air-borne, spread like wildfire. The news had been broken by CNN only two days before it hit my office.

When I arrived that morning I found some of my fellow employees huddled around a Sharper Image catalogue. That in itself wasn't unusual; all of us had bought one thing or another from its glossy pages. The difference was the look on their faces as they perused the contents. Normally you'd see smiles as someone pointed out electronic marvels being offered for sale. This time everyone's face was slack, their jaws hung open vacuously. Some of them had trails of drool glistening on their chins.

My morning greeting went unanswered. I repeated it, but still wasn't acknowledged. The person holding the catalogue turned the page and grunted. The others kept gazing at the open page. Some "ooed" and "ahhed" over whatever they were looking at and pawed at the slick pages. But for the designer clothing they were wearing they resembled some primitive tribe's hunting party hunched over a fresh kill.

Not knowing what else to do, I continued on to my office and shut the door behind me, burying myself in paperwork so I wouldn't have to think about why my co-workers were acting so strangely. It wasn't twenty minutes later when I heard a piercing shriek from down the hall. I leapt up from my desk and raced to the door, flinging it open. Another gurgling cry resounded down the hallway. I followed it to the open door of my colleague Margot Washington's office. The scene that greeted my eyes left me gasping speechless.

An important client, Inoshiro Sumitoma—the owner of a chain of Japanese steak houses in the Jacksonville area—lay sprawled before me. Margot lay on top of him, her face buried in his neck. At first I thought the two of them had succumbed to repressed lust and were getting it on in Margot's office. Sumitoma's eyes were bulging out of his face, as though he was on the verge of cumming. Then Margot drew her face back with a wet tearing noise.

"What the hell?" I croaked.

She turned around at the sound of my voice, a pair of empty, soulless eyes locking with mine. A huge chunk of Sumitoma's throat was clenched between her teeth. Before my horrified gaze, she drew the hunk of human flesh into her mouth and chewed. Blood covered her lips and chin like barbecue sauce. A visible lump squeezed down her esophagus as she swallowed. Her lips curled up, revealing a red grin.

"Sushi," she slurred. *"I like sushi..."*

I stumbled back in shock, my heart leaping even further up my throat when I struck a body behind me. It seemed I wasn't the only one who Sumitoma's scream had drawn into the hallway. I yelped and sprung to the right, turning around to see who I'd bumped into.

It was my best friend, Roger Clemmons. He and I competed good-naturedly, seesawing back and forth on which one of us made the most sales in a month. We competed away from work on the squash courts at our country club as well. We even prowled nightclubs together sometimes, seeing which one of us could score the hottest babe. I liked hanging with Roger. He always had a benignly mischievous twinkle in his eyes, making it nearly impossible not to have a good time in his company.

That twinkle was no longer in Roger's eyes. They stared out blankly from his sockets, as dull and vacant as Margot's. "Sushi," he echoed. "Sushi is good..." Ignoring me, he stepped into Margot's office and knelt down to join in her cannibalistic feast.

Now others were entering the hallway, either from their offices or the lobby where the Sharper Image catalogue had been holding court. Their identical expressions were suffused with hunger, as though there were nothing more to them than a bottomless need to *consume*. A whispered cry of *"sushi"* passed from one pair of slack lips to the next as they converged on Margot's office.

I don't mind telling you; I freaked. I raced out of the office. Even though I was on the seventeenth floor I took the stairs down to the garage. There was no way I was going to stand calmly in the hallway and wait for an elevator. Even with frequent workouts at the club with Roger, I was well nigh winded when I emerged from the stairwell onto the ground floor lobby. Just my luck, I saw a deputy strolling past the front door on the street outside. Summoning more breath into my tortured lungs, I bolted past two men who were also approaching the door and made it to the street before them.

"Officer!" I shouted. "Help, please!"

The deputy turned around, a frown creasing his lips. He looked as if he didn't appreciate my interrupting his day with my plea. He hitched up his Sam Brown belt and strode towards me with a self-important swagger.

"What's the problem, sir?" he asked. His tone inferred he thought *I* must be the problem.

"Murder!" I cried. "They're killing Mr. Sumitoma up in Suite 1708!"

The deputy sprang to attention. "Who is? How many of them? Are they armed?"

"No, they're killing him with their *teeth!* God, they're *eating* him! You've got to get up there and stop them!"

"Just a second, sir. I've got to call this in."

The deputy pulled the radio off his belt and had just placed it up to his mouth when the door opened behind him. The two men I had passed on my race to the door stepped out. I recognized the look on their faces, but before I could open my mouth to warn the deputy, they were on him. He didn't even have time to get out a good scream before they ripped out both sides of his neck. After that, it was impossible—and irrelevant.

"*Pork*," said one businessman as he bent to take a second bite out of the madly flailing policeman.

"*The other white meat,*" his dining partner agreed.

I didn't stick around to see anymore. Overworked lungs be damned. I nearly *flew* to my Beamer and got the hell out of there. I pushed the engine's limits on the ride to my townhouse. On any other day a policeman would surely have pulled me over for my aggressive driving, but it was plenty clear the police had more important things to deal with today.

I locked the door of my townhouse behind me and leaned against it as I collected my thoughts. I'd heard a little something about this supposed Yuppie virus on the news. Surely that was the cause of the carnivorous chaos I had witnessed. But how could the virus have infected the entire suite of Independent Life employees so quickly? Even more curious, why had it *not* infected me? I needed more information. I thwacked on my TV and tuned into CNN.

What they were terming the "Yuppie Madness" was the sole topic of discussion. They already had a logo and theme music for their coverage. Reports were coming in from all across the nation. It had been determined that the Yuppie 25 virus was air borne. Those infected either died quickly or developed a ravenous appetite for human flesh. The major cities were quickly becoming battlegrounds. So far, at least, rural areas were not seeing anywhere near the rate of infection as urban areas. CNN was urging people to stay in their homes, wherever they were. National Guard units were being deployed and there were rumors the president was considering declaring a state of Marshall Law. Things were going to hell in a hand basket very quickly.

I realized staying in my townhouse was not a viable option. Being single, I never did much cooking at home. I made more than enough money to eat out most every day. I was not prepared to survive a protracted state of siege. The news made it clear things were likely to get a lot worse before they got better. Therefore my best bet was to get out of town before Marshall Law was declared and I was trapped in Jacksonville for the duration.

Obviously, the best place for me to go was Hastings. Not only was it a rural area, and as such a much better place to ride out this epidemic, but the thought of my parents having to deal with this situation alone was something I couldn't stomach.

I picked up my telephone. Dead air greeted my ear. The lines were down. This was not a good sign. I tried my cell phone. Having it's own power supply, it was still operative. My fingers drummed on the table as I listened to the rings on the other end. After seven rings it was finally picked up.

"Hello?"

"Ma, it's me. Bill."

"Billy Ray!" she enthused. I had told her not to call me that anymore. I preferred to be plain old Bill. Old habits are hard to break, though, so I let it pass this time.

"Are you okay, Ma?"

"Yes, dear, I'm fine. Things aren't too bad here. There's some trouble in St. Augustine, but Hastings is doin' fine. It seems this here yuppie virus is takin' down all the evil cities, but leavin' us decent country folk alone. What's goin' on up your way?"

"It's bad. I went into work today and... well, it was just awful. I'm scared, Ma. Would it be okay if I stayed with you and Pa until this mess is over with?"

"Of course, Billy Ray. You know your Pa and I love to have you visit. I wish it could be under better circumstances, of course, but we'll take you however we can get you."

"Is Pa there?"

"No, dear. He was deputized by the sheriff to help him out in St. Augustine. It seems there's a few of them yuppies causin' some commotion down there. You jest get in that fancy car of your'n and skeedaddle down here quick as you can. The sheriff was talkin' 'bout maybe closin' down U.S. 1 and keepin' any more of them yuppies from gettin' into the county, so you best hurry."

"I'm on my way, Ma."

I packed up my Gucci suitcases in record time. I didn't take the time to change out of my suit, though. Time was of the essence.

Just as I undid the last of my door locks I heard a pounding outside. I quickly re-locked the deadbolt. That was a wise move, because the pounding was followed by the crack of splintering wood. I heard screams from next door. They were coming from the Martini family, my across-the-hall neighbors. The screams were short lived. I tried looking through the peephole in my door, but the fisheye lens distorted my vision too much for me to make out anything more than the busted down door.

I waited maybe five minutes, then cautiously undid the deadbolt and peeked out. I had an unobstructed view into the Martini's apartment. I wish I hadn't. There were three yuppies inside, dining on Mrs. Martini and her two young children. They were so into their feast they didn't notice me at all. I heard one mutter, *"Three Martini lunch."*

Since the Martini's were well beyond help, I wasted no time snatching up my suitcase and running out to the parking lot. I didn't even bother to close my townhouse door. If they wanted in, they'd get in. That was the least of my concerns at the moment.

I skidded to a halt a few yards from my BMW. There was another blank faced yuppie stroking the hood. *"Beamer..."* it said lovingly. I stepped forward and bashed my suitcase into its head with all the strength I could muster. It flew backwards and landed on its butt. I leapt into the car and started it before the thing could regain its footing. It had just managed to stand back up when my foot hit the accelerator. It flew even further than when I'd hit it with the Gucci. I didn't look behind me to see if it got up again.

I took Atlantic Boulevard to Southside, obeying as few traffic lights as possible. I didn't stop to think that this route would lead me past Deerwood and Baymeadows, two of the more yuppified areas of Jacksonville. I peered into the entrances of these communities as I drove past them. Even at 80 miles per hour I could see that carnage reigned. I didn't slow down to watch more closely. I'd seen plenty already.

Things were calmer on U. S. 1. I saw some figures wandering around a professional plaza or two who might have been infected, but I was travelling too fast to be certain. My travel was unimpeded until I reached the St. Johns County line. You could tell when you were passing from one county to the next even without the signs because the pavement changed from black asphalt to white concrete. I paused a moment to consider the symbolism of that.

A cordon of deputies had indeed blocked off the road to St. Johns County. Some were in uniform and others wore street clothes. These must be civilians brought in to deal with the emergency like Pa had. All were well armed.

I slowed my Beamer to a stop and started to get out of the car. The deputies immediately leveled their guns at me. I quickly stuck my hands up.

"It's one of them yuppies!" a fellow in full hunting gear exclaimed. "Shoot 'im!"

"Wait!" cried another voice before I could protest my own innocence. "We've got to make sure."

I looked around frantically, trying to see who had spoken in my defense.

"Look what he's drivin'" the hunter argued. "Look how he's dressed! That's a yuppie if I ever seen one. We gotta blast 'im 'fore he kills someone."

Many of the other men hooted their approval. I heard several hammers cocking.

"Don't shoot!" I shouted. "I'm okay! I'm not infected!"

"How do we know that?" the hunter shot back, his finger not moving an inch from his trigger.

"Just hang on a minute, Jeb," the voice of my savior responded. "He ain't actin' like none of them others we had to kill."

I was now able to discern who was keeping these rednecks from blowing me away. It was a uniformed deputy. He looked to be around my age. His face was somewhat familiar.

"My name is Bill Masters," I said. "I'm just trying to get to my folks' place in Hastings."

"Billy Ray Masters?" the deputy asked. "Jim Bob's boy?"

"Yeah, that's me."

"Hell, I know you. I was a year behind you in high school."

"You look familiar to me, too. What's your name?"

"Scott Solano."

"Yeah, I recognize that name." Solano, like Masters, was a common name in these parts. "I don't think we knew each other real well, though."

"Not too surprising," Solano responded. "We didn't move in the same circles. You hung out with the geeks, mostly. Never held that against you, though. Your Pa's a respected man in these parts. He's helpin' the sheriff out downtown right now."

"That's what Ma told me."

Grinning, Solano lowered his gun and turned back to his men. "It's okay. I know this guy. Let 'im through."

Amidst disappointed grunts, most of the guns were lowered. Only Jeb the hunter kept his barrel trained on me. "You sure that's a good idea, Scott? Just look at 'im. He may not be showin' no signs of infection now, but that don't mean he won't later. No tellin' how many folks he'll kill if we let 'im in."

"I know his folks," Solano vouched. "They're good people, but they're old. I'm sure they'd be safer if they had their son to look after 'em."

"But he could be carryin' that disease," Jeb insisted. "He could be passin' it on to all of us right now!"

"We done already had some pretty close contact with them yuppie scumbags. I'd say it's just as likely he'd catch it from us."

Jeb grumbled, but lowered his shotgun.

"Okay!" Solano shouted. "Let's move these barricades aside so this man can get through!"

Amidst further grumbling, the men obeyed Solano's order. I shook his hand, thanking him profusely, then got back in my car and drove through the opening. The men wasted no time closing it up behind me.

Surprisingly, there was very little traffic on the road. I continued to ignore the lights, but kept my speed down. The anxiousness that had driven me to return home had lessened appreciably now that I was almost there. I hung a right on State Road 207 to make my way to the farm. I passed the National Guard Armory on the way. There were troops in uniform and others in jeans ringed around the entrance. It appeared the Guardsmen, like the sheriff's department, were also recruiting able-bodied civilians. I half expected to be stopped again, but no one leaped out into the road to stop me this time. I guess none of the psycho yuppies had made it down this way yet. The troops were just a precaution in case they tried.

The Beamer's suspension took a beating as I rode up the dirt driveway. Ma came out of the house as I put the car in park and shut off the engine. Even in her late sixties, Ma remained spry. She was there to hug me the moment I stepped out of the car. She drew back from me, still keeping her hands on my upper arms and smiling.

"It's so good to see you, Billy Ray."

"It's Bill, Ma."

She gave me a light tap on the cheek with her palm. "You may be Bill up in the big city, but you'll always be Billy Ray to me. How was your trip?"

"Not too bad. They've got U.S. 1 blocked off as you enter the county, just like you said. One of those guys wanted to shoot me, but fortunately Scott Solano was there. He recognized me and let me through. Is Pa back yet?"

"Not yet. I'm worried about him."

"Don't worry too much. Pa may be getting on in years, but he always was a tough hombre. He knows how to take care of himself."

"I expect you're right, but I can't help frettin'. With you bein' all grown up an' on your own, he's all I've got left in this world."

"I'm here now, Ma. I won't let anything happen to you."

She nodded solemnly, her attempt at a brave grin less than convincing. "Get your stuff an' come on in. Keep me company while I watch the news."

It was very strange to be watching television with Ma in the middle of the day. That had never happened before. There was always too much work to be done. It occurred to me there probably were some chores that needed doing, but Ma was too anxious about the developing situation to tend to them. Casually, I asked her if the cows had been fed today.

"Oh, Lord! I plumb forgot all about them, what with all this excitement." She stood up to go do it.

"Sit, Ma. I'll take care of it."

Her smile was much more genuine this time. "Thank you, Billy Ray. I just can't seem to think straight today."

"No problem, Ma. You've got enough to think about."

She patted my hand. "You're a good son, Billy Ray."

I went up to my old room and changed into some old clothes. Dressed in thread worn jeans and a T-shirt in the bedroom I grew up in, it was almost as if the intervening years between high school and now had never happened. I had become a different person in that time, but the Billy Ray I once was lay closer to the surface than I was comfortable with.

Indeed, as I lifted the first heavy sack of grain, I was shocked at how easily I slid back into the old routine. It was as though Bill Masters, bang up insurance salesman, was only a dream I once had. That bothered me. I had worked long and hard to become the man I wanted to be. Now here I was again, ankle deep in cow patties, my fancy college degree worth less than the bovine feces I waded through.

I resented that.

Deeply.

And I mulled on it, until the familiar rumble of Pa's Ford pickup truck caught my ear.

Ma was already out of the house and hugging Pa by the time I made it in from the field. Pa broke Ma's strong embrace to reach his callused hand out to enfold mine. The difference in skin texture reminded me again of how different our lifestyles were.

"Billy Ray! It's good to see you, son. I was worried 'bout you, bein' up in that big city an' all. I hear that's where they been havin' the most problems. What's it like up there?"

"It's a nightmare. Yesterday this Yuppie 25 thing was just something we were hearing about on the news. Today I went in to work and I saw..." I paused, remembering Ma's delicate sensibilities. "...I saw some stuff I don't even want to think about. I called Ma and told her I was coming down to look after you. She told me you were off helping the sheriff out in St. Augustine. What's going on there?"

Pa surprised me by grinning. "There was a whole bunch of them yuppie things wandering around St. George Street. Most of 'em was tourists. Always wanted to shoot me a few tourists. Finally got my chance! Some of the merchants also went bad. We had to put down the whole city commission, too—mayor and everything. Always knew them politician boys was yuppies, the thievin' bastards. I took real satisfaction in blowin' *their* heads off."

Ma stepped back in shock. "*Pa!* How could you?"

"It had to be done, Ma. Them yuppie things ain't human. I found one of 'em back in the restored Spanish Village. He was chewin' on some poor re-enactor's guts. He looks up at me and says, '*Chorizo.*' It was all I could do to not to blow my breakfast before I blew off his head."

Ma smacked Pa's arm in disgust. "I do not need to hear that kind of stuff, Jim Bob Masters!"

"Sorry, Ida Mae. It's just that extreme situations call for extreme solutions; that's my only point. We did what we had to do."

"You don't have to take so much pleasure in it."

"I know I shouldn't, but I always hated them greedy politicians and merchants. They got what was comin' to 'em, far as I'm concerned. The Lord God judged 'em, not me. I just put 'em down for the rabid dogs they was. Can't help it if I find doin' the Lord's work pleasin'."

Ma nodded somberly, accepting Pa's explanation. Then her face lit up with a look of surprise that might have been comical under other circumstances. "Land sakes, I haven't even started supper yet! You boys must be famished. Come on in and visit a spell while I get somethin' cookin'."

Pa offered to go light up the grill, but Ma wasn't having any of it. She insisted on preparing the food herself so Pa and I could catch up with each other. She fixed us huge tumblers of iced tea and sat us down in the parlor. When Ma was out of earshot I told Pa what had happened at the office and my townhouse, and how Scott Solano had saved me from being shot by the county's overzealous defenders. He nodded sagely.

"I tol' you nothin' good would come of movin' to the big city. Ain't nothin' there a man needs. They may look all pretty with them shiny lights an' all, but that's just the bait in Satan's trap. Livin' in the city cuts you off from God and the earth. You lose touch with what's important in life. Before you notice, your soul is lost. Now the Lord is rainin' His judgement down on the wicked, just like he done at Sodom and Gomorrah. I'm glad He saw fit to deliver you back to us. Now that you're out of that cesspool of moral decay you can get back to workin' the land like the Good Lord intended."

"Uh, Pa... I do plan on helping you out while I'm here, but I'm not back for good. I'm just staying with you and Ma until things get back to normal."

Pa frowned and was about to retort, but before he could a piercing shriek from the TV distracted us. On the screen, a female news anchor was biting into her male colleague's wrist. He screamed as he tried to yank it from her teeth, but she held on with the tenacity of a pit bull. The sound of his hand tearing off was plainly audible. The man fell out of the camera's sights, spewing blood from his wound. The woman took his hand out of her mouth and casually pulled off the wristwatch that still clung to its ragged stump. *"Rolex,"* she said. The screen went blank. I sat in stunned silence, then turned to Pa.

"My God, did you see that?" I asked.

"Yep. I seen worse than that on St. George Street today. I don' think this is some passin' thing, son. The Judgement is upon us. You might as well get used to livin' here again. I don't think there's going to be any more cities—not for a while, at least."

I wanted to respond, but I couldn't. What if Pa was right? Not about the religious stuff: I'd given all that up as soon as I left home. I wasn't impressed with ethereal promises of a glowing afterlife. I believed in the here and now. I believed in material possessions, things with weight and substance. The idea of toiling away on this farm the rest of my days for no more reward than the food on my table made me sick to my soul. That may be enough for Pa, but it was no kind of life for me. I stewed in silence until Ma called us to supper.

She had cooked steaks, of course. They didn't taste quite as good broiled as they did when Pa grilled them on open flames, but they were still delicious. Mom had slathered it with plenty of barbecue sauce, as always. That was the one aspect of farming life I had never complained about. We always ate well. The simple fare

Ma provided could stand beside any gourmet meal I ordered at the trendy restaurants I frequented in Jacksonville.

The only thing that marred the meal was my own brooding. If Pa was right, and the scene on CNN indicated he might well be, I would be giving up my dream of being a high-powered insurance executive for life as a goddamn farmer. In Jacksonville I was a sophisticated man-about-town-on-the-move with the money to indulge all but my wildest whims. Here I'd be nothing more than a beast of burden. The thought of that depressed me thoroughly. Ma noticed my consternation and asked what was wrong. I pawned off her query by saying I was thinking about what had happened at my office that morning. Not wanting any details about that, she accepted the lie.

After Ma's gut-busting dinner, Pa and I drank a couple of beers together. I'm more the White Zinfandel type myself, but I needed alcohol in the worst way. It was watered down domestic crap, nowhere near as good as the foreign stuff I got when I did indulge. Though I wouldn't want any of my friends back in Jacksonville to see me drinking this blue-collar brew, I was grateful for the buzz it provided. It helped me deal with listening to Pa ramble on about the work that needed doing on the farm.

Bedtime came early, as it always does for farmers. Pa said to be certain I got a good night's rest, as we had plenty to do in the morning. There was a possibility the sheriff might call wanting more help, so he wanted us to get cracking at dawn. I nodded wearily to Pa, gave Ma a kiss goodnight and closed my bedroom door behind me.

The room was stuffy. Ma and Pa didn't get too many overnight visitors, so the room was only used when I visited. I opened the window for fresh air and was rewarded with the odor of cow crap drifting in from the field. The unwelcome aroma depressed me further. It reminded me of what my life would become if the government couldn't get this Yuppie 25 virus under control—*shit.*

I undressed and slid under the covers. I knew sleep wouldn't come soon. My mind was swirling with too many possibilities. How could all my co-workers fall prey to the Yuppie virus while I remain uninfected? It didn't make sense. Perhaps I had some form of natural immunity, but I couldn't imagine why. A part of me even hoped I would eventually catch the virus, if it meant I could escape being the shit-kicking agrarian I'd struggled so hard to keep myself from being.

Even with such weighty concerns bouncing around in my skull, the day's adventures and hard work in the field caught up with me. I was just starting to drift into an uneasy sleep when an electronic twitter drew me back to consciousness. It was the familiar ring of my cell phone. I snatched it up from the nightstand and greeted whoever was on the other end with a tremulous "Hello?"

"Bill."

"Yes, this is Bill. Who is this, please?"

"Roger."

Roger? How could that be? I hadn't recognized his voice because it was devoid of its usual animation. The last time I had seen Roger he was about to make a meal out of Mr. Sumitomo. I found it hard to reconcile that image with the ability to dial a phone. Could the virus have run its course? Perhaps it was one of those 24-hour plagues, and Roger was doing better now. If that was the case, my mourning for the loss of high society was premature.

"What do you want, Roger?"

"Squash."

"Excuse me?"

"Squash game tomorrow. You there?"

I'm not sure how long it took before I answered Roger. The very fact that he remembered our squash date and was capable of calling to confirm it added a whole new dimension to my thinking. Maybe all wasn't lost. Maybe I *could* return to the life I had created. Maybe the virus, if I ever managed to catch it, was something that could be lived with or would wear itself out in time.

I could never be happy if I stayed here. For me, life on the farm represented mere survival. Mere survival didn't interest me, not if it meant I couldn't lead the life I wanted. Certainly returning to Jacksonville to make that squash date was insane. But the alternative was even worse.

"Sure, Roger." I told him. "I'll be there."

"Kick your ass," he promised.

"Well, we'll just have to see about that, won't we? Good night, Roger."

"Yes. Night good," he answered.

I hung up and dressed myself in my Armani. I quickly composed a note to my parents. I didn't want them to freak out when they found me gone in the morning. They'd probably still freak, but at least they'd know I left of my own volition. I knew they wouldn't understand my decision, so I didn't try to explain it. I promised to call later if I could.

I'd been born and raised a Bubba, but I'd taken a different path. In my heart I was a yuppie. There could be no going back. I belonged with my people. It might mean a slight change in diet, but that wouldn't be a big deal.

After all, I'd been raised a meat eater.

Garrett Peck has had short fiction published in the Yard Dog Press anthology *Stories That Won't Make Your Parents Hurl, Brainbox: The Real Horror* (Dreams Unlimited), *Dueling Minds: An Experiment in Terror* (ebooksonthe.net), and *The Red, Red Robin Project* (Lone Wolf Publications). He reviews horror fiction for *Gauntlet* and *Cemetery Dance Magazines, and Hellnotes Newsletter,* as well as various websites. He co-edited the anthology *Personal Demons* with Brian A. Hopkins (Lone Wolf Publications), a collection of essays by horror authors on horror they've experienced in their own lives. He directed the U. S. premiere of Clive Barker's *Crazyface* and the world premiere of F. Paul Wilson and Matthew J. Costello's *Syzygy.* He has also narrated audio books for WyrdSisterS ProductionS, including the Bram Stoker Award finalist, *F. Paul Wilson's Conspiracies,* and *David B. Silva's Sudden in a Shaft of Shadow.* He serves the Horror Writer's Association as chairman of the 2001 Bram Stoker Award Additions Jury.

Garrett lives in America's oldest city, St. Augustine, Florida, which is simultaneously home to large communities of artists and bubbas. The two groups don't see eye to eye on many things. Actually nothing.

THE RECIPE

Robert D. Brown

Harvest time was always difficult on the inmates. Today was no exception. Frank Goodloe drew one meaty arm across his brow; sweat dripped freely. He arched his back to stretch, let out an awkward moan, and leaned heavily against the half-filled cart beside him. The awkwardly shaped knife in his hand was covered in so much goo it made cutting the pods difficult at best.

Squinting against the harsh overhead light, Frank could just make out the edge of the field where it ended at the wall of the building that completely covered the "farm". The opposite end was so distant that the line of the walls disappeared into a single point on the horizon.

"You're fallin' behind, Frank," he said out loud. Despite the higher number of inmates working the fields he feared the harvest wouldn't be finished on time.

Gripping the slippery knife tightly he bent over, reached underneath one of the leathery pods feeling for the toughened stem at its base and found it. He fitted the end of the knife firmly where stem and pod met and twisted hard. The pod separated cleanly with a sickening pop, and he caught it with his free hand.

Like the other pods he had gathered it was warm and pliable in his hands. A small observation glass on the top was the only outward clue that he was holding something manmade, in every important way unnatural.

Frank felt the nub of the stem oozing into his hand, a sure sign the pod had been cut incorrectly. Cradling it, Frank reached with his free hand into the old toolbox

33

perched on the cart, retrieved a patch kit and deftly covered the leaking spot.

Just then the pod squirmed in his hands, much like they all did at this stage, but he gripped it firmly and didn't drop it. Through the thick mucus he could see the small form inside twitch and wiggle in the cocoon, a pair of delicate hands curled tightly against its chin.

He couldn't see if this one was a boy or a girl, but it didn't matter. His heart was heavy as he carefully stacked his prize onto the cart, then moved slowly to retrieve another.

"You there, the warden wants you in his office right now."

Skinner was probably the oldest guard at the farm, and one of the meanest men Frank had ever known. One of the other inmates had joked once that Skinner was really the man's job description. Frank wasn't surprised to hear he'd been found dead in his cell the very next morning.

"Right now, you damn redneck. Let's go!"

"Yessir, Boss." Frank placed the harvesting tool on the cart and took a seat at the front of the personnel carrier, ever mindful of the riot gun steadily pointing in his direction. With a lurch the electric vehicle let out a whine then glided silently down the length of the two kilometer building.

As they passed by the endless rows of gestation pods Frank fell into another one of his dark moods, fighting back the same tears he had held back far too long. He watched blankly as the heads of other inmates bobbed in and out of the sea of pods, accompanied by the ever watchful gaze of the guards.

The whole field was literally a sea of life. Each pod contained a treasure beyond comprehension, a miracle in bioengineering. Children. Human children. A desperate attempt to rebuild the population, gone wrong.

What should have been the salvation of humanity was instead destined for the dinner plates of the mutants.

It was sickening how the Mutants had reduced humanity to food. The virus had driven them to the depths of wickedness. Some of the more rational mutants, those like Skinner and the Warden, kept *their* society going, *barely*.

Frank hardly noticed as they exited the building, crossed the complex to Central Control. He was escorted zombie-like into the building, through several layers of security, until he found himself standing at the door of the warden's office. Skinner knocked twice, opened the door and ushered Frank roughly into the room, then left. The lock snicked softly behind him.

The room was sparsely furnished. The warden was an older man with a skeletal look about him. It was a look common to the mutants, they all appeared not-quite-human. He sat at his desk thumbing through several files. Frank allowed his eyes to wander eventually landing on the nameplate on the man's desk. Mordecai Pickett, it was about as odd a name as Frank could imagine. A little snort slipped out before he could catch it.

"You have something to say, Mr. Goodloe?" snapped the warden.

"Nossir, Warden," Frank replied quickly, trying to sound as repentant as possible.

The warden glared at him with those unnatural violet eyes, a characteristic bestowed on many of the mutants. He squinted as though he could see right through Frank, discover his deepest secrets, or size him up for tonight's dinner. Pickett quickly thumbed over another page or two, gathered the paper together and closed the file neatly.

"Frank Goodloe," the warden recited, "of Bluehaven, Arkansas. Surviving child of Charles and Emily Goodloe, also of Bluehaven, recently deceased. Admitted May

2105, charged with recalcitrant conduct and rebellion. Served six years of a twenty-five year sentence, and now I find you on the top of my good behavior roster. Why is that?"

Frank cleared his throat, choosing his words carefully. "I'm jus' tryin' to make amends, Warden, sir."

"Just trying to make amends," the warden mocked, eyeing the inmate suspiciously. "Still, with the exception of a few minor incidents your demeanor has generally been good and you have an excellent work record in the fields, and now I need your services for a... special... assignment."

The warden pushed his chair back, stood up, crossed the room and faced a smallish portrait hanging on the wall.

"Eighty six years ago," he started, "my grandfather survived the riots of 2025 in the aftermath of the Yuppie-25 plague by virtue of being the only geek in the family."

Indeed, the photograph on the wall was of a man in his late thirties, sitting at a computer terminal, dressed casually, pocket protector complete with two pens displayed prominently. The resemblance with the warden was slight.

"When the Union collapsed many state governments simply folded. Even half-crazed from the virus grandfather saw the opportunity to make something of this area, bend it to his will. He moved here with his son to make a new beginning, and we've been here ever since."

The warden stood directly in front of Frank, arms akimbo and eyes staring disconcertingly at him.

"We haven't had a successful escape from here in a very long time, Mr. Goodloe, and none since I took this position. The last attempt was just two weeks ago." The warden knew he'd scored a point when he noted the surprise on Frank's face.

"Yes, it's true," he continued, "inmates Gleason and Smith thought they could beat the system, get out of their obligation to society. I'm happy to say their capture was a satisfying, and tasty, treat for us all."

"Beggin' your pardon, Warden?" Frank asked.

"Let's just say they made an excellent addition to last Sunday's dinner. The gravy, to be precise."

Frank knew very well what the man was saying. He remembered how several inmates had commented on how good their meal had been. Now he knew why, and he felt a wicked knot of disgust well up inside him. Pickett sneered at Frank as he watched his reaction to his revelation.

"See, there really are advantages to being a cannibal. Which brings me to the point at hand. I'm in a bit of a dilemma, you see, because inmates Gleason and Smith were scheduled for a work detail today, a bit of a field trip I guess you'd say, and with them gone I am forced to look for replacements. You have been chosen."

Frank had heard about the work details, none of it good.

"Yessir, Warden," Frank said reluctantly, "What will I be doing?"

"The latest crop is fully ripened," he said matter-of-factly. "You will load the next trailer full and ride with the bodies to the rendering plant in Metairie, where you will unload them. A guard will be riding along... to keep you company." Satisfied, Pickett couldn't resist a smirk at his own cleverness, and enthusiastically called for Skinner to escort Frank down to the docks.

Frank worked straight through the afternoon, using a run-down forklift to load several crates marked flammable and then start with the pod containers. By the time he had finished it was dark, and try as he might to keep track he still had no idea how many hundreds, how many thousands, of yet unborn human fetuses he was taking to the slaughterhouse. The only free space left in the whole trailer was a small area at the very back where a steel bench was bolted to the floor against one wall and a chair was fixed to the opposite wall, next to what looked like a comm panel.

One of the guards, a surly man with lots of dark red hair and bad breath, handcuffed and shackled Frank onto the bench, then sat down himself facing him. The huge firearm resting on the man's hip clattered loudly against the chair. A second guard closed the big double doors and locked them securely. After a few moments the engine to the big rig revved up, and with a lurch they were moving.

Frank and the guard bumped and swayed in the back of the trailer for what seemed like an eternity, the whining of the dualies underneath almost deafening. Frank tried several times to engage his jailer in idle conversation, how far was it, what would they do once they get there, but finally gave up when he was answered with only silence. After a time, the guard reached up and touched the comm panel.

"What's up, Phil?" asked the driver.

"Checking in. All quiet back here. How far are we?"

"About half way there. Been pretty quiet on the road tonight. Hang on a bit."

The trailer swayed first one way and then the other as they seemed to maneuver several curves in the highway. Frank wondered if the sea sickness he had heard about was anything like what he was feeling. A casual glance at the guard confirmed he wasn't the only one having trouble.

The voice on the comm returned. "Sorry 'bout that, Phil. Hang on, we've got a few more curves ahead. Here comes another one... Oh shit!"

The dualies suddenly locked, followed by the wheels up front, making the trailer buck and bounce violently. It leaned hard in one direction, then abruptly switched direction.

The whole truck flipped sideways top to bottom in a gut wrenching motion that sent Frank flying out of his seat, jerking him hard against his shackles and slamming him mercilessly against the floor. The cargo restraints squealed and snapped just as the overhead lights went out. The sound of cargo crates banging and pounding floor and walls was broken only by a hoarse scream and the sickening pop and gush of bone and meat.

The trailer finally came to rest at a slight angle, the back door popped open and swinging free. Frank's hands and wrists ached badly, and he couldn't feel his feet. He sat there for a moment, shaking his head to regain his senses.

A few of the lights overhead came on dimly, barely enough to see by. The inside of the trailer was a chaotic jumble of bent and broken crates, their contents thrown violently in every direction. Most of the delicate pods had burst open, their contents making a gory human soup. He fought the urge to throw up.

Lying limp and twisted on the floor Frank cautiously felt around to see if he had any broken bones or serious cuts, and was thankful he found none. When he finally managed to twist himself straight, he saw that the guard had not fared so well. What was left of the big man protruded underneath a mound of busted crates and half empty pods. *Only a few inches closer and it would been me*, he thought.

"I gotta get outta here," he said to himself.

He tugged experimentally on the chains, disappointed they hadn't broken loose in the accident. He was still wondering what he was going to do when he noticed a thin layer of blackish smoke working its way down the length of the ceiling and out the back door.

A wave of panic washed over him as he realized the truck was on fire. The flammables he had loaded earlier were sure to go at any moment. He struggled against his chains again, but gave up when he realized they wouldn't budge. Frank watched the thickening smoke roll slowly out of the door, then turned again to the other man's body, wondering how long it would be before he joined him.

Then, in the failing light, he noticed the guard's keys still attached to his belt. He stretched his arms as far as he could, pulling hard enough the that the cuffs bit deeply into his wrists, but the chains were too short.

The smell of the smoke suddenly changed. The trailer itself was on fire. His life was being measured in seconds. Somehow he had to get those keys.

In desperation he took a deep breath, exhaled, and lunged head-first toward the guard, arms trailing behind him. He managed to land close enough to grab a bit of the dead man's shirt sleeve in his teeth. Frank steeled himself against the taste of blood and goo, took another few gulps of air then yanked hard with his arms and legs.

At first the corpse didn't budge, but he kept at it, bunching his muscles ever tighter, pulling so hard he felt his jaw would explode. Harder still he pulled, the sinew in his neck like stiff rope until at last the body suddenly flew out from under the crates, coming to rest draped crosswise over him with a heavy thud.

He retrieved the keys easily from the dead man's belt, unlocked his handcuffs and shackles, then rose to his knees and rolled awkwardly out of the trailer.

He had not run fifty feet when the whole truck exploded in a gigantic ball of flame that lit up everything in sight. The concussion of the blast threw Frank face forward to the ground. Shaken, he rose slowly to his feet and began running as fast as he could even as pieces of the trailer, crates, and body parts began raining down around him.

A line of trees was nearby, and he ran into it without incident. The stench of burnt flesh and chemicals urged him deeper into the woods beyond. He made his way through the trees as best he could in the faint glow reflecting off the clouds overhead, snagging himself on tree limbs, stumbling over rocks and roots, somehow managing to keep moving.

He stopped near a large fallen tree just as the rain began to filter its way through the leaves overhead, slowly soaking both him and the ground below. He sat against the old hickory tree, and allowed himself a short rest.

Frank knew he should be celebrating, but could only think about surviving the night. In some ways being in the woods like this reminded him of the hunting trips he had taken back home. Roughing it wasn't a problem, but the pain in the side of his chest was another matter. He felt his ribs carefully. One rib was cracked for sure, maybe two.

Through the gentle noise of the rain came the rhythmic thumping of a helicopter, at first distant but steadily getting closer. No doubt the warden had figured out there'd been an accident, and had sent somebody to investigate. Frank thought perhaps he should be flattered they would dispatch one of the few working helicopters he had heard of just for him, but quickly shrugged it off. The mutants didn't' think like normal humans did. They were motivated only by hunger or anger. They sent out a copter to check on their dinner. When they saw what had happened, they'd be mad. If they realized he'd escaped, they'd come after him because someone would have to pay for ruining dinner.

Hugging his side tightly he started moving again, a little slower than before. Eventually the rain stopped and the clouds began to thin. The setting moon began to light his way through the thinning woods. He trudged through thickets and briars, adding welts and scratches to his already burgeoning collection of bruises. His prison issue shirt, streaked with blood and water, clung uncomfortably to his skin.

The eastern sky was beginning to glow as he reached the edge of the woods. In the still faint half-light Frank saw a clearing ahead, leveled off and hundreds of acres in size. He crouched behind the last remnants of brush, waiting. As sunrise grew closer he could see a barn and farmhouse at the opposite end of the clearing from his position. Not ten feet away a tangle of razor wire glinted faintly in the approaching dawn.

"Get into that and you're screwed," he said to himself.

The barn seemed the best place to hide for the time being, so he worked his way carefully around the razorwire fence and crossed the open field to the building. At first glance he thought the barn had been long abandoned, but as he approached he was surprised to see places on it where repairs had been made recently. The possibility that the farm was still being used made him suddenly reluctant, but there was simply nowhere else to go.

Frank found the back door unlocked and entered cautiously. Despite the brightening sky, the interior was cloaked in blackness. He made his way carefully, feeling around hay bails and stacked tools, eventually finding a ladder up to the loft.

He climbed slowly, the pain in his side almost unbearable. He searched carefully until he found a relatively dry corner with a thick padding of loose hay. He wallowed out a comfortable nest, lay down carefully and fell asleep.

Frank awoke to an odd mix of noises—shuffling feet, metallic clinks and clanks, and sounds he could not quite identify. He fought to clear his head, acutely aware he might be in danger. The eerie glow of a small light cast weird shadows against the roof overhead as it bobbed and swung around the barn.

His ribs still sore, Frank crept prostrate along the wooden floor to try and see what was going on below, but just as he reached the edge of the loft a loose board gave under his weight.

The form below froze, gasped and ran out of the barn, dropping the lamp to the ground. He heard a frantic voice outside calling out. Within seconds it was joined by another, deeper voice, and footsteps approaching quickly.

He shrank away from the edge to get out of the light just as the door burst open. An older man crashed inside the room wielding a rather large shotgun. A young woman followed close behind him. She pointed in Frank's general direction then quickly ducked behind the man, who looked squinting into the loft until he eventually fixed his gaze directly on Frank.

"Come out whar ah can see ya!" the old man bellowed. He punctuated his words with a blast from his shotgun. Not really at Frank, but close enough to scare him.

"Don't shoot!" Frank cried. "I'm hurt. Jus' let me come down easy, okay?" He slowly arose, his fingers knitted together on top of his head like he had been taught in prison. The muzzle of the shotgun swung around, its dark orifice pointed menacingly at him.

"Git yourself down right dis minute," threatened the old man, the gun wavering a bit.

Frank eased himself over the side and stepped clumsily from one rung to another. He suddenly blacked out, just for an instant, but it was enough that he missed the next step down, swinging him wildly out and away from the ladder. The sudden motion startled the old man and a shot rang out.

The girl screamed as the ladder suddenly exploded in a cloud of splinters and nails. Off guard and off balance, Frank fell to the ground in a heap.

Frank awoke gradually to the pleasant aroma of something cooking. He opened his eyes experimentally, and saw that the young woman was sitting next to his bed. He recognized her as the girl in the barn. She was less girl than woman, that was clear, but still some of both, he guessed.

"Hi," he managed, "What's your name?"

"Hi. I'm Tana," she said with a smile, then ran out of the room, excited. "Grandpa Sly, he's awake!" she called.

In a minute the old man appeared in the doorway, a big toothy grin on his face. "Sleepin' the day away ain't good fer ya. C'mon to the kitchen when you're up an' we'll have some lunch," he said, then disappeared again.

Frank swung his legs over the edge of the bed and eased himself up slowly. His chest was bound in frayed strips of fabric and tied neatly under his shirt. With an effort he managed to stand firmly on both feet and shuffle out of the room, his nose leading his way.

The house wasn't particularly large, but it had a comfortable, almost familiar feel to it, reminding him of his own boyhood home back in Arkansas. The small metal and plastic table had three plates laid out neatly with forks and knives alongside. A bowl of butter, salt and pepper shakers, and a small vase of fresh wild flowers sat in the center of the table next to a short stack of napkins. Frank sat down stiffly, drawing one of the napkins from the stack and folding it just so in his lap.

The old man was standing over an old gas stove scrambling eggs in a black iron skillet. He wrapped a pot holder around the handle, carried the skillet to the table, deposited a big dollop of eggs onto each plate while Tana dropped a few strips of bacon and two biscuits next to the eggs. Frank discovered his appetite to be healthy enough, his mouth watering as he spread some of the butter onto his biscuits.

When he looked up again he was surprised to see Tana standing close to him pouring a generous helping of what smelled strongly of barbecue sauce all over his eggs. He thought at first the combination might well turn his stomach, but one experimental taste of the concoction convinced him otherwise. He dug into the meal with enthusiasm.

"Glad to see you eatin' good, young fella. Sylvester Orophat is my name, but mos' folks jus' call me Grandpa Sly." For the first time Frank looked closely at the old man, whose nearly black skin was wrinkled and thin with deep creases on his face, especially the smile lines on either side of his thin lips and furrows between his brows. His deep set bloodshot eyes spoke volumes of the wisdom that resided behind them. The elderly fellow chewed his food slowly, alternating between his eggs and the bacon, stopping occasionally to daub a biscuit in the runny sauce.

"Don' get many visitors 'round these parts," Grandpa Sly said. "We were wondering what you were doin' in my barn."

It was a fair question, so Frank told them about his work at the flesh farm, about the accident and walking through the woods in the dark, being careful not to leave anything out. By the time he had finished Tana's expression was one of shock and disgust. Grandpa Sly only shook his head understandingly.

"We've heard rumors about that place," Grandpa Sly said. "As far as I can recollect you're the only one ever made it out. Problem now is what to do with you. If they find yer trail they ain't gonna give up lookin'. They'll come here before long, so we better figure something out real soon."

The old man was right. Frank couldn't stay there, but he hadn't put much thought into what he was going to do beyond making it through the night. Now that the full light of day was upon him a decision had to be made, quickly.

When they had finished their lunch Tana cleaned off the table and suggested Frank sleep the rest of the day. She would drop him off someplace tonight while she was out running errands. Frank laid back down in the old man's bed and drifted off to sleep to the sound of Tana working in the kitchen and the scent of aftershave on his pillow. He slept uneasily, dreaming of guards and babies in pods and disease and pretty young girls melting away in pools of slime.

Frank awoke with a start. The room was quiet and through the thin window curtains he saw it was getting dark outside. In the distance he could make out the sound of a door being opened, then closed.

Frank rolled cautiously out of bed, feeling a little better than before. The house itself was deserted. He eventually found his way to the kitchen. A door opened onto a covered wooden porch overlooking an unremarkable yard that was lined by an old wooden fence and almost completely devoid of grass. A clothesline laden with laundry swayed slowly against a gentle breeze that kicked up thin wisps of dust from the barren ground.

At one end of the yard sat a pickup truck which definitely had seen better days. In the opposite corner, furthest away, was a dilapidated old tool shed.

As he stood there taking it all in, he heard a strange noise coming from the old building. He approached the tool shed cautiously, wondering where the old man and his granddaughter were.

The screen door was already ajar, so he pulled it open slowly, expecting the rusted hinges to screech, to his relief they didn't. He walked inside and was surprised to see it didn't look neglected at all. In fact it looked quite clean, with paneled walls and a suspended ceiling overhead. Boxes of tomatoes and other vegetables were stacked neatly to either side, along with several crates of spices. A few of the boxes were stamped "pharmaceuticals", while others were labeled "perishable", but most were simply unmarked.

The back wall was covered by a sturdy work bench, a variety of tools hung from pegs on the wall. In the far corner of the room a second door stood open, a light shining from the other side.

He heard the sound again, a kind of metallic grinding noise he couldn't quite identify. Frank approached the door, but stopped just short, stuck his nose in the air and sniffed experimentally. He immediately recognized the acrid sweet odor of the barbecue sauce he had enjoyed earlier.

Puzzled, Frank peered into the back room, surprised at what he saw. The room was filled with equipment that looked a lot like the fancy moonshine still his uncle Lawrence had built when he was just a boy, only more complicated. The cooking pot appeared to be made completely of stainless steel, with two sets of gauges mounted prominently on its side. Woven stainless hoses were arrayed neatly along the sides connecting the pot to tanks located both underneath and behind. Shiny piping extended from the top of the pot over and down to one end of what looked like a chiller. At the other end sat another tank with gauges on top and a pressure relief valve that hissed steadily. Grandpa Sly was there, observing the gauges.

"C'mon in, young fella," rumbled the old man. Startled, Frank walked into the room unsure of what to expect, but when the old man turned toward them he wore the same wry smile that had creased his features so pleasantly at lunch.

"How d'ya like my cauldron, eh?" he chortled. "My witches's brew. Didn' know I was an ol' warlock, did ya?" He laughed, coughing a bit.

"More like a moonshiner," Frank said, "but my guess is there's more here that meets the eye, ain't there, Sly?"

Grandpa Sly chuckled again, leaning heavily against the equipment. "Pull up a crate and sit a spell. Lemme tell ya a story."

Frank retrieved a wooden crate from the other room and placed it against the wall, then sat down, watching the old man intently.

"A long time ago," he started, "my ol' grandpappy was a pharmacist in a small town not too far from here. A real good one too, the way I recollect it, made up prescriptions for folks all 'round the county.

"The riots didn' come here right away, by the time they did my grandpappy already heard about the Yuppie Madness. Most decent folk were immune for some reason, an' it made 'em feel all safe like it'd just pass them by. None of the town folk made any special plans, 'cept grandpappy, that is.

"They came to regret it later. Eventually them city folk went on a rampage, comin' right through town like the Devil's Plague itself, killin' most those they could catch right away, cartin' the rest off later when they felt like it. There's a bunch of killin's that day.

"Grandpappy took grandma and hid out in the woods for nearly a year, raising what little food they could and stealin' the rest. After a spell, when they figured grandma was gonna have herself a baby, they came out of the woods for good, made their home right here in that rundown old barn what belonged to a kindly old couple. Daddy was born right here on this farm. Years later the old couple passed, and Grandpappy took the farm as his own. I was born here too, you know."

"So what does that have to do with all this," Frank asked, waving his hands at the equipment.

"I'm a-gittin' to all that. I said grandpappy worked a drug store. Somehow he'd heard what caused the sickness, some virus folks called Yuppie-25. He also found out from some doctor far off how the plague had passed us over, why some of us never got sick. Called it the Preservative. It was in the barbecue sauce, of all things, and Lord knows we shore do like our spare ribs."

Frank laughed openly, knowing how well he liked to barbecue.

"More to the point," Sly continued, "He knew how to make it himself. He built all this an' started making Preservative on his own."

Frank nodded his head in understanding, adding "And disguised it in his own recipe so he could send it out to folks all around?"

"That's right. Until those geek monsters caught up to him an' killed him dead."

"And now you're makin' the recipe," said Frank. The old man just grinned.

"Does the girl know?" asked Frank.

"Of course the girl knows!" barked a voice. Frank spun in his seat, startled to see Tana standing right there.

"Tana drives the old truck around to the neighbors," Grandpa Sly chuckled. "Drops off jars of recipe as she can. Helps me some around here."

"Oh, Grandpa!" she scolded.

"It's alright, girl. He found me out soon enough. You all set to take more sauce to the Scruggs widow, an' the others?"

"Almost, Grandpa."

"Good. It's about dark, now, an' we need to get Frank somewhere safe. Take him with you, an' when you're done you can drop him off somewhere. Come back quick. Those Mutants are sure to be lookin' for him round these parts, an' ya never know what they might do."

Tana agreed, and escorted Frank outside as Grandpa Sly went back to tend his gauges. Frank helped Tana load the truck with cases of sauce, arranging them neatly in the bed and securing them with rope. More than once he complained the beat up four-by-four wouldn't be able to handle the freight, each time the young woman reassuring him it would.

When they were ready they slid into the old truck and drove away, waving at the old man as they left.

Their closest "neighbor" turned out to be a thirty minute drive from the house, along disused two lane blacktop and dirt trails through fields in the dark. The rattletrap pickup truck drove fairly smoothly, and seemed to have plenty of power under the dented hood, which surprised Frank more than a little.

The widow Scruggs was waiting at her front door as they pulled up the drive. They got out of the truck, unpacked two cases of the sauce, and carried them inside, setting them in the kitchen where the widow had indicated. A small plate of freshly baked cookies were sitting on the dirty kitchen counter, the smell enticing. The two of them stayed only a moment, each taking a cookie and sipping a small glass of buttermilk. When they were ready to go, she gave them two chickens in a gunney sack—payment for the sauce. They thanked the woman and excused themselves politely, then sped off to their next delivery.

The next few stops were pretty much like the first. Each neighbor was anxiously awaiting their arrival, and each had a treat for them before they left. A slice of cake or pie, some fresh fruit, whatever was handy, and some form of payment—a bag of potatoes, a bowl of butter, the collection was varied. Then with a hug or hearty handshake they got back into the truck and headed off to their next stop. Tana apparently knew the roads by heart, driving more or less directly from one place to another without a map.

They had been on the road for a couple of hours by the time they arrived at the Wallerbe shack, which Tana said was the furthest from home, and the last stop she would make that night. Frank realized it would soon be time for him to hit the road on his own, though he had no idea where he would go and was in no hurry to part company with Tana.

Mr. Wallerbe's shack looked unkept from the outside, but when they carried in the man's order Frank discovered he was a very organized, very clean person. The house reminded him of Grandpa Sly's tool shed out back - ramshackle on the outside, clean and modern inside.

Wallerbe showed them where to put the cases, then with a troubled expression excused himself. They deposited their load then waited in the living room. When he returned the man only frowned.

"I was listening to the scanner," Wallerbe said. "Damn Mutants are crazy mad lookin' for an excaped prisoner they say sabotaged one of their shipments. They've already hit most every house around. The Perkins place, old man Thompson, widow Scruggs. All gone."

Frank nodded saddly, his guilt immediate, but he knew there was nothing he could do now. It was too late.

"Those are the people we already visited. They've worked themselves into a feeding frenzy. It won't make any difference if they find me now, they'll still kill everybody they can."

"Tana," Wallerbe said softly, "I ain't been able to reach your grandfather."

They hopped back into the pickup and sped back to the farm by a different route than before. Tana drove like a crazy woman down roads that were not much more than pig trails, ripe with dangerous curves and deep wheel ruts. It was only by some miracle they were able to make it back in one piece, though Frank's ribs were so sore he could hardly breathe.

Tana approached the drive to her farm slowly with the headlights off. The last few yards of brush and trees hid their approach. Before they got to the clearing near the front gate they could tell something was wrong. She parked the old truck right at the tree line and shut off the engine, then reached over to the glove compartment and retrieved a pair of binoculars. She looked through them for several minutes, scanning for something other than the obvious.

The entire farm was engulfed in flames licking high into the night sky.

Frank asked her for the binoculars, twice, but when she didn't respond he gently pried them from her fingers. In the field between them and the burning house a crowd had gathered. Geeks. Techs. Bloodthirsty mutants. All of them dancing wildly around a separate, smaller bonfire, corralled as they were inside a ring of assorted vehicles.

"This is all my fault. I'm real sorry, Tana. Your grandfather was a good man." Frank slid his hand over hers and squeezed it gently, content to share her silence. He watched the mutants in the firelight, both enthralled and frightened by their ghoulish promenade.

"We can't stay here," Tana said flatly.

She started the old truck and slowly backed away from the clearing. She drove until they reached a fork in the trail, veered down one of the paths and followed it until they reached an old stretch of blacktop, then stopped and threw the gearshift into park. She spoke carefully, obviously trying to hide her emotions.

"What am I supposed to do with you?"

"We could always head back to Arkansas," Frank mused.

"Are you crazy?" she shouted. "You think I should just pick up and leave all my neighbors behind?"

"There's nobody to leave, Tana! You heard Wallerbe, they're all gone. Him too, probably."

"You're right," she sighed. "It's just that my whole life has been with my grandfather, here with these folks making the recipe and handing it out."

"You can do that again," he interrupted. "Back home I was in a resistance group, survivalists really. The mutants aren't totally insane, Tana. They're gettin' smart, and for the first time since the plague they're gettin' organized. We can't just sit back and let that happen, we gotta do something."

"I jus' don't think I could be of any use," she said.

"Well, for starters you could mix up more of that recipe, couldn't you? We can give it out to those that need it and teach others how to make it too."

"No, no, you don't understand! Grandpa said ... well, he said he didn't think that people really needed it anymore. That you're either born with the immunity or you're not. The only reason he kept making it was to give folks hope, a reason to live another day."

"It's a good idea. If we're ever going to get rid of the mutants, we'll need all the hope we can get. We can fight them, Tana."

Despite her apprehension Tana agreed. With her home gone and Grandfather gone, she needed to go in a different direction, and the notion of Frank as a traveling companion had a certain appeal. Tana nodded her acceptance, then put the old truck in gear and started it back down the road.

She smiled and said, "Let's go."

Robert D. Brown works full time selling material handling equipment. In his spare time he enjoys reading, watching movies, hanging out on the Internet and, of course, writing. He got his first taste of scifi in college when a friend gave him a copy of *Nine Princes In Amber* by Roger Zelazny, and he's been hooked ever since. Now, twenty-plus years later, Robert remains active in fandom, and is webmaster for the local fan club and convention.

Being a bit of a Geek himself, he knows how truly tasty a Bubba can be. Robert, his wife and daughter make their home in Little Rock.

EASY MEAT
Mark Shepherd

The Corporate Takeover

Bennet Snort sat behind the wheel of his '25 Ford Excursion, lovingly caressing the fine upholstery as if it were young female flesh, remembering the times before the Virus when he could actually drive the monster, not that he actually had, much. He'd purchased the beast when gasoline was over ten dollars a gallon, which had only enhanced the appeal of its 6 miles to the gallon city (8 highway) rating. Driving the monster in public meant you had arrived, that you were a real human being, risen from the primordial ooze of post-college poverty. It had never occurred to him that someday gasoline might become scarce to the point of non-existence.

Which didn't mean he couldn't just sit in the driver's seat and reminisce. Lately he had been spending much time in the four car garage connected to the three story brick house in the (once) affluent neighborhood. Without pimply faced adolescents and imported Mexicans to mow the lawns, trim the hedges and screw bored, neglected housewives, the sparsely occupied neighborhood had gone wild. The grass and trees raged out of control. An imported South American plant, originally used to border lawns, had thrived the best of all, blanketing houses and entire blocks with layers of green, like kudzu, only with more attitude. Bennet's own backyard lurked under a dense canopy of the stuff, resembling a rain forest on steroids.

Absently, he pushed the garage door opener, half-expecting the door to open. Yet the opener didn't have any batteries, and electricity to the neighborhood had been terminated years ago. Nothing happened.

"Shit," Bennet said, tossing the opener aside with a snarl. Nostalgia turned rudely to hard, cold, present-day reality. In his now dismal mood he considered that he was the only homeowner on his street, the others having long since succumbed to the Virus. He tried to cheer himself with the knowledge that he had never seen his neighbors anyway, with only the annual passage of Halloween reminding him there were even Others nearby. After all, he always had preferred isolation.

Since adolescence, Bennet had been convinced that every little infectious organism out there had targeted him for destruction, and was waiting for an opportunity to attack. Washing his hands ten times a day and bathing in full-strength Listerine did not suffice. Total isolation was the key. This, of course, made dating difficult; even online liasions ended when the other party realized that online screwing was all Bennet was interested in. He never married, even after pointing out to several prospects how inexpensive an online wedding would be, compared to the real thing.

But in 2015, his obsession with germs carried into his professional life. Encasing his office cubicle in a sheet plastic tent had been the last straw, but because he was a dedicated and valuable employee, his supervisor gave him the option of telecommuting instead of firing him outright. Bennet seized the opportunity with both hands; it was what he had been pushing for all along!

He never left the house. Bennet did all of his personal business on the net, including grocery shopping. His paycheck was handled through direct deposit. He spent many long, happy years home, alone, and would have been content to spend the rest of his years in this situation had the shit not hit the global fan.

He started seeing disturbing reports on CNN about the new, deadly virus, Yuppie 25. It spread rapidly and infected almost everybody. Someone was working on a cure, but not much progress had yet been made. He bought all the canned food and water he could, which was quite a bit, given his healthy bank account, stashed everything in the garage next to the Excursion, and nailed his doors and windows shut.

In the following weeks, the cable TV channels had gone blank, and his only contact with the outside world had been an FM receiver. It finally went, too, followed soon after by the electricity. Still, Bennet stayed inside, and he had seen nothing and no one. He'd estimated his food supply would last a few years, if he was careful.

How long had it been? Three years. And last night he'd had his last can of beanie weenies. His food had run out, along with the bottled water. It was time to go into the office to see what the hell was going on. He dreaded going out, but knew he had no choice. He filled his bathtub with Listerine so it would be waiting for him when he returned; a *thorough* decontamination would be required.

Death and destruction lined the roadways as he drove the Excursion to WillTell, located in the Williams Tower downtown. He saw maybe half a dozen people, lurking in the shadows and cradling large caliber firearms, and lots of skeletons lying about in various agonizing poses. Very strange. Particularly alarming was the pack of feral (not to mention ungroomed) Pekingese who tried to chew his tires off the rims; fortunately he had non-flattening tires, standard on all "new" Fords. And the dogs did make an interesting popping sound when he ran over them.

All the way in, none of the traffic lights worked. After a while he started ignoring them, as there was no traffic to speak of anyway. As he pulled up to the WillTell parking garages, he saw that the Williams building seemed to be closed. *Was* this a holiday?

The doors were open to the spacious, marble covered lobby, but before he reached the elevators, three of his co-workers, carrying cardboard boxes of what appeared to be personal items, were coming out of the stairwell. Their ties were loosened, and they were sweating profusely. The elevators were out too!

"Look, its Bennet!" Frank said, and they changed course towards him.

"Does he still work here?" another asked. That was Lars.

"None of us work here now," a third, unidentifiable person said. But he was white, male and middle aged like the rest.

"Hi, Frank," Bennet said, realizing how much older his co-worker looked. Frank used to have a full head of dark hair; now it was gray and thinning. Bennet's eyes wavered to the boxes of personal effects they were carrying; it wasn't a good sign.

"Say, what's been going on?" Bennet asked, feeling like he should have asked this question a long time ago.

They stared at him blankly. "We've been bought out," Frank said. "Didn't you know?"

"No, I didn't. Is something wrong?" Bennet asked, for the first time realizing something really horrible must have happened. Maybe those skeletons he saw were an indicator of a deeper social problem. "I mean, there aren't that many, you know, *people* around."

They looked at him as if he had just urinated on their shoes, *and* declared that he was a Democrat.

"He doesn't know about the virus?" the generic white man said incredulously. "How can he not know about the virus?"

Frank, patient as always, explained the dismal situation to him. Three years ago the world had succumbed to Yuppie 25. Some people seemed to be immune to it, like, anyone who might still be *walking around.* Then Lars pointed out they probably had it too, but a mutated strain that didn't kill them, at least not right away.

Taking a second to really look at them, Bennet realized they didn't look well. Not well at all.

It also came out that the four of them were what was left of the company. "Except for one... Lars began, and the others glared at him until he shut up. The rest of humanity, and what was left of the company, had died in the riots, whenever the hell *that* had been, or had succumbed to the bug, or just plain disappeared. *Come to think of it, some of those skeletons were wearing suits.*

But the very worst of the news was that their company had been bought by an upstart called Joe's Bubbateria. The name gave no indication of what the company actually *did,* but then neither did any other company names.

"Can we roll our 401k over without any penalties?" Bennet asked, and received blank stares. He sighed and rolled his eyes. *Management just doesn't think this stuff through enough.*

"But... we do have jobs!" Frank assured him. "Which is more than most people can say today," he added somberly. Lars and Generic Man nodded and made thankful noises.

Bennet was *not* looking forward to updating his resume, not to mention circulating it in a job market that was probably all shot to hell. But having something now would at least give him enough of a financial buffer to find something better.

"Well, Bennet, now that you know," Frank said. "I think we should get started walking to the new digs," Frank said, going to the revolving doors.

"Walk?" Bennet said. And without thinking, added, "I drove here."

All three stopped in their tracks.

"Yeah, but does it still have any *gas* in it," Lars said with skepticism. He sounded like he had been taken in by this joke before, and was not about to let it happen again.

"But of course, I got..." Bennet replied, then stopped. He had bought the Excursion with the intent of having the biggest, baddest gas guzzler on the road, short of a Peterbuilt hauling a double trailer full of Hummers—not so that he could actually transport large groups of people in it. In fact, the other fifteen seats were all still virgin territory, and he wanted to keep it that way, lest he infect his precious sanctuary with germs! Thus the dilemma.

"No, I don't think, so," Bennet said, also realizing that if he got there before they did he might get the biggest office cube. Then felt incredibly stupid. He didn't know where the new company was, and they did. *Maybe I can call directory assistance...*

From his box of personal effects Frank had pulled out an old Colt six shooter Bennet remembered seeing on a plaque in his office.

Frank tracked him with the gun's barrel. "Yes, I *do* think so. Take us to the wheels, Bennet."

Bennet tried to look amused when he said, "Oh, come on Frank, that's a replica. Everyone knows that."

Without taking his eyes off Bennet he aimed the gun at the distant ceiling and pulled the trigger. The deafening report rang like a bomb in the marble lobby.

"No," Frank said calmly, leveling the gun on Bennet as bits of ceiling tile and dust rained down on all of them. "It's *not*. Let's go. We need to beat the rush hour."

Resigned, Bennet turned and led the party towards his Excursion, hoping Frank would at least poke him in the back with the gun. Then he might be able to file a sexual harassment complaint.

Last Chance

Last Chance, Oklahoma, was a sprawling metropolis of around three hundred mobile homes, mostly double wides but a few of the old fashioned kind that could actually go somewhere without having to split 'em in two. It was established shortly after the Virus hit, when it became apparent that some of *God's people* would be spared the catastrophe, and allowed to live in this tiny corner situated off Keystone Lake. Last Chance resembled a military base, which was no small wonder as several army bases had been ransacked, and their wealth of weapons of every imaginable variety and ammo to go with it now lay in the possession of Last Chance's militia, which numbered a hundred and fifty.

All told, five hundred of God's Chosen lived at Last Chance, led by the wisdom of Preacher Hickey, a holy man of unknown denomination, possessed with military knowledge and armed with God's word. Along with seven wind generators and a simple oil refinery located in the back of a 1969 Airstream, which processed a trickle of crude from several wells in the area, the community regained some of the technological ground lost when the world had gone to hell in a hand basket. They didn't take kindly to outsiders, not that there were many outsiders to take kindly *to*.

Clem Helms was a member of the Militia's elite force, The Sappers and Gatherers, who went forth to scavenge the barren wasteland of useful items such as food, car parts, ammo, medical supplies, ammo, propane, matches, ammo and ammo. He drove a four wheel drive Chevy Silverado, with an M60 mounted over the cab, and kept with him a pistol grip Smith & Wesson shotgun and a wire stock AK47. And lots of ammo. The truck ran, sort of, on the questionable gasoline produced by Last Chance's mini refinery. It was crappy gas, but it was all they had. The engine sounded like someone either gargling or choking on mouthwash.

After all, the Lord provides our needs, not necessarily our wants, Clem thought. Adjacent to his trailer was a small ranch, and he regarded the livestock of cattle and emu roaming it. To call the emus free range poultry was stretching things a bit, but it seemed to be the best way to keep them. Half the militia's duties centered around guarding the livestock from rustlers. The ranch was well protected by surveillance towers armed with guns considerably more powerful than Clem's M60. Which was a good thing because lately the rustling had taken a ugly turn. Seems these folks from the city wanted to go hunting for people too, saw it as some kind of sport, no tags required, and no bag limit. Besides, when they tried to rustle the livestock the emu's would kick the living shit out of them. Turned out people were easier to round up. Clem supposed them folks would eat any ole kind of meat, something which he could identify with to some degree, though his diet would never include Aunt Ethel, no matter how slow she ran. These city folk were scientist types or something, and wore black framed glasses and drove some of the purttiest trucks around, but had next to nothing in the way fire power. They hunted people down and tied them over the hoods of their trucks like deer, and high tailed it out of there. At first, Clem found this hard to believe. Then he did some math. A full grown man could feed a family of five for at least a week, maybe more, depending on what was considered eatable, and what wasn't. Still, it was a concept he had trouble wrapping his brain around. The rumors persisted, and few were allowed to go beyond the sheet metal barricade which surrounded the more vulnerable stretches of the community.

Clem was closing the front door of his Fleetwood Pioneer, carefully holding the top hinge together as he smoothed the duct tape over it, when none other than Preacher Hickey came sauntering down the narrow alley between trailers.

"Praise Be, Clem," the Preacher said. "How are you this glorious morning of the Lord?" Hickey was a tall, thin man, who spoke as if his jaw was always clenched tight. Old enough to be Clem's grandfather, his skin was dark and leathery, as if he'd spent years in the sun, but there weren't much sun in a church, Clem figured. Dressed in a somewhat soiled black suit, and wearing his usual jet black Elvis Presley wig, sprayed with so much Just for Men and (when that ran out) spray polyurethane it could double as a helmet, he looked as if he'd just stepped down from the pulpit.

"My needs are fulfilled, and I ask only what I can do to serve the Lord," Clem intoned. It was a standard reply to just about anything the Preacher, or his minions, said to the common folk.

The Preacher smiled. "I see you're going on patrol today. If I could ask you a favor... my daughter went out to the east fields to check on the sheep and tobacco. Last night she said somethin' about feeling like she was being watched by someone when she was out there before. Probably ain't nothin', for sure the girl's got an active imagination. But could you swing by there and make sure she's okay?"

Clem agreed easily, and tried not to let his surprise show. Sammie Jo Hickey had just reached child bearin' age. She had bleached blond hair, and boobs the size of really big cantaloupes. She'd taken to wearing ragged little miniskirts and tank tops, allegedly because of the heat, and had enough curves to make any male in Last Chance over the age of thirteen trip over their tongues or something. She also packed two .357 Ruger Security Sixes, one on each hip, and a .45 Derringer between her boobies... or so the rumor said. Why she was out there, alone, escaped him, until he remembered the sheep. She had raised some of those lambs by hand. No wonder she was a bit fussy over them.

"Why yes, Preacher Hickey. In fact I was goin' out there right away to check on one of the oil wells. Pump was actin' a might strange. Yes, I'll check on your daughter, just don't you worry about it none."

The Preacher thanked him and continued on his way, and Clem walked a little faster than usual to the truck. Jimmy Bob usually rode shotgun when he went out on patrol, but he was laid up with a sprained ankle he got on a drunken toot, slipping on some fresh chicken shit on his porch. So Clem was alone. And so was Sammie Jo. He forced back the smile that threatened to rip his face open.

At the main gate, flanked by two large anti-aircraft cannons pointed toward the hills, more or less permanently parked with guardhouses built onto them, Clem waved at the two guards as he drove by. A portcullis of old iron beds, their tips sharpened to spears, hung by chains over the gate. On either side the rusted sheet metal walls meandered into the woods, out of sight. Clem made a beeline for the east fields.

The road that twisted tightly through the hills was mostly dirt with a few stretches of stubborn asphalt. The east fields were the most isolated, but least protected, of the town's holdings. That's where they grew tobacco and herded a few small flocks of sheep. Raiders had come and gone in years past, but their numbers had dwindled, and the guard turned their resources to more aggressive gathering in the city. Now it looked like they might have to to back to making security rounds again.

At the edge of the east fields he heard gunshots, and drove a little faster. The engine sounded like it was trying to throw up at this speed, but the truck plodded on until he saw Sammie Jo behind a huge dead tree trunk, shooting at something beyond. Clem pulled the truck up beside the trunk and scrambled out, AK47 in hand.

"I swear I'll shoot the balls off those mother fuckers if they give me a chance!" Sammie Jo said, sitting with her back against the tree trunk as she reloaded the six shooters. Sammie had a sharp, sassy tongue, and wore too much makeup, unbecoming to a preacher's daughter, but Clem couldn't have cared less. Across the field an old Chevy Blazer was parked, and two guys in ragged business suits were carrying a goat by the legs and tossing it into the back of the truck. Off to the north sheep ran off in a dead panic, and four or so goats lay on their sides, legs stiff, apparently dead.

The weirdness of the situation froze his finger over the trigger. "They've killed your goats?" Clem asked in vexation. One of the men pointed a short stubby machine gun in their direction and opened fire. Clem ducked as splintered wood cascaded around them.

"No, they're not dead! They're faintin' goats," Sammie Jo wailed. One of her boobs had fallen out of her tank top, but she didn't seem to be paying no never mind. "Special goats. They freeze up when they're scared. I run them with the sheep so the coyote get *them* instead. Nothing really wrong with them. They just freeze up and fall over when they get frightened or excited." Sammie peered over the trunk, and carefully, and fired. A branch near one of the men's heads exploded, and he ducked behind the Blazer.

Clem edged around the gnarled roots of the dead tree and pointed his AK47. The ground exploded in a ring of dancing dirt snaking up to the Blazer, missing the men, but taking out a window. The men had seized the legs of another stiff goat, and tossed it into the back of the Blazer like a sack of potatoes, then jumped in the truck and sped away.

"We gotta go after those mother fuckers," Sammie Jo said, looking up at the truck bed, where the large machine gun stood on a tall tripod. "I'll take the M60."

Which sounded fine to Clem. They were just a few damned goats, but if he could impress her with his driving skills, all the better. And if he hit enough bumps, then that other boobie might fall out! She leaped behind the M60 and slapped a belt on it as Clem jumped into the driver's seat. Overhead the M60 erupted, the spent rounds tinkling on the top of the cab. In theory, the spent shells were supposed to land in the truck bed, to be reused later, but they hadn't quite worked the bugs out of that yet. Clem tried to start the truck, but the engine just turned a few times, coughed, and farted. No good. It had plenty of gas, but really shitty gas, its shittiness ever so apparent now in their moment of need.

The Blazer drove away, with a little more speed now with an M60 spitting at their backside, and vanished into the woods.

Sammi Jo climbed into the cab beside him. "Faintin goats," Clem said, mystified. "What the hell do they want *them* for?"

"Ain't no good for eatin'" Sammi Jo pointed out. "That's fer damn sure. Lately those rustlers seem more interested in the goats than the sheep."

The Chevy finally started.

Sammi Jo whooped and hollered and prepared to resume her station behind the M60 when Clem pointed out, "If you shoot that truck with that thing, you might hit your goats. We ain't goin' after them no how... "

"Oh yes we are, sugar pumpkin," Sammi Jo said, with renewed urgency. "We gotta know where they're takin' our livestock!" She leaned forward. She hadn't bothered to tuck her boobie back into her tank top, either. "You do this for me, and tonight when we get back, I'll fuck you silly."

Clem dropped the Silverado in drive, and floored it. The hand of God pressed them back into the seats with the sudden acceleration.

Bubbalicious, Inc.

The corporate main offices of Joe's Bubbateria were in the upper floors of a gold plated, high rise monstrosity called the City of Faith. It had been built in the early eighties by evangelist Oral Roberts, in part through donations raised at revivals. It was to be a large hospital, attracting patients from around the world, where Oral and students from his nearby medical school would dispense a combination of faith healing and traditional medicine to the sick, and rake in piles of money. But the expected avalanche of patients had never materialized, and the hospital never opened. While pristine and beautiful on the outside, the inside had never been completed, and had remained mostly vacant for decades. On the building was a large, hand painted sign that said, "Joe's Bubbateria."

Bennet groaned when he realized this was their destination. There was a high razor wire-topped chain link fence surrounding the building's acreage, and as Frank inserted a card into a box at the gate, he heard the tell-tale drone and odor of diesel generators. He was already in a funk; perhaps they'd let him telecommute. But if this was going to be his new place of employment, he'd better start developing a positive attitude about it. It didn't look like he had much choice.

"Turn in here," Frank said, and they pulled up in a huge parking lot with maybe a dozen cars. At a small loading dock a white Chevy Blazer, clearly having been shot to hell and back with large caliber weapons, had backed up, and two men were unloading what appeared to be dead goats, tossing them up on the dock with a thud. Amazed, Bennet watched one of the goats come back to life and struggle to its feet, then regard its surroundings as if nothing had happened. Bennet frowned, his hope that this would be a "normal" kind of job fading rapidly.

Frank led them past the reception desk, where the secretary smiled and waved them through. They took the elevator to an obscene height and got out. Bennet's ears popped as he stepped on the sleek marble floor. The others stood about, clutching their cardboard boxes. At some point during the trip Frank had thoughtfully returned his firearm to the box.

"Bennet!" said a familiar young voice from deep within a lavishly appointed office. "I didn't know you were still on the payroll. Good of you to join us." A young man walked out from behind a mahogany desk the size of an aircraft carrier. Bennet recognized him instantly as Joe Furnier the mail boy, formerly employed by WillTell—the kid had never really worked that Bennet could remember. He always managed to screw up the mail and lose important documents. He had spent most of his time at a computer in a vacant office playing Quake Seven until his eyes threatened to pop out of his head, and would get rather pissy if anyone interrupted his game and actually asked him to work.

The boy, who looked a few years older in a suit, might have been all of nineteen.

"That's the new boss," Frank murmured, half apologetically.

Bennet grimaced, but before he could say anything Joe clapped his hand twice, and from hidden compartments in the walls scantily clad serving girls flounced into the room with silver trays ladened with food and drink. The heavenly scent of grilled meat reminded him he hadn't eaten all day, and having lived on canned food for the last three years he'd forgotten how good fresh, cooked meat could smell.

"Have a Bubbaburger!" Joe invited, flashing a boyish smile. "We're in the foodservice business now, guys." Bennet bit into an incredibly tasty burger as Joe continued, "We have seventeen restaurants in the Midwest, serving what's left of the high tech industry in

Texas, Kansas, and here in Oklahoma, with more to open in California. Even with the world gone to hell, I've still managed to pull a business together." The serving girls deposited their trays on enormous coffee tables and vanished back into the compartments, like smoke in a wind tunnel.

"Computer... techs?" Bennet began, doubting the boy's claim to the title.

Joe smiled dourly. "I've played through every version of Quake, and beat them all. That takes a lot of time in front of the computer. But since I *am* the boss anyway, that doesn't much matter now, does it?" The words carried a hint of threat, quickly glossed over by that radiant smile.

Bennet finished the burger and started another... damn, they were good! The kid had something here. But Bennet remembered something Frank had said during the ride over about the infrastructure of society turning to shit, and nothing, including farming and ranching, remained. The remaining world population scavenged the ruins of grocery stores and Wal-Mart Supercenters for nonperishables like canned goods, potato chips, Velveeta and in particular, Spam. Where did the fresh meat come from? Remembering the goats, he wondered if the Bubbaburger was a combination of fresh meats, or just goat, or something else. Having had one, and deciding it was good, he didn't much care what the origins were. Times were tough, and he could overlook the unsavory details.

A short little Chinese man came into the office pushing a janitor's cart laden with cleaning supplies. In an amazing flurry of activity, he went to work vacuuming floors, polishing furniture, and emptying the little trash cans with startling urgency. It looked like a martial art, and he moved as if his life depended on it. Bennet wondered what Joe had done to win such enthusiastic loyalty.

"That's Hwong," Joe explained. "He was a Chinese businessman caught over here when the Virus hit. Ever since then he has cleaned and picked up everything in sight." Hwong continued around the room, which didn't appear to need cleaning at all, muttering to himself in barely audible Mandarin. With a final, vigorous polish to the large desk, Hwong bowed deeply to Joe and scurried quickly out of the office as if his ass were on fire.

"In spite of the collapse of the banking system, there is currency, of a sort," Joe continued. "We've managed to salvage a few of the e-dollar systems and use smart cards to store credits. The currency is backed by a commodity, much like gold was used for so many years in the old U.S."

Over the mouthful of burger, Bennet mumbled. "What commodity?" What could possibly have any value *now?*

"Computer games, of course!" Joe exclaimed. Some of the computers in his office were showing paused games of Quake, Diablo, Deer Hunter, and others he didn't immediately identify. "It's value can be a little slippery, but since there's a big demand—me—it's the most stable standard we have."

Joe led them to a hallway adjacent to his plush office, where the place took on an immediate scientific research-and-development aura. Techs in white coats darted back and forth with clipboards and test tubes, and burst through large white doors marked with various placards reading, "Lot 5," "Lot 6," "Lot 7," "More Secret Stuff," and so on. Frank and Lars frowned and dodged the techs with their boxes of belongings.

"This is where we perfect the meat blending techniques," Joe announced proudly. "And the packaging, and a few other details that are kept secret for now. After you've been with us for a while," he said with a sideways wink, "I might let you in on it. But for now your job is to monitor the quality of our product.

Not much computer expertise required there, I'm afraid, but it's the only thing I have open right now."

Lars muttered, "so much for the corner office." Bennet decided he'd better go over his job description with a fine toothed comb before he signed *anything.*

Joe led them through a door marked with nothing at all, and the cacophony of bleating goats greeted them as they entered. Hwong was already hard at work, mopping the floors, and already had half of it done, muttering away in his native tongue. Along the wall were about ten pens full of goats, and in the center of the room on a short metal examination table stood a full grown male goat. Though it appeared to be perfectly capable of standing on its own, it was supported in several straps that were connected to a harness. It reminded Bennet of a puppet on strings.

"So. We're preparing goat meat," Bennet said. "What's so hush hush about *that?*"

"No, it's not goat meat. No, no, no... not by a longshot. If you would take a look at the hints, up front and staring you in the face... " Joe said, not unkindly. "This is a project which is designed to help us in ... harvesting." Joe walked up to the goat, leaned over, and in its face shouted *BOOOO!*

The poor creature bleated once, its eyes rolled up in its head, and it went completely stiff. It teetered to the right on the rigid legs, like a plastic horse caught in a high, lateral wind. If not for the harness, it would have toppled completely over.

"You killed it!" Bennet exclaimed in horror.

"No, not quite," Joe said, turning back to his audience of four. "Scared stiff, perhaps. These are a special breed of goat. They are born with a genetic defect which makes them go paralytic when frightened. Any loud noise or sudden movement would do. You see," Joe said, indicating the goat. "He's coming around already."

The goat came out of it paralysis, stumbled a bit until it found its footing on the slick metal surface, and regarded the humans as if nothing had happened. Joe continued, "In these goats we've narrowed the search to five different neurotransmitters, similar to acetycholine, which govern the communication between the brain and the rest of the body. One of these neurotransmitters is responsible for the paralysis you've just witnessed. We have been able to identify it, and once we determine how to isolate it we can put it to use. Once introduced in a goat or, *perhaps*, a human, the condition is permanent."

Frank, Lars, Generic Man and Bennet all looked at each other, with the same blank expression.

"Towards what end?" Bennet asked suspiciously.

"Like I said, *harvesting,*" Joe said, a touch impatiently. He stepped aside while Hwong mopped where he had been standing, mop handle bobbing past energetically. "Here, let me show you the meat processing facility. Maybe that will answer your question."

The meat processing plant was on the lower floors. The swift ride down in an express freight elevator placed them precariously on the edge of zero gravity, and nearly made the bottom of Bennet's stomach drop out. The others seemed not to notice; the doors opened on a scene of death and carnage Bennet was not likely to forget for the rest of his life.

"You didn't see the morning delivery," said Joe, loudly over the machinery. "The truck is already back in the field, harvesting more raw material," Joe explained cheerfully. "We found a storage tank farm containing about half a million gallons of diesel, which gives our collection truck *quite* a range."

The processing facility took up the space of a good sized Rapid Lube, at one end equipped with a forest of meat racks, with beheaded human bodies, each rather round and overweight, dangling from meat hooks. "The brains are a delicacy," Joe explained, "and are packaged in another area. Here, let me show you." A hallway led past an observation window, where bodies were being systematically beheaded by an industrial grade guillotine. "We've developed a process to make human brains look and taste like caviar. After a little creative blending in a food processor." Joe rubbed his stomach expansively, still managing to look reserved. "Delicious!"

Bennet lagged behind the tour group a few paces so he could vomit in relative privacy.

"And here," Joe said, opening large double doors, "Is the dock where the deliveries are made." On the large concrete platform were several flatbed carts, arranged neatly in a row. At the far end were several 45 gallon trash carts full of refuse. Hwong was busy sweeping the area with a push broom.

How the hell did he get down here so quick? Bennet wondered. He must have taken the elevator right after they did. His sweeping had taken on a frenzied pace.

Joe brought them back to the main facility, where workers in white coveralls, hairnets and paper face shields fed the bodies via conveyor belt into a large machine that looked for all the world like a Hobart dishwasher, but clearly wasn't: the hacking, gurgling, splooshing, and bone-snapping sounds of mechanized slaughter coming out of it could *not* be the sound of foodservice tableware being sluiced clean. It sounded more like a whole chicken being shoved down a disposal. Marching from the other end, spread out neatly on another conveyer belt, were inch-thick meat patties, each imprinted in fancy letters with the curious phrase *"Bubbalicious!"*

"This is the Bubbamatic!," Joe announced proudly. "We converted it to its current use from... another industry." The admission seemed to make him uncomfortable. "And, we found a whole shitload of Lawry's Seasoned salt in a Wal-Mart food distribution center," Joe added, pointing to a forest of pallets beyond the meat racks. One of the workers emptied a carton of brownish salt into an orifice on the machine.

Frank stepped forward timidly. "This raw material," he began cautiously. "Is... alive when you... collect it?"

Joe looked puzzled, then comprehension dawned on his youthful features. "Of course it is, nothing but fresh meat. Shame on you for suggesting otherwise," the boy admonished with mock severity, and with downcast eyes Frank looked appropriately chastened. "I'm just setting things right again. It's unfair that good people got sick while the lower class lived. Can you think of a more useful purpose for trailer park trash?"

Bennet flinched at the derogation. As a child he had lived in a double wide while his father completed his B.A. He remembered the family barbecues; now the families were being barbecued. They'd moved into an apartment by the time he was eleven, but still, the term rankled.

Joe continued, swelling into a rant, "This is only the lower caste of deranged white trash that is immune to Yuppie 25. They are multiplying, and growing stronger. Eventually their armies will overtake the dubious stronghold we geeks have on the remains of civilization!" A satisfied smile brightened his face. "So, instead of taking them on directly—we don't have *near* the numbers for that—we conquer them subtly, like wolves nipping at the edges of a large flock of sheep, and then come back and strike again, with no casualties."

"Huh?" Generic Man articulated.

"How exactly do you... nip?" Bennet wanted to know.

"Until now, we've been using large traps of various designs. Nets, when sprung, pulled up into bubba-bags. Loops of rope that snatch the feet from under them. Dumpsters with spring-loaded lids, like Have-A-Hart traps. Many different types of bait have been implemented, but the most effective has been pork rinds, in single-serve bags. Moon Pies, beef jerky, and butane lighters with the Confederate flag on them are a close second, but they just go *ape shit* over the rinds. We are working on a new system, which is so far classified. But someday you'll be let in on it, provided it works."

"I see," Bennet said, knowing full well that the classified secret had everything to do with the goats. *But how?* Regarding the patties on the conveyor belt with undisguised fascination, he said. "You said our new job involves quality control. What, precisely, does that entail?"

"Ah, so we get to the *meat* of the matter," Joe said, chuckling at his own stupid joke. "You'll notice the patties are each stamped with the word, 'Bubbalicious.' Sometimes that doesn't quite take, and we just get 'Bubb' or 'licio' or whatever. We run those patties back to the retry bin, here," he said, pointing to a wide orifice, next to the Lawry's slot, on the Bubbamatic. "Simple. Great entry level work."

Lars was glaring at the kid. No doubt he was considering Joe's dismal performance at WillTell in his "entry level work" of delivering mail.

Bennet cleared his throat, and said before anyone else, "I'll take the job. Where do I sign?"

Faintin' Goats

Clem pursued the rustlers to the nearest highway, keeping a considerable distance from them, to avoid detection. He wove between dead carcasses of automobiles, some burned to a crisp, and enormous potholes which had already swallowed a car or two.

The Silverado consumed the "gas" at an alarming rate, but so far it left them with plenty in the second tank to return. The Blazer was a tiny white square in front of them, and if they knew they were being pursued, they made no sudden maneuvers to indicate it.

"They're getting off there," Sammi Jo said, deftly reloading her revolvers as she watched the Blazer. Clem followed them through the remains of downtown, then to Riverside drive. She checked the other weapons for ammo, replaced the AK47's clip, and topped off the shotgun with pumpkin rounds. Clem mentioned the Glock, with five extra clips, a pair of binoculars, and a fresh roll of gray duct tape, all in the glove compartment. She pulled them out and set them on the seat between them. Her eyes barely left the Blazer as her hands expertly worked the weapons by feel. He sure hoped he never pissed her off.

The chase ended at 81st and Lewis, at the doorstep of what was once the City of Faith building. Across the street from it were the ruins of a Mcdonald's, complete with Magic Playground populated with life sized Mcdonaldland characters. Giant mutant thistle clogged the grounds, growing stubbornly from cracks in the pavement. Clem pulled up in the Mcparking lot, turned the engine off, and began a careful study of their objective across the street.

A ten foot chain link fence, topped with razor wire, surrounded the acreage of the City of Faith complex. The Blazer pulled up to a gate, inserted a card in a box on a stick, and the gate opened; it continued along a recently poured gravel road. Clem was always amazed when he saw stuff work that shouldn't.

"Well, now what?" Clem asked. "Now we know where they're taking them." He was contemplating the other half of their deal, and was searching for a common plan that would expedite getting laid. "Maybe we should go back now... "

"Now, jes' *wait* a minute, Clem. We just got here. We don't even know what this place is. Don' look like no meat packin' place to me."

"Looks more like a research center or sumthin'," Clem said, scratching his head. He had no idea what the place might be, but thought he sounded intelligent making a guess.

Sammi's attention was on the gate. "Look, someone's comin' out." Up the same road the Blazer had gone down came another, larger pickup, with the unmistakable engine-gurgle of diesel propulsion. Inside sat two people, a man and a woman, in white uniforms. "They're leaving."

It required a bit of convincing to get Clem to follow them, but after she took her top completely off, the truck was in motion before the garment hit the floor.

Twenty minutes later *they* were wearing the white lab coats, complete with pocket protectors. The two scared techs had put up no fight whatsoever once they saw their impressive arsenal. They were now naked and duct-taped securely to a neon green jungle gym in the Magic Playground, the grim countenance of a fiberglass Hamburgler scowling down at them disapprovingly.

"Now jes' take that card and stick it in the slot," Sammi Jo instructed. "An none of your rude comments, either." The gate slid open without argument, and Clem drove the truck on through. "Remember. We *work* here. Act like you own the place." He knew this would be a trick, but the prize at the end of the tunnel maintained his enthusiasm. Besides, he was starting to get a might curious about the place himself.

Clem parked close to the front door and backed into a spot with a quick escape in mind. The roll of duct tape went into a coat pocket. Sammie Jo shoved a clipboard with papers in his hand as they got out. "With a clipboard and a friendly wave, you can get into any building in the world. Or at least, it used to work."

They strode past the receptionist, who glanced up briefly, then nodded with a smile. For lack of a better plan, they wore the picture ID badges they'd found on their victims, and it appeared the plan would work, provided no one looked too *closely*. And if someone did, he had his Glock holstered under the coat, and Sammi Jo had her Rugers under hers.

They nearly collided with a little oriental guy pushing a cleaning cart. He scrambled over the receptionist's desk with a rag and a can of Pledge; the receptionist got out of the way, quick. His actions nudged a sheet of paper over the edge of the desk, but the guy ran around in front of it and caught it before it hit the floor. Apparently finished, he seized the cleaning cart and pushed it away at warp velocity. The receptionist sat back down, and grinned at them weakly.

"Now what do we do," Clem whispered under his breath, fighting back a wave of uninvited panic. The little oriental guy disappeared around a corner at a dead run.

"We figure out what this place is. And what it wants with mah *goats.*" Sammi Jo replied stubbornly. Another man in a white coat was snarling like a dog at a clipboard as he walked their way. "Excuse me," Sammi-Jo said, all hint of her usual drawl gone. "How do we get to the fainting goats department?"

"Nineteenth floor," the man growled. He had a glazed expression on his face, and didn't look up from the clipboard. "Elevators back there," he motioned behind him.

"Shit, that was easy," Clem said, as they entered the elevator, and Sammi Jo pushed *19.* "You work in an office or sumthin'?"

"Farm Bureau," she said absently. "One thing I learned is no one pays much attention to you once you're past the front door. Help me remember how to get out of here."

The elevator opened on a hallway encased in white marble. Immediately across from it was a large fancy office. A kid in a business suit was sitting at a computer destroying hordes of Ogres with a joystick.

"Sir? Where do we find the faintin goats department?" Sammi Jo asked politely.

"Eat shit and die, pig sucking peons," the kid said, eyes still glued to the computer screen.

Then Clem heard the muffled bleat of goats, somewhere down the hallway, and pulled Sammi Jo away from the doorway. "I hear em'!"

She nodded, and they followed the bleats to an unmarked door. They went in, and found the goats milling about in several pens. A roundish woman with thick, black framed glasses and a picture ID badge that said "Margie," looked up with a sour face, reminding Clem of a fat bug. She stood beside a low metal exam table with a goat standing on it—or rather, it was supported there by a harness. The goat had apparently just fainted.

Surprisingly, the tech smiled at them. "We finally isolated it!" she said, walking over to them.

"Why, that's wonderful!" Sammi Jo exclaimed, casting worried glances toward the goat as it came out of its seizure. "What was the secret?"

"Urine!" she exclaimed. "Faintecholine is found in highly concentrated amounts in the urine of fainting goats."

"I see," Sammi Jo said, inching toward the exam table. Distracted by the new arrivals, the goat stared at them quizzically.

Then, evidently recognizing Sammi Jo, the goat strained against the harness as it lunged forward, bleating excitedly, "Maaaa Maaaa!"

Sammi's smile remained frozen in place.

"And this little bugger," the tech continued, apparently noticing nothing as she indicated the struggling goat, "has the most faintecholine of all."

Clem had no idea what they were talking about, but Sammi Jo seemed to have the situation under control—as she did in most cases, it seemed.

"Maaaa Maaaa!" the goat bleated again.

She smiled at the tech, giving the goat a surreptitious scritch to calm it down. "I'm curious to see if we can find some other use for *faint choline,*" she said, stumbling a bit over the ten dollar word, "Aside from the primary purpose. Which is precisely what I came to talk to you about," she said, putting an arm over the tech and walking her over to a computer.

On the screen passed a screensave scrolling marquee reading "Bubbalicious!" Clem did not like that word at all; it conjured all manner of disturbing images.

"We've isolated the neurotransmitter," the tech continued. "The problem now will be developing large quantities of it."

"But the earlier results indicated this wouldn't be a problem, or so it was reported to me," Sammi Jo said, still not making much sense to Clem.

"That was a false lead. Wrong neurotransmitter; *that* one just made the little buggers horny. This is the one that causes the paralysis."

"And... ?"

"All we have to do now is devise a way to deliver it through the air."

"Why?"

"Because a voice in my head told me to."

Sammi Jo stared at her blankly a moment, then asked, "What else did the voice say?"

"Just that it must be an aerosol delivery of some kind. That's the next step. So we can spray the trailer park trash. It'll make hunting them so much easier!" The tech frowned, as if something disturbing occurred to her. "But you should know this." The frown deepened when she glanced at Sammi Jo's badge, then her face, then her badge again. "Hey, who are you guys anyway?"

"Trailer park trash, sweet cheeks," Sammi Jo said, raising one of the Rugers to the tech's nose. "And ah do believe I got the drop on you. Make one more sound and your brains are gonna decorate that wall." She raised an excessively penciled eyebrow. "It would be real tacky."

Despite the threat, subduing this one proved a little more challenging than the first two. Then it appeared the voice in her head had told her to settle down, allowing Clem to duct tape her mouth shut, and her hands behind her back. A broom closet at the rear of the lab made for convenient storage, complete with locking door.

Quality Control

Dressed in an all-white sani-suit, a hairnet and paper face shield, Bennet studied the row upon row of Bubbaburgers, looking for flaws in the imprinting as they marched past in neat rows of ten. In spite of the precautions, he tried not to think about all the germs he was being exposed to here. From there the conveyor belt vanished into a slot in the wall, which presumably led to the packing stage. The incidence of incomplete "Bubbalicious!" stamps on the meat was extremely rare; he'd been at this for two hours, and had only found one that needed to go to the recycle bin. The tedium let his mind wander, and several disturbing notions about this job occurred to him. First and foremost was that what he was doing was not really necessary. In a world where civilization had entirely collapsed, quality control of this nature seemed trivial. The only other reason for his position might be for the gratification of Joe' ego, or some other twist of his personality that needed fulfilling, since after all the boy had once been the lowest of the low, and openly regarded as such.

Secondly, and in all likelihood more importantly, was that everyone in the company was stark, raving mad. In particular, Joe: when he wasn't wandering around the company patronizing his employees with false praise, he was at one of his computers hacking away at critters in one of several games he had going simultaneously. Joe had commented that it was essential he keep as many games in play as possible, so that the world currency would not devalue.

As for the other employees, well... there was the woman standing in the corner of the plant, arms in the air. When asked what her duties were, she replied she had none, because she was a banana tree. When asked why a banana tree would talk, she replied that she had been genetically altered to have vocal cords, to scare away the monkeys who would steal her fruit. Other techs would occasionally walk by with clip boards, either barking like dogs, engaged in deep conversations with people who weren't there, or singing, out of tune, "Yellow Polka Dot Bikini." Then there was the one he saw in the hallway, carefully counting each square of floor tile, and periodically diddling with an old fashioned slide rule and shouting "More, More!" for no discernible reason.

There was no evidence of drug use on the premises.

Which brought him to the brink of a rude awakening.

Am I the only sane one here? The thought came unbidden. Then, *If I am sane, why am I here?* The answer to that was obvious. He needed to eat, and he needed a job to do that. Here he had a job of a sort, and it was probably the only real job available. Anywhere. And it would probably keep him from being eaten.

Having a job meant security. It meant a regular paycheck, it meant house payments, health insurance (sort of-the HMOs were next to worthless even Before), a retirement plan... in effect, all his worldly needs, met by higher, unseen forces, intangible, yet real. That Joe's Bubbateria lacked these benefits didn't matter so much, Bennet had a *job.* A buffer between him and the rest of the world, so he wouldn't have to deal with it. Much.

Yuppie 25 killed every one but the techs, but made techs crazy (the evidence around him was overwhelming). Why did he have *his* shit together?

Processing human beings for food might be a little distasteful to some, but it was fulfilling a real need, feeding the hungry. Bennet hoped that the virus wasn't just incubating in his bloodstream, waiting to manifest in some bizarre way later on. He was cultivating a routine, which made him feel normal. Safe, if a bit boring.

After Joe sent Frank, Lars and Generic man downstairs to Personnel, he showed Bennet where his locker was. A thin, pale elderly woman in a cheerleading uniform walked by wearing an aluminum foil hat, spraying Glade in a wide arc. When Joe asked what she was doing, she explained the aluminum kept the aliens from reading her mind, and the spray was alien repellent. *"The Grays in particular hate Rain Forest,"* she informed him dutifully. Joe seemed to think this was a good idea, *"...provided we give to United Way when summer rolled around. Save the rain forest, and all that."* Bennet glanced around furtively. So far, the repellent seemed to be working.

Oh well, it was only his first day, and he was already tired of that goddamned song.

It was an itsy-bitsy teeny-weeny yellow polka-dot bikini, that she wore...

Goat Piss

"Can you be-lieve this shit, Clem?" Sammi Jo said as she scrolled through several Maxisoft Word version 79.9. documents. At first he thought she was talking about the fifteen times they had to restart the computer because it had "locked up." Someone had thoughtfully replaced the Maxisoft startup logo with a picture of a large ass with a screw sticking out of it. *These techs are weird, kinky kind of folks,* Clem thought with a shudder.

But the unbelievable shit Sammi Joe referred to was what they planned to do with the goats. "Look, it says here, 'several trailer parks have been identified as fertile hunting grounds. In particular is the small community of redneck folk called Last Chance. It is estimated that only nine gallons of fainting goat neurotransmitter would be needed to prime the entire population. This could keep the Bubbateria supplied with raw material up to a year as the rednecks are processed into patties. This is a cost effective measure, as it would concentrate our efforts into one target area, instead of over several hundred square miles.' Jesus fucking Christ!" she exclaimed, angrily jabbing the page down key. Clem ducked as a Lee Press-On nail flew over their heads.

"We already knew they were hunting us," Clem said, uncomfortably shifting his large posterior on a little round stool. "I jes didn't know they had perfected the process of ... mass processing."

"Well here it is," Sammi Jo said, pulling up a picture of the meat processing facilities. "It's down on the lower floors. Look, the bodies are stacked up here, and they're feeding them into the thang like it was a wood chipper. With no waste, no by-product. The inclusion of bones and organs in the meat grinding process, seasoned liberally with Lawry's Seasoned Salt (or equivalent generic knockoff), gives the product the distinctive flavor we call *bubbalicious.*" She made a sour face. "Yuck!"

"What are we gonna do now, Sammi Jo?" The noises from the closet had dwindled to nil. Clem wondered if there was enough air getting in there.

She was already digging through more documents. "Here's a map of the geek tech communities. Seventeen, all around us." Sammi Jo smiled and sat back from the screen, and regarded Clem with an expression that turned his blood to ice. "At least, they *were* coming after us. I got a plan. We'll see who dances to whose tune!"

"What are you talkin' about, Sammi Jo?" Clem edged off the stool, which sighed audibly with relief. "We got to get out o' here. There's too many of them. An' we don' know what the hell we're doin'—"

"No, *you* don't know what the hell *you're* doin'," Sammi Jo said fiercely, stabbing him in the chest with a finger, the Lee Press-On Nail threatening to draw blood. "Go ahead, take off, leave if you want to. I'm stayin' till I get this thing done. First we need to find some kind of gas mask or," she looked around, her eyes coming to rest on a large metal cabinet in the corner. On it was a neon orange symbol with the words HAZMAT under it. "That might do..."

She opened the cabinet. "Hazardous materials suits! That's perfect! Here, put this on," she said, flinging a suit at him. "One size fits all."

One size didn't fit all, at least not well. Clem wedged himself into the suit with great difficulty, feeling like a tightly wrapped sausage by the time Sammi Jo zipped him shut. His head poked through an enclosed hood, and peered out of a plexiglass visor. "These have filters that keep out diseases. They'll let you breathe just fine. I hope they're enough. We're jes gonna have to give it a try."

After Sammi Jo wriggled into hers, she went through the lab, looking for the fainting stuff they had found in goat piss. In a refrigerator she found a plastic beaker with a rubber stopper marked "Faintecholine, Batch #3."

"It looks like goat piss," Clem commented, his words muffled but intelligible through the suit.

"It *is* goat piss. Highly concentrated goat piss." Further searching turned up an empty spray bottle, into which she poured the Faintecholine, Batch #3. "This shit had *better* work," her words were tinged with uncertainty.

On another table was a collection of noise making devices, cap guns, plastic party horns, firecrackers, bells, gongs, and various squeaky toys sorted by size. One item in particular caught her attention.

"Perfect," she said, handing Clem a large aerosol horn. "Remember when we used to blow these suckers at football games?" She gave it a shake. "Feels like its full, too." She handed it to him.

Clem remembered, and gave it a blow, a few inches from Sammi Jo's butt. She jumped about a foot in the air, a surreal sight in the hazmat suit; she looked like a bug hopping on a hot porchlight.

"Dammit, Clem!" She slapped his arm, hard. "Quit screwing around! We got thangs to do!" Armed with a spray bottle of goat urine, she marched over to the storage closet and unlocked the door. The tech was still struggling in there, sweaty and flushed.

"Get her and stand her in the middle of the room."

"What fer?" Clem wanted to know.

"We gotta know if this stuff works! Come on, time's a wastin!"

The suit made the task difficult, but Clem succeeded in standing her in the middle of the room as instructed. Her arms and mouth remained taped. She gaped at them fearfully, apparently wondering what horrible redneck torture they had devised for her. Sammi Jo sprayed her square in the face with Faintecholine, Batch #3, better known as goat piss. The tech's eyes watered, and she looked ready to scream, but of course could not.

"Now, buttercup. Honk that horn of yours at her."

The horn ripped off a peal that could strip paint off the walls. The tech's eyes rolled up in her head, her legs stiffened, and she just fell right over, flat on her back. The rigidity was total, as if she were frozen solid. Sammi Jo leaned over and examined her. "She's still conscious. Just like the goats! The stuff works, sweet pea!"

"Holy Moly," Clem exclaimed. "Now what?"

"Remember that mangy old tomcat Jimmy Bob had? Would piss all over the place markin' its territory?" She held the bottle up. "I claim this entire damned building *my* territory. And everyone here is gonna get a face full of Batch #3!"

Batch #3

Margie lay on the floor, paralyzed from head to toe. Knowing full well she was the chief scientist developing Batch #3 did not douse any of her fury at being the first human to be exposed to it; particularly in the *way* she was exposed to it.

Then what would you expect from a couple a rednecks? her thoughts raged. *At least they didn't sodomize me.* The opening chords of the Deliverance banjo-guitar duet strummed in her brain.

The paralysis ... It's only temporary... it's only temporary... it's only temporary. . ." she repeated to herself, an impromptu mantra designed to calm her, perhaps hasten her recovery. When she felt the paralysis slipping, she breathed a sigh of relief, the only physical action she was still capable of. She wiggled her feet. Soon it would be ...

...but we're being overrun with rednecks! They have guns! They're crazy...

This made her afraid again.

And the paralysis locked down tighter than ever.

Good heavens, she thought. *I can't think alarming thoughts! Or I'll stay paralyzed! How did the goats ...*

Then she saw how the goats slipped out of the paralysis. They were too *stupid* to think alarming thoughts, to know anything was even wrong. They had little in the way of memory, long or short term. Humans, on the other hand...

As the paralysis slipped away again, she braced herself against thinking frightened thoughts. And failed miserably. Her body remained rigid as a lamp post.

Maybe if I can sleep... she thought, at the same time knowing that she wasn't about to go to sleep, not anytime soon, maybe not ever.

The Hunt

Mack pulled the truck to a stop, and radioed to the sniper, Phoenix, perched up on the roof.

"See *anything?* Anything at all? Over."

A pause of static. Then, "Not a damned thing. Recon was full of shit about all the Bubbas out here. I don't see so much as a pork rind bag."

The remains of the small town was overgrown with dense weeds and mimosa. An old town, with brick building ruins. And not a soul in sight. And not a single catch in the back of the Class 6 Mitsubishi Fuso. The refrigerated truck, with the slogan "Bubbalicious!" painted lovingly on the side, was frugal with the diesel, but if they came back empty handed they could be in deep shit. Joe could either bitch up a thunderstorm, or not even notice, depending on his mood. Too bad there wasn't a computer store to ransack. A cache of unopened computer games would smooth over any sticky upper management problem.

Phoenix sat atop the Fuso in a crows nest of half inch thick armor plate, peering through the scope of good ole Army M21. Ammo for the antique was easy to come by, and several boxes sat nearby. Nervously, he scanned the sky, the sun would set in about an hour. Not a good idea to be caught out after dark.

Phoenix radioed back, "Don't know, Mack, I think we oughta head in. This place is a lost cause. I'd rather face the music when we get back than deal with the crazies that only come out at night."

"Roger that," Mack said, putting the truck into gear. Why don't you come down here where it's cool?"

Phoenix considered this, then replied, "Naw, I might see something on the way in. One catch is better than nothing."

"Now, you know he doesn't want non-bubbas," Mack warned.

"If they're stripped naked, how the hell would he know?"

"We'd know," Mack said. "We can't use diseased flesh, and we can't eat our own. Everything would fall apart then."

Phoenix didn't say anything for a long moment, then the truck lurched into motion, it's turbocharged diesel gurgling to life. "Might see a Bubba," he said, not knowing if Mack heard him or not. If he started seeing things that weren't there, he might as well ask for a transfer to packing. If he were to lose what was left of his mind he didn't want to be holding a military spec sniper rifle.

He was at least sane enough to consider *that*.

Joe's Bubbateria

The hazmat suit was getting hot. Clem considered removing it for a moment, then saw the tech, frozen solid, laying on the floor. *Don't wanta end up like that,* he thought, and started collecting various odds and ends about the lab that he thought might be useful to their mission. Sammi Jo finished whatever she was doing on the computer and stood up.

"Its showtime, luv muffin," she said, and Clem perked up at that particular endearment. Rumor had it that when she said that, she was about to jump your bones. *But in the suits? I don't think so, at least not yet!*

"First one I want to get is that little peckerwood down the hall," she said, and Clem followed her out the door.

The kid was still sitting at the computer. He didn't look up.

"Hey, dipshit!" Sammi Jo's muffled words came through clearly.

"Hey, what—" the kid said, looking up, just as she hit him with the *eau de* goat, Batch #3. "Hey!" he said, startled, taking a whiff and wrinkling his nose in disgust.

Clem lit a string of firecrackers with his Confederate flag lighter and tossed it into the office. The hazmat suited bubba hurried out of the office, hands over his ears, as the firecrackers started exploding on the floor; the boy froze, stiffened, and fell over on his face like an overturned statue; the firecrackers continued to pop away, inches from his head.

"Clem, you stupid idiot!" Sammi Jo screeched. "Use the *horn!* Use the firecrackers for *large groups!*"

"But I've got more, Sammi Jo," Clem protested, over the deafening roar of firecrackers, holding up another long string of Black Cats.

"That'll bring the whole damned building down on us!" she shouted over the blasts. "What if they have security guards? *REAL ones?*"

"They don't, or we would have seen them by now," Clem replied, grateful, and surprised, that his words made sense.

"We'd better hope not," she said, and turned her attention to two techs hurrying down the hall. She sprayed them as they turned to enter the office, where the string of firecrackers had a ways to go before burning out. A moment later, the paralysis seized them, and they toppled over just like the kid.

"You know, it occurs to me we might want to find the owner and president, Joe Furnier," Sammi Jo said. "Take him out, and the whole authority pyramid collapses."

Clem looked up at the open door, with the sign, *Joe Furnier, President, Joe's Bubbateria.* "It think it was the kid."

"Well, don' that jes' beat *all,*" she said, taking in the sign on the door. She pulled the kid's head up by the hair. "Next time, sugar plum, be a little nicer to your employees. You never know when they might rebel." She let go, his head making a painful sounding *thump* as it bounced on the thin office carpet.

Faintecholine

But I'm the boss! Who are these fuckers blowing up bombs next to my face? I can't move. I can't even think. I think I pissed my pants I think I'm still at WillTell. No I'm the boss of my own fucking company and these fuckers have come in and SPRAYED PISS IN MY FACE I wonder if it was Faintecholine? Yes it must have been Faintecholine look what it did to me. Now they've left and the bombs have stopped going off and no one's here except that Chinese fucker Hwong. Come over here and help me. Yes that's right. No that's not right. Don't load me on the cart. I'm not trash don't clean me up. I know that's what you do best... I'm the boss for crissakes!!*

The Bubbamatic

Bennet shooed the old woman in the cheerleading uniform away from his rows of meat patties. She sprayed the alien repellent in ever widening arcs, to keep an alien invasion at bay. But he didn't think that alien repellent, cleverly disguised as Glade Rain Forest air freshener, would be terribly healthy to eat. Though it was probably lo cal and lo fat, this just was not that important after the fall of civilization. Quality control was, after all, *his* job.

He had returned to his task when he heard the blood curdling scream from the cheerleader: she stared in horror at two aliens, one holding a spray bottle, one holding a ray gun. They stood at the main entrance calmly regarding the humans.

"Spray them!" Bennet shouted, but the woman was hysterical. *The room is full of the stuff anyway, why wasn't it working?* he thought, then saw why the repellent wasn't working. The aliens had a counter-repellent! They sprayed the cheerleader, who staggered backwards, then they hit three other techs in white sani-suits and hairnets who had come running, evidently responding to the scream.

What the FUCK?

Hwong the Chinese cleaning man scurried in with a flatbed cart, ladened with four lab-coated bodies of Bubbateria employees. He stopped at the aliens to wipe their faces clean (the traitor!), and scurried off before they could spray him. As usual he was amazingly spry for a little old guy, pushing the body cart as if it were nothing.

One of the aliens lit something with a Bic lighter and threw it in the middle of the room. A grenade!

"Hit the deck!" he shouted, not waiting to see if anyone heard him. Bennet dove behind the Bubbamatic just as the grenade went off. And went off. And went off. Strangely enough it sounded like a string of Black Cats, but perhaps that was just a clever ruse, to fool the humans into *thinking* it was just a string of Black Cats. He stayed secreted behind the Bubbamatic for a long time till long after the grenade had finished exploding. When he emerged from his hidey hole he found his fellow employees, all lying dead, and apparently suffering early rigor mortis. The aliens were nowhere in sight.

And the Chinese guy, unscathed by the alien's weapons, was dutifully picking up the bodies and placing them on a flatbed cart.

"Hwong!" Bennet shouted, but Hwong ignored him. "You've got to run! The aliens have invaded. They're taking over the world. They're taking over the Bubbateria!" Then a horrible thought came to mind. They're taking over the Bubbateria to convert humans into patties! But wasn't he doing just that, mere moments ago?

Then finally, Bennet's mind, frail to begin with, snapped.

Hal the computer in 2001: A Space Odyssey, had a similar reaction to conflicting orders. Bennet's brain shut down, and on a sort of autopilot, just walked off the job. He didn't even ask for references. He drove home, barricaded himself in his garage, and wept.

Clean and Sanitized

"Now what do we do?" Clem wanted to know

"Well, honey bun, looks like we wiped out the Bubbamatic crew, but this place, I don't see how to get in." They were in a hallway adjacent to the room they just cleared out, watching a grisly scene of headless bodies behind thick, wire-reinforced glass. The white suited techs within seemed oblivious to the "raid." Sammi Jo couldn't figure out how to turn off the Bubbamatic, the main controls being somewhere else, perhaps with these guys in white suits calmly decapitating corpses on what looked like a giant carrot slicer. After a moment's deliberation, she said, "Forget these guys, we've got to get the rest of the executives. These are just the worker bees. We need the Queens."

They were headed back towards the Bubbamatic when the little oriental guy nearly ran them over with a cart full of paralyzed techs, stacked up like firewood.

"Sugar, where are you going with that?" she said to him, putting a hand on the cart handle and gently stopping it.

"Ah! Lay them out near the dumpsters. Must clean! Must *sanitize!*" he replied excitedly.

"If they're paralyzed like that first one upstairs," Clem pointed out. "They won't go far, wherever he takes them."

"Yep," Sammi Jo concurred. "At least they're out of the way." She hooked a thumb over her shoulder. "Go on. Git."

The little oriental guy bowed expressively, and continued toward the loading docks with his load.

The Catch

Mack and Phoenix pulled up to the dock and parked the Fuso, dejected and worried about their failure to catch anything.

"You know," Mack said, his words dripping with remorse. "Maybe we should have stayed out until we caught something. Joe ain't gonna like it."

"Joe don't have to know," Phoenix said, looking at something on the dock. "What do we have here?"

There was a row of dead bodies in white tech suits, fifteen in all. "Don't know what happened to them, but it don't look like they're diseased to *me.*"

"Me neither," Phoenix replied, his spirits lifting with their find. "Won't say nothing if you don't."

They weighed each one on the scale, tagged them and sent them through the chute to Processing. The tallied weights of each, along with a falsified report on where they found them, went into a computer. Had they recognized their boss, Joe, among the bodies they might have rethought their plan. But they'd been taught from infancy not to play with their food.

Mack frowned, sniffed, and looked around. "Do you smell piss?"

Yuppiegeddon

About a month later, Clem was backing the Mitsubishi Fuso up to the dock to unload the rich load of techs they'd rounded up at a Joe's Bubbateria restaurant near Dallas. It was only the third of the seventeen tech communities which had declared war on Bubbakind, but it was a good start. He got a laugh when he'd come back from the first expedition and found the big hand painted sign on the building modified to read "Sammi Jo's Bubbateria."

"Sugar Pumpkin!" Sammi Jo said as he climbed out of the truck. She threw her arms around him and kissed him but good. "How'd it go?"

"Never knew what hit 'em," Clem said, reaching around and grabbing Sammi Jo's firm buttocks with two meaty fists. "Which reminds me, we need to come up with some more firecrackers."

Mack and Phoenix, who as it turned out were really immune Bubbas with identity crisis', opened the back of the truck and started unloading the bodies, each taken down with one clean shot from the M21. They didn't bother weighing them anymore, just popped them in the chute. Clem might have felt a little bad about the whole thing had he not seen first hand the massive slaughter the techs were planning to wage on Bubbakind, starting with Last Chance. The Bubbateria's designs to infect them all with Batch #3 was just the beginning of Bubbageddon. The techs had neutron bombs in readiness, and would have used them if things hadn't … *changed.*

Although it was a shock to Clem and Sammi Jo when they realized the first round of techs they had paralyzed with Faintecholine Batch #3 had been inadvertently sent (alive) to the guillotines in Processing, it did relieve them of the burden of dealing with them, *and* it gave Sammi Jo a grand idea of what to do next. Bubbaburgers made out of techs was just as tasty, if a little lean, compared to the real thing. They sold them to the tech communities by the cases, after first treating them with Batch #3. Then a week or so later, Clem would come along with his sharpshooters, toss a string of fire crackers in the middle of the Bubbateria and watch them topple over. Easy meat. Sammi Jo estimated they would have conquered all of them within a year.

But the best thing of all, Clem thought, was that Sammi Jo had delivered the goods, and what's more, she *liked* puttin' out to Clem, and *only* Clem, so much that she accepted his proposal to get hitched, permanent like. The entire town of Last Chance breathed a collective sigh of relief. Sammi Jo was a scandal waiting to happen, and everyone, including her daddy Preacher Hickey, knew it. He married them with his blessings, and sent them back to the Bubbateria with a dowry of large caliber weapons (and lots of ammo) to complement the M21 pea shooters they already had.

As Clem clutched Sammi Jo tightly, he felt the painful stirrings of a full blown erection squirming to escape a tangle of pubic hair. It had been four days, after all.

Does it get any better than this? Clem wondered as he scooped her up in his arms and carried her inside.

It's Bubbalicious

Bennet Snort woke himself from the daydream, sitting upright in the driver's side of the Excursion, which was more or less permanently parked in his garage. He remembered little of the previous year, only that one day he'd come home and ransacked his dead neighbor's houses for supplies. He did have lots of canned goods, bottled water, sterno, and a variety of large and small caliber firearms. There was a small problem with his situation, though.

He was sick and tired of eating canned food, and some of it was starting to go bad.

The mutter of a distant diesel engine grabbed his attention, and he ran to the garage window and looked out.

Bennet knew the rednecks had found a bunch of diesel somewhere, so a diesel engine was a sure give away. He didn't *think* they knew where he lived—but then again, they might.

Sure enough, a little white refrigerated truck chugged by without stopping or slowing... and something dropped off the back of it, right in front of his house. It was a white cardboard box, no markings. Bennet waited about an hour to see if it would blow up. When it didn't, he crept out to the box, picked it up, and ran back to the house. He opened it and found twenty meat patties on waxed paper, each imprinted proudly with the word "Bubbalicious!"

He had a vague memory of a company somewhere, a meat packing place (or was it a restaurant?) where this might have come from. It was long ago.

Even so, the meat was fresh, and he was hungry.

Bennet went out to the back yard and fired up the grill.

In 1990 **Mark Shepherd** began collaborating with Mercedes Lackey on the SERRAted edge urban fantasy series with the novel *Wheels of Fire*. Another collaboration with Mercedes followed, *Prison of Souls*, and a solo project, *Escape from Roksamur,* both novel tie-ins based on the bestselling role playing computer game *The Bard's Tale.*

His first published solo work, *Elvendude,* is an elves-in-the-mall urban fantasy set in Dallas, Texas. Within weeks of its release it appeared on the Locus magazine bestseller list. The sequel, *Spiritride,* set in Albuquerque, New Mexico, came out in April of 1997.

His newest novel, *Black Rose Avenue,* a speculative fiction dealing with an AIDS epidemic in all-too believeable United States controlled by the religious right, was released in May of 2001 from Yard Dog Press.

How does he know about bubbas? He attended high school in Jenks, Oklahoma. Enough said.

BUBBA'S, PICKLES, AND THE YOMBIES FROM HELL
Ed Cain

So I reckon yall's wontin' to know 'bout how we country folk came to take over the world. I gotta admit, I ain't so sure sometimes how all this come to be myself, my memory aint' what it used to be, but I figure what I'm gonna tell you is close enough.

Near as any of us can tell, that there flu bug they called "Yuppie 25" hit in the summer of 2025. Me and Shirlene was watchin' the five o'clock news one night when the newscaster lady just up and went crazy and started tryin' to eat the weather feller. We thought she didn't look none to good before, but our T.V. was kinda old at that time, and we just figured the color'd done gone out of the set again.

After that, we started hearin' bout how all the summer folk that come down here to Virginia Beach was goin' crazy, rammin' their SUV's into buildings, lootin' and a riotin'. Hell, none of us folk ever went down there anyway, so we actually kinda laughed when we started seein' it on the news, which by the way, was now fully staffed with what we've come to call "Yombies," that's half yuppie, half zombie.

The area of the beach with all them fancy hotels is pretty much surrounded by country, but other than seein' the tourists on occasion comin' out to the produce stands we pretty much just stayed away from 'em, and they kept away from us. Then one day Earl Bodkin had just brought up a fresh load of onions to the stand when some of them Yombies got out of their mini-van and just 'bout tore ole Earl to pieces. It left a terrible mess. We

99

didn't find nothin' of him but a bloody John Deere hat and his favorite Dale Earnhardt memorial tee-shirt.

Now I'm gonna tell you that nothin' makes us madder than havin' some damn family from New Jersey rollin' up into our produce stands and eatin' the proprietor's. Hell, we never minded doin' business with them tourist's before, but that's just down right rude. So after that, we all just kinda closed our stands and stayed away from the populated end of town. Some days you could see smoke comin' from all of the fires down the oceanfront, I guess all them fancy hotels was goin' up one after the other. We'd been watchin' the news every night, and I guess that flu bug was goin' round and round pretty much everywhere.

I don't know why none of us never got it. We thought Billy Rae Mason had come down with it once, and Cletis Barns had run a pitch fork clean through Billy before we realized he was just havin' an allergy attack. We still chuckle when we see Billy limpin' along the street.

I'm kinda wanderin' around here, ain't I? Well let me tell you what happens if'n you should get Yuppie 25. First of all, we ain't real sure how you get it. We'd heard it was some kinda chemical that the Army was workin' on, but Cletis come up with an idea one night while we was deer huntin' that I thought made more sense.

Cletis says the French did it. He thinks that all that fancy cheese them yuppie folk was always eatin' was poisoned on account of the fact that them French folks ain't to fond of us'n over here. Think about it, all them cheeses with names that end with that funny e with the thing over it. Them yuppies ate that stuff like it was goin' out of style.

Anyway, Yuppie 25 killed normal folks out-right, but it turned yuppies into a kind of zombie. Actually, other than the fact that their skin turns kinda green and gray, and they eat other people, they're pretty much the same. Near as we could tell, most of the country got it. The news went right out, and other than Hee-Haw re-runs and that Lawrence Welk feller, there weren't much on T.V. in those days, even NASCAR races had been postponed because some of them network fellers was interviewin' Jeff Gordon, Jr. and one of 'em tore off his good drivin' arm.

After a couple of months, pretty much every city in the country was destroyed, and the disease had done spread all around the world. For the most part, us country folk was all okay (another reason we thought Cletis may have been right about that cheese thing), but the world sure was gettin' to be a strange place. All the malls was closed, they was half eaten bodies everywhere, hell, we was afraid to go out at night lessen' they was five or six of us and we had our guns with us.

We went down to Munson's to get some gas one night when a mini-van and one of them SUV's pulled in. Well them doors opened up and two whole families of them "Yombies" jumped out and started headin' over to our truck. They was all grey lookin' and smelled rotten, but I gotta admit, they still dressed pretty nice and it looked like one of the ladies was feedin' her kids an arm. It still touches my heart to see folks takin' good care of their kin.

Anyway, this old boy comes staggerin' up to us lookin' at Cletis like he's a Thanksgiving Turkey. Slobber started runnin' all down the front of his shirt (you know, the shirts with them little 'gators on the front of 'em) so Billy Yates fetched his shotgun and met old boy 'bout halfway to the truck. Well you know that feller tried to grab Billy's gun, and as everybody 'round here knows, you don't ever touch Billy's gun, specially if you got some grease on your hands cause it smudges the blue'en on the barrel. Well Billy just went off. He hit that old boy up side the head with the butt of that gun (why not, he was gonna have to clean it anyway). The feller's skull split wide open (Billy made his stock outta alderwood, ain't much harder out there), and his brain's just kinda fell out of his head and onto the ground there. Well, no sooner did that guy hit the ground when his wife, all them folk from the mini-van, and them kids was all walkin' across the parkin' lot at us. I gotta admit, I ain't never been afraid of much, specially city folk all dressed up, but when you got two car loads full of flesh eatin' well-dressed people starin' at ya, ya do what ya gotta do. We pulled our guns out the back of that truck and just a started shootin'. Now I hate killin' folk, but if'n it comes down to me or them, well, we just thought of it as kind of a mercy killin'.

One day Willie Wilkin's come up to the house an asked me if'n I wanted to go for a ride. Shirlene was over at the Smith's house a quiltin', so I grabbed my gun and off we went. Willie said he had a theory (that's like an idea, but more important) 'bout how come we ain't gettin' sick like them folks, and he wanted to prove it. He said we was goin' to Portsmouth, which is a city a little ways north of here. He said he ain't seen too many colored folk comin' down with it either, and Portsmouth gotta lotta colored folk livin' there so he thought we could go and see for ourselves.

It was quite a drive. They was wrecked vehicles all over the roads, and dead and half dead folks was everywhere. As long as we kept movin' we was okay, but we had a close call when some lady drivin' one of them German cars (BM somethin') and a talkin' on her portable phone tried to ram us. Ole Willie had put one of them railroad ties on the front of his truck some years ago, and although I think them German's build a fine automobile, nothin', and I mean nothin', can stand up to an old Ford pickup with a railroad tie front bumper. Willie hit that car right in the middle and just about broke it in two. The lady must not have had her restraining belt on, she come straight through the windshield and went skiddin' across the road. We didn't stop to see if'n she was dead, we just kept right on.

So we got into Portsmouth, and sure enough, they was colored folks all out and about. We went into a neighborhood and got stopped by some young feller's with them hankies on their heads. Willie tipped his hat, and the feller started twistin' his fingers and hands in some kind of strange ritual. Willie and me tried to communicate with this young man by givin' him all of the hand signals we knew, like "O" for Okay, "V" for Victory, and even the finger through the hole. I think he was kinda mad (even though we wasn't implying nothin' with the finger through the hole), but then some other feller come up and asked us what we wanted. We told 'em 'bout what had happened to the yuppies, and that we was just seein' if'n anybody else had gotten sick. He said they'd seen the same thing, even had one of his, what'd he call them "homies", eaten by some woman with a Gucci hand-bag. We nodded and told 'em what we'd seen.

Well he sure was a nice feller, and he asked us if'n we was hungry. We was so he said follow him and he and them other nice colored folk all piled into this big old Chevy and started off down the road. That car kept jumpin' up and down, and me and Willie had to chuckle 'cause we knew them shocks of his must be terrible broke, but it looked like he liked the car so we didn't say nothin' to him.

Anyway, we pulls into this little road-side restaurant. The sign said, "Best Carolina Bar-B-Que in Virginia." Now I know most people think that country folk and colored folk ain't got much to say 'bout each other, but I think we got more in common that most people realize. First of all, none of us really liked yuppies anyway. Sure the grocery stores start carrying more stuff when they come to town, and the woman do smell nice with their fancy French perfumes (there's them French again), but they was always somethin' not quite right about 'em anyway, and I think the colored folk pick up on it same as us.

So we sit down with these nice feller's and a nice old woman come out the back and takes our order. The colored feller that seemed to be in charge of the others said we should try the baby backs, but I likes them pulled pork sandwiches, so I had that, and old Willie had him the Brisket. All the colored folk got the Baby-Backs. We passed the time while the food was a cookin' talkin' bout how this disease done wiped out civilization. The nice young feller with the car's name was "Mookie," and he said that no colored folks he knew of had been down sick with this thing.

I lit up a cigarette, and one of them other colored folk lit up what looked like a little cigar. It sure didn't smell like no cigar I've ever seen, and the smoke smelled down right funny. He offered it to Willie, then to me, but I gave up cigars on account of the missus. It must have been real good, 'cause that feller would hold the smoke in for a long time then blow it out while sayin' "Yeah, yeah." Anyway, the food come out, and it sure was good. I tried some of Willie's brisket, and on of the young boys gave me a couple of his ribs.

The sauce tasted familiar, and Willie asked the waitress what kind of sauce was they usin'. She brought out the bottle, and me and Willie had us a good laugh. It was none other than "Pickle's Pig Pickin' sauce", simply the finest Bar-B-Que sauce on this earth. Pickle was a crazy old man who had been makin' that sauce as far back as anyone can remember. Everybody who knows anything 'bout good sauce uses nothin' but. Both me and Willie complimented them on their good taste, and Willie commented how he'd seen Ol' Pickle not too long ago headin' down to the grocer on his tractor.

I looked around the restaurant, and other than some more old black folks at the counter weren't no body in there. We finished our meal, and treated them nice fellers by pickin' up the check. When we was on the way out, one of the young fellers gave us one of them cigar's and said we should have it on the way home, and he also told us to make sure we inhaled. I knew the missus would be madder than hell if'n she knew I snuck one, but we'd been married too long for her to fuss too much, so Willie and I shared it on the way back into town.

I tell you that cigar weren't nothin' like anythin' I've ever had. My head felt kind of fuzzy, and me and Willie almost wrecked his truck twice 'cause we was laughin' so hard, at what I don't know. 'Bout half-way home we had to stop cause we was cravin' Doritos for some reason.

We came up on one of them 7-11 places, and pulled into the parking lot just in time to see the poor feller behind the counter being attacked by some of them damned Yombies. So we fetched our guns from the rack behind us and went on into the store. The poor clerk feller had had it. They was a woman in khaki pants, and some nice sunglasses that was feastin' on that man's innards by the time we got to her. Her husband was over by the cooler stockin' up on some of the local wines that they sold there. Willie chambered a round, and that woman looked up, a piece of the feller's guts still in her mouth. Willie fired just as her husband came 'round the corner behind him. I pushed the bolt forward in my trusty Springfield and let him have it. His head come clean off, and he dropped the two bottles of wine and the big jar of Mayonnaise he was a carryin'. Willie'd hit the lady right between the eyes, and her head came off too.

Now, I don't want you to get the impression that me and Willie is some kind of killer's, we's regular folk just like you, but sometime's you just gotta do what you gotta do. We left money for them Doritos on the counter (you don't just steal somethin' cause the clerk got eaten by zombies, gotta have standards) and we left.

As we was havin' them Doritos, Willie finally told me 'bout his theory. Whereas Cletis thought the French had given us the bug with the cheese, Willy thought maybe it wasn't what the Yuppies was eaten that gave it to them, maybe it was what we was eaten that was keepin' us from getting sick. Well, that Willie is one smart feller, and that set me to thinkin' what was we eatin' that them city folk weren't. That's when it hit us. Yuppies don't know nothin' bout good Bar-B-Que. They buy that stuff in the grocery store, neither one of us had ever seen none of them buyin' good sauce. They sure are hell don' know nothin' 'bout grillin'. Then Willie mentioned the colored folk, and we agreed that they also have very good taste when it comes to Bar-B-Que sauce, and that Bar-B-Que is kind of a food staple for both of us kind of folks.

We decided to pay Ol' Pickle a visit before headin' home. Now Pickle is a funny man. Like I said, he been makin' that sauce most of his life. While we thought he just sold it around town, apparently his youngest son got him up on this thing called the "Internet". It's got somethin' to do with computers. Now I ain't too swift on them computers, I can't type, but I guess there are people who shop on it and damned if Pickle didn't have him a big house and a nice car from sellin' lots of his sauce.

So we knocks on the door, an Missus Pickle opened it up a crack and stuck the barrel of a shotgun out before she peeked around it. She saw us, apologized, pulled the barrel back in and unchained the door. Boy, that sure was a nice house. We talked with Pickle for awhile over some beers and some of them Doritos, and Pickle gave us ten jars of his best. Willie even told him 'bout his idea that it was his Bar-B-Que that kept us from getting ill, Pickle just laughed and said somethin' 'bout them yuppies getting' sick cause God was punishin' them for bein' such snobs and all. We all laughed at that, and thanked Missus Pickle for her hospitality, and headed on home.

We pulled up in front of my house, and Willie got him another idea. He wanted to catch him one of them "Yombies" and make it eat some of Pickle's sauce to see what it would do to them. I thought it was kind of dangerous, but things had been slow and if somethin' good could come from it, I guess we had to try it. I told him me and the Missus was goin' over to our son Earl's house for dinner the followin' evenin', but after that I was free. Willie suggested that maybe Earl would like to come along too, and I said I'd ask him.

The next evening we pulled into Earl's trailer park about 5:00. The folks livin' there had piled up a bunch of old cars at the entrance, and they was about five or six feller's with guns watchin' out. I didn't think yuppies would come to a trailer park, but better safe than sorry.

Now I love my son, but he ain't the brightest bulb in the box if'n you know what I mean. His wife Betty Sue done give 'em four of the dumbest kids I've ever known. I'm a proud grandpa, but these kids are slower than molasses runnin' out a tree stump in January, if'n you know what I mean. Betty Sue done blowed up to about four hundred pounds after squeezin' all them kids out in just three years, their trailer done taken a permanent lean to one side where their beds is, but he still loves her and she's a good momma to them kids. Shirlene says that Betty don't keep a good house, and she don't like goin' over there to eat cause they's always bugs in the food. She does it cause she loves Earl like I do, but she'd rather have them come over to our house. Anyway, Betty made up some good food, and I gave her a couple of Jars of Pickle's sauce and without describin' too much, just told her to cook with it a lot and make sure them kids get some in their system. I figured Willie got just as much a chance of bein' right as wrong, and why tempt fate.

After dinner me and Earl went fishin' at the pond in the park there. He caught him a couple of cat-fish but I had to give up when my hook got stuck on the roof of an old car down the bottom of that pond. I told Earl 'bout Willie's idea and asked him if'n he and some of his boys would like to come along. Earl said he'd be over the house round 6:00 tomorrow night. We left Earl's house round about 9:00, poor Shirlene had a cockroach crawl up her leg and just couldn't stay there any longer.

Well, Earl showed up on time with some of his buddies. They was already about a case of beer into the evening (which meant they'd probably only been drinkin' for 'bout an hour) and they pulled up next to the house a whoopin' and a hollerin', they'd even put a big ol Rebel Flag up on the aerial of the truck they was in. They were in fine spirits.

Willie showed up 'bout half an hour later, and we all piled into Earl's friends pickup and headed into town. We hadn't been anywhere near the town in months, boy it was a mess. They was dead people everywhere, and the stink was terrible, but the line at Bennigan's was out the door and them Yombies seemed to be goin' on like nothin' was different.

Willie had a plan, and lord it was a goodin'. We was gonna set up a free wine tastin' in the field across from the Bennigan's, complete with some of that French cheese them folks like so much. Willie got him a big box from a refrigerator, we folded it back out and put the wine and cheese underneath it on a nice tablecloth and set the box on a stick with a string attached to it. It seemed simple, and I didn't think none of them Yuppies would bite, but sure enough, some feller with penny loafers come staggering out of Bennigan's and was lookin' at his beeper when he noticed the set up. He came over slowly, kind of sniffin' the air, but me and all the other fellers was hidin' in the tall grass, and he didn't see us. Well, he bent down to pick up that cheese and some of that wine and Willie pulled the string. The box fell down on top of this feller and we rushed out to make sure he didn't claw his way through.

It was quiet when we got to the box, but when we listened a little closer we could hear that feller a munchin' away and sayin' something about that brie cheese not bein' heated to the right temperature. I think that steamed Willie a little bit, he prides himself on bein' thorough. Anyway, Willie didn't quite figure out what to do once we'd trapped this feller, but Earl and some of his buddies got some rope from the back of the truck, and while one of them flipped over the box, them boys got that man tied up in no time. He was hoppin' mad too, mumblin' something about him not being able to finish his appetizer.

So we got us a "Yombie" prisoner. We took him back to our barn and tied him up in a chair. His damned cell phone kept ringin' and he was beggin' somethin' terrible to get it, sayin' something 'bout mutual funds, but Earl took it off this feller's belt and threw it up against the barn wall, and it went quiet.

When Willie approached him with the Bar-B-Que sauce, the feller started squirmin' in his chair, turnin' his head this way and that and tellin' us that eatin' that stuff was gonna "ruin his palette". We didn't know what the hell he was talkin' about, so Earl grabbed his head and Willie just stuck some of the sauce in this guy's mouth with a big spoon. The fellow squeezed his eyes shut, then he licked, then he opened his eyes and looked at us and said, "This isn't bad, it's a little heavy on the vinegar, perhaps some balsamic would go better." Again, we didn't know what the hell this feller was sayin' so we just kept feedin' him the sauce. After he ate 'bout half the bottle, we left him alone for the night. Earl double checked to make sure he couldn't escape, and we put a blanket on him so he wouldn't freeze, then we left him till morning.

I asked everyone to stay the night, so we could see what the sauce would do, if anything, in the morning. We had a good old time that night, Earl's boys had brought enough beer with them for everyone, and I woke up the next morning for the first time in twenty years with a hangover. Well we went out into the barn and checked on the feller, and damn if'n he didn't knock over his chair and he'd caught him a rat in his mouth and was eatin' away when we opened the door. The sauce was a failure, so we thought, but Willie had another idea. What if we cooked up some ribs with the sauce and tried that. We agreed, and I fired up the grill with some nice hickory that I keep on hand for just such an occasion.

We slow cooked them ribs for hours, drinkin' some more of the beer that Earl had. Willie remembered that them young colored kids had given him a phone number, so we called them up and asked if'n they'd like to come out and see what we was doin'. That young feller said somethin' like "word" and hung up, I didn't know what that meant but I hoped they'd come out, and maybe they'd trade some beer for another one of them Cigars.

Well, 'bout an hour later they come down the drive in that car of theirs, still hoppin' around like a rabbit on a hot griddle. Now Earl and his boys don't like colored folk much, and I suspect them colored folk weren't too fond of Earl, but this was science dammit, and we just had to put our differences to the side.

We' made plenty of ribs, and finally about 4:00 they was done. Shirlene had made up some of her best potato salad, and them nice colored kids had stopped by that restaurant we'd eaten at and bought some greens with 'em. Well, that yuppie feller looked just terrified when we brought him them ribs. He demanded a knife and fork to eat them with (these people are stranger than I could have ever thought) but we said no, on account he might cut himself free with the knife and eat one of us, thus bringing a nice day to a bad ending.

Earl tore some of the meat off and one of his buddies forced open the feller's mouth. He spit out the first bite, and Earl hauled off and punched him one, so the second time around he was more open to the idea. He chewed 'em up, and swallered, and suddenly his eyes got big as saucer's.

He fell over in the chair and was a layin' on the ground twitchin' and gaggin', then after about a minute of that he just kinda stopped. We kinda stood 'round him in a circle, waitin' to see what happened next.

Now I gotta admit, even though most of them yuppie folks was kind of annoyin', I think everyone of us was hopin' that this feller was gonna get better. We gathered on up around him, and damn if'n he didn't lash out and try to take a bite out of Willie's leg, all the while mumblin' 'bout how them rib's done lost their "texture" on the grill.

Now nothin', and I mean nothin' makes me madder than to see a feller show no appreciation for a good meal (one of them black fellers called it "givin'props," although what this whole thing's got to do with airplanes I don't know).

So, we took that feller and stuck 'em back into the truck and took him back to the Bennigan's where we first caught him. Earl and his friends kept their guns on him, and a couple of them colored folk had some guns too, but they was all holdin' 'em sideways. We didn't figure they could hit nothin' a holdin' 'em like that, but damn if that yombie didn't jump at one of them boy's and they just all opened up and filled him full of holes.

Now, like I said before, I think all of us wanted that feller to feel better, but it just didn't happen. That don't mean that Willie still ain't a smart feller for figurin' out that Ol' Pickles Bar-B-Que sauce done stopped most of us from a turnin' green and eatin' people, it's just that sometimes life don't work out the way you want it to.

Well to make a long story short, the world now pretty much consists of us and them, and in some ways, it ain't that much different than it used to be, except we don't sell them folks no produce no more. There's a lot more country music on the radio these days, and NASCAR is more important than Presidential elections. Oh, and we nuked the French (apparently we wasn't the only ones who thought it was the cheese causin' all this mess).

Some good did come of it, though. We got some nice colored friends now, even Earl has been seen around town with some of them boys we met in Portsmouth, and I have started smoking them little Cigars again, but only the ones them feller's sell me, Shirlene doesn't seem to mind.

Ed Cain was born and raised in the suburbs of Washington D.C. His first book, titled *13 Stories*, has been nominated for the 2000 Bram Stoker Award.

Ed feels to understand the Bubba, one must *be* the Bubba. "Childhood experiences include going fishing in a pond in a trailer park and getting my hook stuck on the roof of a car in the pond (it's sad, but true), and having my next door neighbor, who worked for the Sewer Commission, bring home a huge snapping turtle he found in the sewers and keeping him in a metal trash-can. Well, if that ain't Bubba, nothin' is."

ERLENE
Ajax

Jerry Springer had said "Take care of yourselves."
While Erlene continued cleaning the shelves,
After doing the dishes and wiping the counter,
A smirk on her face, hoping Cecil would mount her.

It was the fourth time this week he had gone fishing,
Had returned empty handed, sad, and left wishing.
Cecil'd left early when the catfish was jumpin',
It was odd, Erlene thought, how fish controlled humpin'

Erlene cracked a beer, hung her rag on the sink,
Sat down on the sofa, and took a big drink.
Sally-Jesse was bitchin' at some loose-nutted boys,
When from way down the road Erlene heard a good
noise.

There was a hoopin' and hollerin' and yee-hawin' sound,
Then the squealing of brakes and boots on the ground.
"Erlene!" Cecil called, "Help me bring in this mess!"
So she jumped off the couch to prepare for the sex.

Erlene grabbed a fresh beer and the filletin' knife,
Cecil ran up the stairs and embraced his wife.
"Erlene, my darlin' you is purty as a dove!"
Erlene squeezed Cecil hard. He was ready for love.

I ZING THE BUBBA ELECTRIC
Selina Rosen

In the year 2025, when the great plague broke out and ravaged the earth a group of ten scientists had been living in an entirely enclosed environment engaging in an experiment called Earth Dome. This dome was an artificial world that would, hopefully, prove capable of sustaining human life indefinitely, with nothing leaving the plastic domed world, and nothing being brought in.

An earlier attempt had been a total failure, but this time they had done everything right; their experiment was a success. On the day before they were scheduled to leave the dome they waited breathlessly for a news team to show up to cover the event. None came. All attempts to reach anyone by phone or radio having failed, they turned on their TV to see what occasion had preempted their amazing, earth-shacking event. The small screen was filled with nothing but news about the air borne plague that was infecting the Earth outside their bubble world.

Wishing to remain uninfected, they decided to remain in the dome. When the last of the television and radio signals died out with no news of a successful vaccine, they knew that they were the only humans alive—saved and protected by their world under glass, or sophisticated plastic as the case may be. It was decided that they would live there indefinitely and keep humanity alive.

But now fifty years have passed. While they have been careful not to over populate the dome, they realize that as it currently exists the environment cannot contain them. A meeting has been called to discuss the problems currently facing the dome, and the future of the human race.

Jason Roberts was and always had been the leader of the colony. Now in his early seventies, his mortality glares at him daily from his reflection in the mirror. He regards the group of five people through squinted eyes that hardly see. He and four of the others are the only ones remaining from the original group. The fifth is the oldest of the children born into the colony, and even though he is forty-five, and both of his parents have died of old age, they still consider him to be *the kid.*

"We are running out of room," Jason said discarding the whole speech he had been going to give. "The dome as it exists is crumbling around us. Ever since we lost Earl there is no one to fix things."

"What are you saying?" Janet, a still spry sixty year old botanist, asked, a touch of panic entering her voice.

"I'm saying that while you passed on your skills, and I passed on mine, so on and so forth, Earl didn't pass on *his* skills," Jason explained. "Our short-sightedness has left us with no one to either add onto the dome or to maintain it as it stands."

Benjamin Gold, still pompous at seventy-five, laughed. "Earl was a moron! For God's sake, he was the maintenance engineer. Not even a scientist. I wasn't even sure half the time that he was speaking English. He was a glorified janitor, nothing less, nothing more."

"Yes ... that was what we all thought, so we didn't let him reproduce, and we didn't let him teach, and now he's gone and the whole place is falling down around our ears," Vivian, the chief robotics engineer, said. Even at eighty she was also the chief bitch of the group, a fact which no one had ever really decided was a plus or a minus. "I tried to tell you when Earl first started failing, but you were all so sure that anybody could do the things he was doing. What now, weenie boys? The dome is falling apart, and we need more room. None of you even knows how to go about putting in a God dam screw!"

"But *you* do, Vi," Justin the kid said. "You could fix things—teach us to fix them."

"I build robots, kid," Vivian said. "I don't know the first thing about construction, plumbing and the likes. None of us does. We all thought we were too damn good to do that sort of work." It was well known that Vivian had always had a fondness for Earl, and had resented the fact that the others wouldn't let him be the father of any of her children.

"Maybe ..." Mark fell silent. Now in his late sixties, and the youngest member of the original team, he just wasn't ready for the same crap he'd heard over and over again for the last fifty years.

"Maybe what, Mark?" Jason all but screamed. "If you have an idea, just spit it out."

"Well only ... how do we know it's not safe out there now?"

"Christ! How did I know he was going to say that?" Benjamin screamed. "How many times do we have to go over this? The virus is air borne. It may have mutated, gotten more deadly, but it probably hasn't just gone away. All of our attempts to create a vaccine for ourselves have ended in total failure.."

"We live here in this man made hell, wondering how we are going to live to the next decade, and none of you will even consider the fact that we might be all right outside," Mark said angrily. "You're all so scared that you won't even consider leaving this bubble in a suit, maybe taking some samples for God's sake. Hell, Earl went out there to repair things all the time."

"Yes, and Earl wound up dying in quarantine of an unknown virus," Jason reminded gently. "Probably a mutated strain of Yuppie 25."

"He was an old man," Justin said. "He might have died of a normal flu. Something that younger, healthier people might have lived through."

"You want to be the guinea pig, kid?" Ben asked smugly.

Justin just looked confused; he had no idea what a guinea pig was.

"I'd do it," Mark said boldly. "I'd do it just to feel the sun beating down on my face and the wind in my hair one more time. I'd gladly die to get out of this bubble. I'd risk my life on the chance that perhaps my children and grandchildren could actually enjoy a world that they have never known and that I have almost forgotten."

"Are you serious?" Jason asked cautiously.

"Yes, dead serious. Send me outside with testing equipment. I'll collect samples. I'll use myself as a test. I'll stay in quarantine when I get back inside. Whatever it takes."

After three hours of discussion, Mark walked into the air lock and then outside, drew in a deep breath, looked up at the sun, smiled, took three steps and fell over dead. As the siren blared, indicating that his heart had stopped, the stunned group just stood and stared in horror. Only Justin was willing to don a suit and go out to get Mark, but the elders wouldn't allow him to do it.

Another meeting was called.

"The environment has become so toxic that Earl was infected through his suit, and Mark was out mere moments and died," Jason announced.

"Christ!" Justin exclaimed. "Mark wasn't out long enough to have died from any virus. He must have died of something else, maybe a heart attack. I can't believe we're just going to leave him out there. Everyone else got composted, and poor Mark just has to lie out there and get wasted."

The elders all looked at each other with a certain amount of guilt. Need had prompted them to teach their off spring that you honored the dead by composting and reusing them, but they all knew that just wasn't right. Was in fact worse than letting Mark rot outside the dome. At least Mark was where he had wanted to be.

An argument ensued between the elders and the kid.

Jason tried to ignore them and think about their real problems. His eyes caught a glimpse of the robotic sprinkler system, and suddenly he had the answer. He coughed loudly. It didn't work; they didn't even stop arguing long enough to say bless you.

"Shut up!" Jason screamed. They fell silent looking at him in shock. "This isn't solving our problems. Ben, you're the shrink," this in itself was more irony than Jason wanted to consider at the moment. "What sort of person was Earl.?"

Ben was thoughtful for a moment. "He was hard working, a problem solver, as long as the problem could be solved with a pipe wrench or hammer. Not one of the great thinkers of our time. I'm sure that we all remember his quest to make a Twinkie. However he did finally succeed in making beer." He smiled broadly then. "He was a *bubba*."

"Where is this going, Jay?" Vivian asked.

"I can program a computer to do damn near anything," Jason said. "You construct a robot that matches Earl's height and body mass with complete hand, foot, body, leg, and arm movements. I will feed the design program of the dome into the computer, pictures of all Earl's tools. The contents of all his manuals. All the information contained in those handyman and mechanic magazines that Earl horded all these long years. You, Ben, will then feed the computer Earl's personality."

"A robot would be able to leave the dome and scavenge for materials in the most contaminated areas.

It could then be decontaminated with a simple washing," Vivian said thoughtfully. "It could bring us the components to build more and better robots, and in time we could have a real work force."

"Let me get this straight," Ben said in a tone of utter disbelief, "Are we really considering making a robotic Earl?"

"You have any better ideas?" Jason asked hotly.

Ben shook his head reluctantly.

"Then let's get to work."

They cannibalized equipment to complete the project. They worked in shifts around the clock. Finally, after six long months, the project was complete. Jason looked around at the entire community, waiting anxiously for their savior to be activated. Jason took a deep breath, discarded the speech he was going to make, and just flipped the switch.

The robot powered up with something that sounded a whole lot like a fart. The elders all turned to glare at Ben, and he smiled and shrugged. The robot rose to his full height and turned its glowing laser eyes upon the crowd assembled. It scratched absently at the place which could only be explained as its crotch, made a loud belching type noise, and then spoke:

"I zing the Bubba Electric. I kin not die. I'll take keer of all yer buildin' an' fixin' needs. I won' never leave y'all."

Selina Rosen edited this mess and created this universe. I think that says about all you need to know about her.

(NOTE: She has also written over thirty novels and dozens of short stories. You should check out her work.)

SHOP N' SAVE ZOMBIES
Gary Jonas

Zombies shambled across the street from St. Joseph's hospital to the Shop N' Save where I worked in the Before Time. Wonderful. My wife and I were supposed to supply the food for Ned's barbecue bingo party and we were running late. The living dead weren't going to shave any time off our food run, that's for sure.

"Damn zombies are already out," I said as I parked the truck. "We could have been here and gone if you hadn't spent an hour on your makeup."

"Don't start in on me, Junior," Vette said.

We ran to the door ahead of the zombies. I went to put my key into the lock when I noticed that the door was slightly open. I looked at Vette. "We locked this yesterday, right?"

"We always lock it."

"It ain't locked now."

She looked at it. "Looks locked to me. Just ain't closed."

She was right. The bolt stuck out from the side of the door. The metal jamb was twisted all to hell. I pulled out my pistol and motioned for Vette to stay behind me.

We eased into the store. I looked around, but the place was darker than my dead mother-in-law's moods. I could see the registers standing in line across the front of the store with the magazine and candy racks beyond them, but other than that, just darkness.

121

"I'm gonna head over to the office and turn on the lights."

"Whoever's in here will know we're here," Vette whispered.

"Probably already knows."

"What if he's carrying a machine gun?"

"What if it's Elvis?" I said.

"If it's Elvis, I'm asking for his autograph."

We moved to the stairs that led to the office.

"You think the burglar is upstairs?"

"Hell if I know. He could be up there waiting to kill me and rape you."

"What makes you think he wouldn't want to rape you?"

"Sissy boys ain't burglars," I whispered as we continued upstairs.

"Junior, that's one of the stupidest things you've ever said."

"What?"

"Gay guys can break into places."

"You're right. Just last week, Billy Ray complained about a sissy boy breaking into his trailer to redecorate."

"That was his wife and she didn't redecorate, she cleaned."

"She moved stuff around. That's redecorating."

"Stop it. The burglar could be up here and you're—"

"Shh!" I said. "I think I heard something."

We held our breath and listened.

After a moment of silence, Vette whispered, "What do you think you heard?"

"Nothing. I just wanted to see if you could shut up for a second."

If she tried to hit me, she missed. I was already moving down the dark hall. I ran my hand along the wall until I reached the office door. It stood wide open, so I crept inside. I knew the computer desk with a chair stood to the left and the main desk sat over by the window with the cool one-way glass.

I reached out to steady myself on the computer chair, but my hand closed on an arm. I jerked away and the chair shot backwards to smash into the desk.

I screamed and jumped back, slamming into Vette. She yelled and shoved me forward. I fell right on top of the person in the chair.

"Uhhhh!" yelled the person.

I scrambled backward and then there was light.

The intruder whipped a flashlight around, blinding me. Between the flashes of color before my eyes, I could make out a small woman.

"Who are you?" I asked, trying to shield my eyes.

"Uhhh!" she said.

"Great," I said, fear dropping away, "a damn zombie."

I walked over, punched the zombie in the nose and took the flashlight. Zombies, as a general rule, were slow and stupid. This one was no exception. They didn't feel any pain and most couldn't talk or do much thinking. I mean, they might be able to think, *hey I used to shop here*, but long division was out of the question. Not that anyone around here could do long division on a good day, but there you go.

The zombie leaned back in the chair and the weirdest thing happened. She started tearing off her clothes. I pointed the flashlight at her as she yanked on the flimsy hospital gown she wore. Her flesh was all rotten and once the gown dropped, she exposed far more than I'd ever wanted to see. I'm talking ribs poking out and big gaping holes and pustules swarming with maggots and I'm getting woozy just talking about it. She started to spread her legs and I moved that flashlight away.

"Junior?" Vette called from the hallway. "You all right?"

"I think I'm gonna be sick." I ignored the zombie's movements and sounds as I walked around the desk to get a clear shot. Normally I don't waste bullets on them, but in the confined space of a small office it's too easy to get trapped even by a slow zombie. One bullet to the brain and all her movement stopped.

"It's safe now, Vette."

I powered up the generator and the emergency lights came on.

Vette moved into the office and stopped when she saw the naked zombie sprawled on the chair like a perverted offering. "Oh my God. Who was she, one of your dead lovers?"

I looked at the zombie's face. "Well I'll be," I said. "It's Mrs. Norton. She was an old customer. Few bricks shy of a load if you ask me." She used to come by every time her husband was out of town so she could screw Mike, the other assistant manager. Back in those days, she was hot and Mike was only too happy to pass around Polaroids.

"Was she good looking ... before?"

"She was uglier than a bag full of assholes."

"You think she could have pulled that door open all by herself?"

"Well, I did until you mentioned it."

I punched up the security cameras and flipped around checking the store. "Aisles are clear," I said.

"What about the backroom?"

"Ain't got cameras back there, Vette."

"Margot always said there were cameras everywhere since management didn't trust the employees."

"Margot also said Clint Eastwood was her second husband."

"Just because she was crazy didn't mean she was wrong about everything."

"You go on believin' that. Meanwhile, I'll check out the backroom while you grab the Spam, Twinkies and chips."

"I think we're out of Spam."

"Already? Grab some vienna sausages or something then."

"Whatever. Give me your keys."

I looked at her. "Huh?"

"You heard me. Give me the damn car keys. If you get killed back there, I want to be able to get away."

"I ain't gonna get killed."

"You don't know that. Give me the keys."

"You watch too many scary videos."

"And they taught me that if I'm ever in a situation like this that I'd be an idiot not to get the keys from you. A zombie in a hockey mask could be back there with a butcher knife and I ain't gonna risk being stuck here if you die."

"Fine," I said and gave her the keys. "But don't you even think of leaving me here."

"Now there's an idea I can snuggle up with."

"Snuggle up with it all you want, just don't go home with it."

So we split up and while she gathered up the food, I went to the back to check things out.

As I pushed through the doors to the back room, I caught a whiff of something nasty. Made me think Edgar Dean had come back from the dead to break wind in the back room like in the old days. I swear, that man could clear a building in five seconds flat and you'd know it was him because of that shit-eatin' grin of his.

Thanks to Vette, images of zombies with butcher knives and hockey masks flashed in my head. I kept my pistol ready as I crept back there waving the flashlight around.

My flashlight didn't show me much back there and the generator only provided lighting on the sales floor. I edged along, trying not to breathe. I stumbled across a pallet with an open case of barbecue sauce. Well, it wasn't *real* barbecue sauce. It was that godawful fancified New York Gourmet Bar-B-Q crap that Earl and Mike were addicted to.

That might have accounted for the smell, actually, since there were a few open bottles. I didn't want to get close enough to find out. Stuff looked, smelled and tasted like three-day-old diarrhea. I tried it once at Mike's place and I about puked. Makes you wonder about some folks. I mean, here we were in the heart of barbecue country and they ate that nasty-ass shit. What were they thinking?

"Anybody back here?" I called.

No answer.

Over by the delivery docks, there were three doors. One was an emergency exit, the other two were roll up delivery doors.

The emergency exit was propped open by something. As I moved closer, the flashlight revealed a leg. I figured a zombie had fallen down, opening the door and got stuck, but as I drew even closer I saw that it was just the leg. There was no body to go with it. The leg was all decayed and it had a scuffed brown penny loafer on its foot.

I pushed the door open and kicked the leg outside. Then I poked my head out to check behind the store. Just a bunch of backhaul. Stacks of pallets. Bales. Milk crates. Empty racks from Frito Lay. And of course, the giant trash compactor.

The door to the compactor stood open and a man stood reaching into it. My first thought was that I'd come across a dumpster diver. We used to have those losers going through the trash to find rotten produce to eat. That was why we got the compactor. We could lock it up to keep the divers out.

The man tried to crawl inside.

"Hey!" I yelled.

The man hopped backward. He only had one leg. I guess he'd used the other to prop open the exit door.

"Uhhh!" he said holding up his bottle of New York Gourmet. His St. Josephs gown flapped in the breeze.

Great. Another damn zombie. And I was right about that smell.

I looked closer. "Mike?"

"Uhhh?" he asked.

"Yeah, it's me. Junior. You don't work here anymore, man."

"Uhhh!" he said.

"No you don't. The store is closed. And you ... well, hell, man, you're not even alive!"

"Uhh!" he said with some force.

"You're a zombie. I don't know what the deal is, Mike. Why are you here?"

He hopped toward me and landed on a piece of broken wood. It threw off his balance and he fell sideways. He tried to catch himself with his arm, but it broke off and skidded off to the right. The Bar-B-Q bottle shattered and spewed brown gunk on his severed arm. A huge rat raced out, sniffed at the arm with that nasty sauce on it, shook its head and scurried away without even a nibble.

"You okay, Mike?"

"Uhh!"

"Yeah, you lost your arm there. Does it hurt?"

"Uh."

"I didn't think so. See, you're a zombie. Tell you what, I'll go ahead and put you out of your misery." I moved a rock over to keep the door from closing since it couldn't be opened from outside—no handle—then I walked over and pointed the gun at his head.

"Uhh!" someone said behind me.

I spun around and saw Earl, the store manager standing in the exit door and wouldn't you know it, he had an open bottle of that New York Gourmet crap, too. He shambled outside and his foot knocked the rock away.

"Catch the door!" I said.

Too late. It slammed closed and now I was locked out. I could have opened one of the delivery doors, but Vette had my keys.

"Jesus, Earl. I thought you were dead, too. I guess you are dead, actually, but why are you guys up and about?"

"Uhh."

"I didn't catch that, Earl."

At that moment, Mike grabbed hold of my ankle. Zombies had one-track minds. Food. I knew he was fixing to take a bite out of my leg, so I shot him in the head. "Sorry, Mike." I turned back to Earl. "How many other employees have come back, Earl? You have them punching the clock?"

"Uhh." He walked toward me, arms outstretched like a monster in an old horror movie.

"No offense, but you ain't the manager here anymore." I didn't want to shoot anyone else since I was low on ammo. I pushed him aside and started to walk around the store to the front. I figured the front door would still open since the jamb was all jacked up.

Earl followed me. I looked at him, but kept walking. He was slow, so I left him behind in no time.

At the front of the store, a bunch of zombies kept walking into the front door and bouncing back. None of them were bright enough to pull it open.

I saw Vette peeking through a gap between boards on the window. Her eyes pleaded with me to help her.

"Got the food?" I called.

She pushed a box of Twinkies into view.

I pointed toward the front door.

She pointed behind me. I nodded and stepped forward avoiding Earl. Several zombies started toward us. They reached for Earl's Bar-B-Q sauce. He held it away from them and they started moaning. I motioned toward the door again and Vette disappeared from the window.

I didn't have my car keys, so I couldn't run the zombies over. I didn't want the zombies to see that the exit door opened outward, so I had to distract them while Vette escaped the store. I rushed over and grabbed the bottle of Bar-B-Q from Earl. He complained, but he was a zombie. What could he do?

I held up the bottle. "Hey there, folks! Anybody hungry?"

Most of them turned toward me. I upended the bottle letting the sauce glop out to splat like sewage on the ground. Unfortunately, I got some of that crap on my hand. I wiped it on my pants and made a face.

The zombies all said, "Uhhh" and started toward the mess.

I stepped backward and they fought each other trying to get some of that sauce. It was an awful sight watching grown men and women in various states of decay dropping to all fours to lick sauce off the pavement. Each of them wore tattered green hospital gowns that opened up to show their ass ends.

Vette pushed through the door and ran to the truck.

"Don't leave without me," I said.

Vette started the truck and rolled down the window. "We got problems, Junior. I was right. There's no Spam left in the store."

I hurried to the truck. "Did you snag a substitute like I told you?" The zombies moved toward us, so I tossed the empty bottle in their direction and they converged on it like flies to shit, which wasn't too far from the truth.

"All that's left is a bunch of Tuna and cans of Salmon. That ain't gonna make good barbecue. We need some kinda meat."

I looked back at the zombies. As they fought, pieces of rotten flesh flew all over the place. I smiled. "I think I got us covered, and it will solve two problems at once.

Them zombies are falling apart so much already, they ought to grind up pretty easy. Ned ought to forgive us for being so late if we bring plenty of good food. After all, a grill and enough sauce can make *anything* tasty."

Vette looked at the crowd of zombies. A smile stretched across her face, and she turned the truck to face the zombies. "Works for me," she said and stomped on the accelerator. "Tonight we'll bring Sloppy Joes."

Gary Jonas' work has appeared in numerous anthologies including Robert Bloch's *Psycos, Horrors! 365 Scary Stories, Fantastic, Murderous Intent,* and *Stories That Won't Make Your Parents Hurl*—just to name a few.

Gary says he once dated a girl who had the childhood nickname "Bubba", and he figures that gives him as much right to write about bubbas as the next guy.

CANDYLIGHT AND THE THREE BUBBAS
Laura J. Underwood

Once upon a time, in an old shack in the woods, there
lived three Bubbas.

In truth, their names were Hank, Chuck and Bill, and
they lived in the backwoods of Morgan County,
Tennessee. They spent all their time hunting and
fishing, and naturally, everything they caught, killed,
skinned and scaled, they threw on the grill with great
quantities of their favorite barbeque sauce and ate. It
was a good life, though Chuck sometimes wished they
had a TV set. But since there wasn't anything left on the
air to watch except for the Home Shopping Network and
the Public Television Station, he didn't say anything
about it more than once or twice a week.

Hank, the oldest and surliest of the Bubbas, was a
disabled veteran who fought in Desert Storm when he
was a teenager. Sometimes, he thought he saw Saddam
and a herd of camels in the trees, but this was generally
connected to the number of cans of Millers he had
consumed.

Chuck, the second of the Bubbas, was way too young
to have fought in Desert Storm, but he'd once had a wife
and a trailer over by Claxton in Anderson County. That
was before the Yuppie 25 Virus came and wiped out
most of civilization several years ago. His wife was a
computer programmer who worked at the Y-12 Plant
where they made nuclear waste. One day, she just
upped and went mad. Starting acting like a Yuppie,
getting all dressed out for work in power suits. Chuck
didn't mind this too much, until she tried to eat him...

literally. He lost two fingers and his favorite hound dog Blue, but he managed to get the hell out of Claxton before he could lose any other body parts.

And finally, there was Bill, the youngest and quietest of the Bubbas, and there were times Chuck hinted that maybe Bill should have been named Bruce cos he made real good biscuits. Of course, Chuck didn't suggest that too often since Bill owned the shack. Bill once had a wife as well, but she ran off with a Fuller Brush salesman just before the virus came. Bill had no idea if she survived, but he rather doubted it since she didn't like barbeque.

One crisp autumn day, Chuck gassed up the Chevy with methane and decided to take a trip over to Wartburg to see if there was still some Spam left on the shelves of Missus Tucker's General Store. He'd hardly been gone thirty minutes when Bill, making hushpuppies to go with the mess of catfish he caught that morning, heard the truck pull back up the gravel drive. Hank, who sat out on the porch nursing a Millers and shooting squirrels out of the hickory with a pellet gun, said aloud, "Will you look at that!"

Bill sauntered out on the porch, hands in his pockets, to see what had Hank so excited. Chuck was crawling out of the Chevy, and he wasn't alone. He ran around to the passenger side, giddy as a school boy let out for the summer, and pulled open the door. The first thing to slide into view was a pair of long legs, followed by firm hips, a slender waist and a pair of hooters that would have put Dolly Parton to shame. Atop this loveliness painted into tight designer jeans and a tank top that left little to the imagination sat a perky, sweet face, bewitching blue eyes, and a cascade of long blond curls caught back in a red bandana. She had lips the color of blood, and a lot of white teeth. Bill looked at her and felt a shiver of dread.

"Hi, ya'll," she said and waved a hand full of perfectly manicured nails painted a passionate crimson. "I'm Candylight..."

"Oh, I bet you can delight," Hank said and she giggled. The pellet gun came up and another squirrel hit the ground with a dusty *whump!*

Candylight clapped her hands. "Oh, you're good with that thing," she said cheerfully. "Here, I'll get that for you..."

With high heel mini-steps, she wriggled over to the hickory and with two dainty fingers, she picked up the squirrel by its tail.

"Just where in the hell did you find her?" Hank asked.

"Found her down the road a piece," Chuck said with a grin that made Bill think of a tomcat in heat. "She was walking along, so I offered her a lift. Being as she had no place in particular to go, I brought her back here..."

"She was just walking?" Bill asked suspiciously.

"Yep," Chuck said. "She tells me she'd run away from Sevierville. Her daddy got ate by the Yuppies..."

Bill frowned as he took in the high heels, the tight jeans, the tank top and a tan that seemed to occupy every inch of exposed flesh. "Just how did she get past Knoxville?" he asked. "I hear tell it's full of flesh-eating Yuppies these days..."

Candylight had reached the porch and tossed the squirrel down next to Hank, wiping her fingers on her jeans. "Oh, I hitched a ride with a nice trucker from Mobile," she said cheerfully. "Look, he even gave me a box of Twinkies cos he said I was the sweetest thing he'd laid eyes on in a long time..." She hopped back over to the truck and pulled out a corrugated box labeled "Hostess."

Hank's eyes lit up like the Fourth of July as she held it out for his inspection. "Twinkies," he said, salivating. "Too bad he didn't give you any Spam..."

"He didn't have any," she said. "Look, if you boys don't mind, I'd really like to freshen up a bit... and I have to tinkle..."

"The outhouse is out back," Bill said, jerking his thumb in the general direction.

A faint glimmer of disgust crossed her face, and Bill suspected he was the only one who saw it since Hank and Chuck were busy pawing through the box of Twinkies.

"Thanks," she said and started around the shack. "Chucky darling, would you fetch my backpack out of the truck, please?"

"Oh, sure," Chuck said and bolted for the truck as she disappeared.

"Hey, Chuck, think we could convince her to stay a while?" Hank asked as he tore open one of the Twinkies.

"And just where is she gonna sleep?" Bill asked.

"Oh, I don't think *that* will be a problem," Chuck said as he came back on the porch carrying a knapsack that clinked a bit. He elbowed Bill in the ribs. "First dibs!"

Bill rolled his eyes. It wasn't that he didn't miss having sex, and there were times he felt as horny as Chuck—who seemed to stay that way all the time—but this whole affair was starting to bother him.

Candylight eventually returned, looking smug and sweet. Bill went back to finishing his hushpuppies and frying that morning's batch of catfish on the woodstove. He watched Candylight from the corner of his eyes. She sat at the table with Chuck and Hank, and chattered away liked some little magpie.

She told them how the Yuppies came to their home and broke through the windows and doors, and how they ate her daddy, her momma and her two brothers. She had barely escaped through the woods and ran all night until she found the road and the trucker. He offered her a lift, but he wasn't going to Clay County where she had kin, so he let her off in Anderson, and she had been walking the road for days.

Chuck made sympathy noises, then offered her a beer, which she drank too quickly. Suddenly, she was all giggly. As Bill threw supper on the table, she reeled back and forth between Chuck and Hank, alternately teasing and tickling them.

Bill had just finished his meal when Candylight suddenly hopped up, ran around the table trying to avoid Chuck's clutches and plopped her tight ass right down on Bill's lap. He grunted and tried to push her off as she wiggled like an insane eel.

"Hmmm," she said after a moment. "This one's *too* soft..."

Hank choked on his Millers. Chuck winked and made smooches with his lips. Candylight tumbled out of Bill's lap and staggered around to Hank. His eyes bugged in their sockets and an idiot grin spread across his craggy face as she fell into his lap and started her little dance again.

"Well, not hard enough," Candylight said, then kissed Hank on the nose and hopped out of his lap.

"Hey, give me a minute!" Hank said. "I'm an old man with a war wound..."

"And very tender," she said, tweaking his cheek. "I likes 'em tender..."

Chuck guffawed and reached over to punch Bill in the arm. Then Chuck pushed back his chair and patted his lap. "Come on over here, sugar..." he said. "I'll give you something hard..."

Candylight twittered and practically threw herself on Chuck, straddling his lap and planting a big kiss that included a lot of tongue. Hank continued to laugh. Bill felt downright disgusted. When Candylight stopped kissing Chuck, she pulled back. The gleam of a predator filled her blue eyes.

"Now that's what I call just right," she said and started to unbutton Chuck's shirt. "Come on," she whispered, "Let's go outside someplace more private...."

She slid seductively off his lap. Chuck followed like a lamb, grabbing a couple of the beers and a blanket. Candylight seized up her backpack and smiled as she followed Chuck to the door. She cast a coy look at Hank. "Keep working on it, old man, cos you're next," she said and blew him a kiss.

Chuck caught her around the middle. "Don't be dawdling, woman," he said. "Besides, there might not be enough of you left when I get done..." He wagged his brows. Candylight squealed as the two of them whirled out into the night.

"I don't like this," Bill said in the wake of the silence that filled the shack.

Hank flapped a hand in dismissal. "Hey, just because you were *too soft*," he said.

Bill crossed his arms in anger. That had nothing to do with it. She was attractive, but there was something too phony about her that set him ill at ease. Too manicured for Bill's taste. Granted his wife Alice used to tell him that he didn't have any taste if it wasn't beer or barbeque.

Bill sighed and crawled out of his chair, collecting dishes and throwing them in the makeshift sink. Through the window, he could hear the high-pitched giggles and the guttural chuckles of the two as they made their way through the woods, heading down to the river. *Oh, Jesus, Chuck, don't take her to the bend!* Bill groused. That was his favorite fishing spot, and he'd be hard pressed to concentrate on his angling if he knew Chuck had been humping that woman down on the banks. Bill could almost imagine finding her butt imprint in the sandy clay of the shore, and every time the river swelled and retreated, those imprints would become twin pools of muddy water...

Whunk!

Bill paused from the dishes. That had sounded just like a hollow lead pipe popping a skull. He'd heard the same sound when his grampa once hit a mule between the ears with a truck axle.

"You hear something?" Bill asked.

"Hear what?" Hank said and ripped open another Twinkie. "I don't hear nothing..."

Neither did Bill now. Night birds and crickets and the distant song of the river rolling down towards Wartburg. But no giggles or coos or laughs or growls. It stayed that way as Bill finished the dishes.

"Something is wrong," he muttered.

"Oh, come on, what's got you all nervous as a cat," Hank said. Half a dozen Twinkie wrappers littered the floor at his feet.

"That woman," Bill said. "She just ain't right..."

"I'm starting to think Chuck was right when he said you didn't like women," Hank said.

"Hey, I like women just fine," Bill said. Hell, sometimes, he even missed his wife. "But that woman gives me the willies..."

"So how come you can't get your willie up for her?" Hank scoffed.

Bill gnashed his teeth and headed over to his cot. *You stupid old son of a bitch,* he thought. *You're blinded by her Twinkies!* He plopped down on the edge and leaned over so he could reach under and pull out his compound bow.

"And just what in the hell are you gonna do with that?" Hank said.

"Depends," Bill said. "Don't hurt to be cautious. And if Chuck doesn't come back soon..."

"Well, now, he might be out there for a while," Hank said and wagged his brows.

"We're talking about Chuck," Bill said. "Mr. Pop His Cork at the sight of an underwear ad in the Sears catalog."

Hank frowned. "Yeah, well at least he can pop it... and so can I, so even if he does finish quick, that just means I'm gonna be in quicker than a...."

The clatter of high heels on the path silenced them. The door of the shack burst open, and Candylight stumbled though. She was dirty, disheveled and wet.

"Oh, Hank, come quickly," she said in a desperate voice. "Chuck went down river to take a pee, and he hasn't come back, and now I can't find him..."

"Maybe he's passing a stone or taking a dump," Hank said.

"Oh, please Hank, I'm so scared," she said. "What if he fell in the river... what if Yuppies got him?"

"There can't be no Yuppies around here," Bill said, and for a moment, Candylight looked as though she might refute him. She blinked her eyes, and tears came tumbling down her cheeks, ruining her mascara.

"Please, Hank. Come help me find him," she begged once more.

"Oh, all right," Hank groused as he crawled out of his chair and reached for his old shotgun in the corner. "But if he's taking a dump, you're mine, okay?"

Candylight nodded, waiting for him at the door, her baby blues swimming. Hank sauntered out, carrying a flashlight in one hand and the gun in the other. Candylight shot a look back at Bill... just a flicker of a predator's smile, then followed Hank out into the woods.

Bill stayed where he was, counting his own breaths. He could hear Hank calling for Chuck and Candylight echoing the cry. They moved towards the river, then faintly, Bill heard a curse, followed by another "whunk!"

Then silence.

Bill scrambled to his feet, clutching the bow and his arrows. He hit the door at a run. He knew the path to the river like the back of his hand, but rather than follow it, he stepped off into the woods. Bill had hunted enough deer to know how to move silently through the autumn undergrowth even in the dark.

Up ahead, the river's clatter did not hide the voice now speaking at a cultured clip. "Yes, you might as well come on up with the SUV. I've killed two, and one is already dressed for the freezer. I'm going to have to wash this second one in the river before I dress him. God, I don't think this man has had a bath in a couple of years."

Bill hid by the old pine and peered around the trunk towards the riverbank. The flashlight that Hank had carried now lay in the mud, throwing a wide beam of light across his face. Hank's eyes stared from beneath the cowl of blood springing from his caved-in skull. Beyond him, dangling from the limbs of a tree like a field-dressed deer was Chuck. And between them stood Candylight with a bloody pipe in one hand and a cell phone in the other.

"There's only one more little pig left to be slaughtered, darling, and then we can go home," Candylight said. "Yes, dear, I think we'll have more than enough meat from these three for the party this weekend. I know this is an important affair, Charles. Your boss and half his staff will be there. That's why we need to get these carcasses back to Knoxville as soon as possible. I'll probably have to marinate them in merlot for the rest of the week just to kill the gamy flavor. These backwoods Bubbas sometimes have a nasty taste. All right, dear, but I'm telling you right now, the next time, you can stand on the road and I'll drive. I'm going to be feeling the first ones hands on my backside for weeks... No, we didn't get that far. Now be a love and tell Mindy that Mommie loves her and I'll give her a goodnight kiss later... Love you too. Bye, dear."

Candylight folded the phone with a click. She slipped it into the backpack, and in the light of the flashlight, Bill saw that the handles of several wicked chef knives protruded. Candylight pulled one out and squatted over Hank to slit his shirt.

"You Yuppie bitch," Bill muttered and nocked an arrow on the compound bow. He drew the fletching to his cheek, and used the sights to zero in on her neck.

And fired.

She apparently heard the twang of the bowstring, because she jerked around, then twisted to dodge the arrow. It caught at an angle on her collarbone. Shrieking madly, she rose and tried to jerk the arrow out of her skin with one hand. Bill quickly pulled another broad head from the quiver and set the nock to the string.

Candylight suddenly came at him like a demented fury. The broken shaft of the first broad head bobbed up and down in her chest. She was close before Bill knew it, moving with pain-maddened speed. Before he could even release his arrow, her knife slashed across and severed the top string. There was a twang as the tension broke at angles, sending his second broad head flipping back. Bill felt the steel nick his cheek. Minor pain compared to what he would feel if he didn't moved. That knife was heading straight for his heart.

"You little bastard, you stinking little bastard!" Candylight screamed. "You have ruined my neck!"

Bill ignored the rant and focused on just dropping out of harm's way. He snatched up the bow and flung it at her face, then ran for the woods. Silence was not his friend, but distance was. Candylight came crashing after him, shrieking at the top of her lungs.

He made it into the shack, shutting the door in her face. The blade of her chef's knife penetrated the wood by several inches. Bill threw the bolt and backed away. Outside, Candylight screamed and battered at the walls.

"You bastard, there's no place to run!" she screamed in a demented voice. "You just wait until Charles gets here!"

Bill stood in the center of the shack, feeling like a trapped rabbit. He couldn't wait. Candylight was bad enough. Charles was probably worse to deal with face to face. As for the two of them together, he doubted he would have a chance. Damn, he should have paid attention to his own instincts. He should have tried to poison her... or blow her away...

His eyes darted about the cabin in search of a weapon. There wasn't much ammo left these days. Hank refrained from actually firing that .12 gauge too often. The pellets he used on the squirrels were scavenged from their peppered flesh. Chuck had a pistol somewhere, but the .38 no longer had bullets. Bill had learned to use the bow because one could always reclaim arrows, or make new ones. But his compound now lacked a string...

The window over the sink suddenly shattered as Candylight threw a rock through it, and now she used a log from their winter wood to clear the debris. "You might as well give up, meat boy, because there's no place left to run," she said. Her blonde locks flew like Medusa's snakes around her face. With a snarl, she heaved herself through the broken window, quick as a cat. Bill ran for the door. He barely got the bolt undone and threw himself outside before she lurched across the room. He held the outer handle for dear life as she screamed and jerked from inside the door, and waited until he felt a good hard tug before he let go. The door whacked her in the nose. Blood spurted as she was knocked on her rump.

Bill ran, this time heading for the river by the path. Behind him, Candylight filled the night with throaty screams of rage, almost drowning the mute purr of a Nissan Pathfinder spitting gravel from under its tires.

Oh, hell, Charles was here! That thought spurred Bill to go faster.

At the bank of the river, Bill snatched up the flashlight and scanned the clay soil until he saw the gun Hank had carried. Grabbing it up, he popped open the chamber. One cartridge...

Candylight shrieked as she exploded out of the woods and ran at Bill. He swung the .12 gauge around and pulled the trigger. The close range of scattershot put a hole in Candylight's chest big enough to contain a man's fist. The force threw her back and dropped her at the edge of the woods. She hit the ground and did not move.

"Maureen?" a man's voice called from the woods. "Maureen, darling, where are you?"

"Oh, shit," Bill said and backed off, raising the gun as a tall, willowy man in a nice suit rushed into the clearing. He stumbled over the corpse and cursed.

"Maureen!" he cried and suddenly flung himself down at Candylight's side. "Damn it, Maureen! You should have waited for me!"

He pulled her close, but she was a rag doll in his grasp. His gaze flashed over to where Bill stood holding the empty gun.

"You... you killed my wife," Charles said. "Why?"

"Hey, it was her or me!" Bill said. "Just look at what she did to Hank and Chuck..."

The Yuppie cast his watery gaze on the corpses. "Yes, well, Maureen does get a little vicious when we have an important dinner party... but then... *so do I!*"

Charles dropped his dead wife and charged. Bill slammed across with the butt of the shotgun, catching Charles in the nose. The Yuppie fell down, smearing blood across his face with his sleeve. "Damn you, this is an Armani and it's ruined! I'll never get the stains out, you low-life animal..."

He lunged from the ground, grabbing Bill's leg and sinking teeth into his thigh. Bill tumbled backwards, reaching for anything that would make a good weapon. His hand found the lead pipe. With a cry, he brought it down on Charles' head with every ounce of strength he could muster. Brains and bone splattered. Charles died with his teeth still locked in Bill's thigh.

It took Bill some effort to finally break free, and his leg wound was pretty bad. The blood loss made him ill and light-headed, but he managed to stagger back up the path. He reached the drive and nearly tumbled, catching himself on the hood of a pretty sky-blue SUV with a luggage rack. Bill sighed and opened the door to see if there was a first aid kit he could use to bind his wounded leg.

A small head of long blonde curls rose from the passenger seat, and a sleepy-eyed cherub of a five-year-old girl rubbed her eyes. She looked at Bill and smiled.

"Oh, shit, a kid," Bill said and closed his eyes.

And opened them just as the precious little goldenlocks lunged for his throat.

Once upon a time, there was an adorable little Yuppie who lived alone in a shack in the woods, eating her Mommy and Daddy and the three Bubbas to survive...

But that's a whole 'nuther story.

Laura J. Underwood is the author of numerous short stories in the field of fantastic fiction, which have appeared regularly in such publications as *Marion Zimmer Bradley's FANTASY Magazine,* SWORD AND SORCERESS, *Adventures of Sword & Sorcery, Dark Regions,* SUCH A PRETTY FACE, CATFANTASTIC, and many others. Laura's chapbook, *Bogie Woods,* was released by Yard Dog Press in March of 2001, and YDP will be releasing her novel based on the characters from *Bogie Woods* early in 2002.

Laura is a born and raised East Tennessean who has found much inspiration while hiking her native mountains as well as from her travels through England and Scotland. By day, she is a librarian, and her fields of expertise range from Scottish folklore and fencing (she made a recent appearance at WorldCon as a SFWA Musketeer) to playing harp. She is, in fact, the owner of the original Glynnanis who has appeared in a number of her Harper Mage tales. For information concerning her recent publications, visit her website at http://www.sff.net/people/keltora.

A lifetime of residence in Tennesse more than explains her knowledge in the field of Bubbatology.

BUBBAS VS. SLIME DEVILS

James S. Dorr

"Hal-l-o-o-o—weenie!" Bobby Joe called out from the roof of his 80x17. "I ever tell you boys the joke about how come warlocks can't have no children?"

Jethro looked up from where he was packing the beer into ice in his own kids' old wading pool. "Can't say you have," he said, though the truth was that Bobby Joe had told that old creaker every year from at least since the last time a Southerner was president.

"It's 'cause they got *hollow weenies*," Bobby Joe called down. Then he cursed some, because he'd just mashed his thumb with the pliers he'd been using to try to adjust his TV antenna.

Lynette popped out then. "You hold down that language, you hear?" she said. "Ain't no reason to carry on that way, even if John Boy and Earl and the others are down to town doing their trick-or-treating. So how you coming there?"

Bobby Joe looked sheepish as best one could tell, what with the sun being nearly down and all—which was a good thing when you figure we were fixing to have us a Halloween party, which are traditionally held after dark. Lynette had confessed she hoped the kids would bring back something good from the yuppie part of town, down past the hollow, where she'd sent them to do their kid thing, looking all cute and waif-like, like little Draculas and witches and zombies, all big-eyed and hungry like.

Then Caleb called out—speaking of zombies. "Hey Bobby Joe!"

145

"Yeah, Caleb?"

"Thought it was zombies had the hollow weenies. You know, like they're all rotted out and such. Comes from their being dead."

"You hush up, too, Caleb," Lynette said as she flounced back inside, letting the screen door slam behind her. "It's not as if I don't have things to get ready, too …"

"You got the Twinkies, Bro?" That was Lester's voice, down around the other side of his and Cindy Lou's trailer, kind of on the outskirts of the trailer park out past the wash house. "You know, in case the yuppies' kids come up *here*."

That got everyone laughing. The city folk—Yankees, most of them—generally avoided good old boys like us. Shoot, most of them just hung around their computers and didn't hardly go out at all, geeks and geekettes mostly. They certainly wouldn't let their *kids* come up here, those that even had kids, not without supervision and stuff like that. Even at that they'd probably take anything their kids collected down to the sheriff to run through his radar, whatever it is they use to make sure there's nothing *inside* the stuff that shouldn't be inside. They even had a program about that once on the TV.

Except that was why Bobby Joe was up on the roof of his trailer, his being the only working big-screen TV in the whole park these days and, even at that, for the last week or two there'd been something wrong with the reception.

But right then, Bobby Joe must have been still thinking on what Caleb had said to him. "Nope," he finally said. "Don't think it's zombies. In fact I'm sure the way I heard it it's warlocks got the hollow weenies. I got to admit, though, Caleb, you make a good argument."

"Maybe it's warlocks and zombies both," Caleb said. "Anyhow, I sure ain't heard of no *zombies* having kids, either."

"Who'd want to *do* it with zombies anyway?" Lester called out.

"You hush up," Lynette's voice echoed from inside.

"Maybe it's Slime Devils," Jethro suggested.

That got Bobby Joe mad.

"You hush about Slime Devils. *The Invasion of the Slime Devils* is one of the finest movies ever made, don't you forget that. And if I can get this antenna adjusted, it's going to be right on our local TV here, at a special midnight showing—they announced it in the Supermarket Shopper a week or more ago, last time Lynette was down to the Piggly Wiggly—so if you want to watch it with the rest of us ..."

Then Lester called out again, but this time his voice was all serious. "Bobby Joe," he yelled, "look out here, down the slope a ways. You see—where the lights are just coming on over there? What do you make of that?"

Some of the rest of us looked out too, though without as good a view as Bobby Joe's. Nonetheless, those that were closest reacted.

"For God's sake," Caleb said. "Get the womenfolk inside!"

"We're inside already," Lynette's voice drifted back.

"Then *stay* inside, and close the storm door, too. The rest of you women, too. Jethro, you get your shotgun loaded."

"Can't rightly do that. You know I've been cleaning it."

"What is it you guys *see*?" I piped in with that one.

Caleb answered first. "Zombies," he yelled. "Zombies—and maybe some warlocks, too –just like in that movie, the one about living dead."

"Ain't no such thing as zombies," Jethro said. "That's just in stories. Ain't that right, Bobby Joe?"

147

Bobby Joe had been silent up to then, but now he screamed at the top of his lungs, *"Slime Devils!* Just *like* in the movie—you'd see for yourselves later on tonight if I could just get this thing adjusted. But this isn't a movie. They're coming up the hill, just like Lester says, sort of shambling and shuffling. Caleb's right, keep all the womenfolk inside, and, guys, you climb up, like I am, up on the roofs here where we can all watch 'em—make sure they don't try anything funny. Maybe that way they won't notice we're up here."

"Ain't much light here, Bobby Joe," Jethro answered, "to see if they're doing much of *anything*." But Jethro, even as he protested, had already scrambled up to the top of his trailer as well and was hugging onto its roof so hard that afterwards, when it was all over, Caleb swore he could see Jethro's thumbprints permanently stamped in the aluminum.

"To see they ain't molesting our womenfolk," Caleb shouted back, he, like the rest of us, having made roof level in what must have been Olympic record time. If they *keep* records on stuff like that—you know, practical things, and not those fairy sports nobody *really* does, like with those little sleds in the winter, or somersaults and stuff.

But anyhow, Caleb was up with the rest of us, me having got up the fastest of all, except now he also remembered about the beer.

"Jethro... ?" he began.

Jethro looked down, as did we others, first to the wading pool filled with ice, with at least two cases of long necks buried under it. Then we turned our gaze toward the wash house and where Lester's trailer was, where the zombie-warlock-Slime Devils, whatever it was they really were, were already milling around in circles, hundreds of them at least, some of them pressing on further into the park.

"Well...," Caleb went on.

"Don't look at me," Jethro said, "not with them *things* there. Anyway, when Bobby Joe shouted for us to all climb up, he didn't say anything about me bringing the beer up with me."

"You pipe down, all of you," Bobby Joe broke in. "Thing is, we got to make us some plans now. We're being invaded by genuine Slime Devils, just like in the movie, except in the movie they brought in the Army while—unless you paid your phone bill recently, Caleb—we're going to be on our own."

"I brought the Twinkies up," Lester said, hopefully. "I can toss some over in case anyone gets hungry."

By then the Slime Devils had spread all through the park, fast and relentless, sort of like kudzu on a warm, sunny day. Except this was nighttime and, what with it being the end of October and all, it was more kind of pleasantly cool—a nice night to party and dip in those long necks except, of course, we were being invaded—and, unlike kudzu, these Slime Devils seemed to stick to ground level, not trying to climb up or even, for that matter, to bash the doors in of the trailers to get at our womenfolk. It was, in fact, almost like Bobby Joe said, that maybe they didn't notice us yet.

It was as if maybe they were just confused and, in fact, as they came closer, some of them shambling right under the trailer lights, some of them almost looked a bit familiar.

It was Caleb who noticed it first. "You know," he said, "some of these Slime Devils look just like yuppies. The geek kind, I mean. All pale and buggy-eyed from their computer screens. Smelling like ... well, you know. Crazed-looking, tongues hanging out like they *want* something ..."

That was when one of the Slime Devils whispered: "Meat." Others took up the chant, slow and low-voiced, but nonetheless with a certain persistency: "Treats for us. Human flesh!" Except they still milled around, as if they hadn't figured out yet where to look to find it.

"Well, now you done it," Bobby Joe said then. "Caleb, why'd you have to go and start talking? They *was* ignoring us ..."

That's when the nearest of the Slime Devils turned and looked up toward Bobby Joe's trailer's roof.

"Meat," one repeated. "Up above, in the sky. Human flesh. Up *there*."

"Hey!" That was Lester's voice. "Hey fellas, think maybe they'd like some Twinkies?" He started to toss handfuls in the direction of us others on the roofs, most of them close enough that we could catch them, but some falling to the ground. Some fell into the Slime Devils' midst, where the nearest ones grabbed them—exept that their fellows tried to grab them, too.

"Meat!"

"Fingers!"

"Long, fat toes!"

"Plump and marrow-filled, tender and juicy."

The Slime Devils began fighting over the Twinkies. The light was poor—unwrapped they *did* look a little like fingers. Fat, juicy fingers.

Lester and Caleb threw more into the milling Slime Devils, starting new knots of fighting here and there. Then Caleb had another idea.

"You know, fellas, if we could throw these just right, to draw them away from the ice and stuff down there, maybe then Jethro could scramble down real fast and rescue our beer ..."

But that was when Lester shouted again, his voice rising real squeaky-like in panic: "More monsters! Reinforcements from down the hill. Coming our way, too. Doom! Destruction!"

Bobby Joe shouted back. "You mean more Slime Devils?"

"Even worse," Lester yelled. "Vampires and witches! Frankenstein monsters and big, round-eyed zombies ..."

"It's our own *kids*, stupid," Lynette's voice answered, drifting out from her chrome-trimmed double-wide, its storm door still locked tight.

But the Slime Devils had heard Lester, too. They started to back away.

"Zombies," one whispered.

"Not good to eat. Not fresh, like human meat."

Now the Slime Devils were shouting themselves, drowning out even Lester's panicked voice.

"Zombies eat *our* flesh. And Draculas drink our blood!"

"It's on the Internet—witches and vampires!"

"Then we must *flee.*"

Thus, as quickly as it had begun, the invasion of the Slime Devils ended. The final remnants disappeared down the hill, circling, oddly enough, back around toward town where the yuppies lived, where our own kids had gone for their trick-or-treating. But now our kids were back—Lynnette was right!—their costumes glowing luminous in the dark, their zombie-eyes black and fake-gore encrusted, their vampire fangs dripping red food-color blood. But their treat bags still empty.

"It was like a ghost town," John Boy said. "No one was home at all."

"Yeah," Earl added. "We knocked on their doors. We even soaped up some of their windows, but nobody even yelled at us to go away. It was like maybe something had *happened*—something terrible, maybe, that we didn't know about ..."

Bobby Joe chuckled, finally back down on the ground with the rest of us. "Nah," he said. "They're probably just off somewhere having a party. Just like we're going to have ourselves, right fellas?"

"Darn right," Lester said. "I've even got more Twinkies."

"And we're getting the barbecue started up," Cindy Lou added, standing beside him. "We got delayed a little with, you know, all that excitement, but we womenfolk have it under control now. Isn't that right, Lynette?"

Lynette nodded, while Jethro reclaimed his post by the wading pool, pouring in a new bag of cracked ice into the water and ice that was already there, miraculously undisturbed, considering. "Ain't exactly a washtub," he called out, "but it ought to do us. Anyone ready for bobbing for long necks?"

'Course the kids had Cokes. Even if Earl was nearly thirteen, and they *had* saved the day—Lynnette drew the line there. But even if they hadn't brought treats from town, they shared in the barbecue when Cindy Lou finally had it just perfect, and, it being Halloween, they got to stay up past their bedtimes as well. But then, at midnight, the hour of witching, John Boy asked Bobby Joe: "You going to bring your TV out for that *Slime Devil* movie? The one you've been talking about so much these past two weeks?"

Bobby Joe shook his head. "Never *did* get that antenna fixed quite right." But then his face brightened, as if a sudden thought had come to him. "Anyway, we had enough of Slime Devils ..."

That's when Lynette kicked him. "Ain't no use scaring the kids, Bobby Joe," she said.

Bobby Joe nodded. "Guess there ain't, Lynette. Anyway, maybe they'll show that movie again next Halloween. Like they did last year. But you know the one thing that's *real* funny? I'd been working to adjust that antenna practically all afternoon and nothing I could do brought in *anything*—almost as if the TV stations, for some weird reason, just stopped broadcasting."

James S. Dorr's book, *Strange Mistresses: Tales of Wonder and Romance*, is a 2001 release from Dark

Regions Press, while other work has appeared/will appear this year in the anthologies *Children of Cthulhu, The Darker Side, Bloodtype,* and *Tales from the Teeth Park* (England), as well as such magazines as *Fantastic Stories* and *Carpe Noctem.* He is past Anthony (mystery) and Darrell (stories set in the U.S. Mid-South) nominee, winner of the Best of the Web 1998 award, and has been listed in "Honorable Mentions" in *The Year's Best Fantasy and Horror* for eight of the past nine years.

Ah, alas, poor Mr. Dorr! An intellectual with the soul of a Bubba. Perhaps someday modern science will find a way to help him, but hopefully not before he writes many more pieces of fine Bubba fiction.

THE WIZARD OF BEER
Mark Fewell

Everybody knew that the Wizard had a knack for brewing beer. Because of this, the Yuppies didn't try to eat the people in the Munchkin Village Estates. If the people there hadn't supplied the Yuppies with alcohol, they'd have all been supper by now.

It's no wonder Danny Gale was pissed when he found Jim Bob asleep at his post; his shotgun lying on the floor where it had fallen. The old man was supposed to be guarding the Wizard and his stills, not doing his imitation of a large chain saw. Danny looked around, hoping to spot the Wizard, but he was nowhere in sight.

Danny sneaked up to Jim Bob, watching the ground as he moved. He wanted to be sure Jim Bob wasn't sawing logs because he had lowered the Wizard's production. He put his face close to the other man's and coughed, but not because he smelled like alcohol. Smelled more like Jim Bob had died.

Danny took a step forward and slapped Jim Bob upside the head.

"What?" Jim Bob jerked, reaching for his shotgun.

Danny kicked it out of the way, too early in the morning to have a hole blown through one's middle. "Where's the Wizard?"

Jim Bob hopped to his feet and searched the area, his right hand over his face, shielding his eyes from the sun. "I don' see him."

"Of course, you don' see him. You been sleepin'. On guard duty!"

"You ain't gonna shoot me, are ya?"

155

"Nah. Leastwise not yet. I'll be needin' yer help to find the Wizard."

But the wizard was long gone. The Yuppies hadn't even tried to hide their trail, as if they were teasing them with the knowledge that they had the Wizard.

"Looks like we're gonna hafta call all the families together," said Danny. "You go tell everybody ta meet at my place."

"You ain't gonna let them hurt me, are ya?"

"I should let them string ya up, but we'll probably need all the help we can get ifin we hafta fight the Yuppies. Ya ever fight Yuppies, Jim Bob?"

"Can't say that I have."

"Me neither, but my grandpappy fought them right after the virus first hit. Came right out of their office buildings looking for human flesh, all hungry and crazy like."

There are three rows of twelve, eleven, and ten trailers apiece in the Munchkin Village Estates. Danny lived at Lot No. 1 at the start of Row No. 1, the only double-wide in the park. He was proud.

Danny claimed the largest trailer since his grandpappy had been managing the place when the Yuppie 25 virus broke out and changed the world.

It was the first time Danny had called all the people together, and they all huddled uncomfortably around his porch.

Danny got right to the point. "The Yuppies have taken the Wizard."

Everybody started shouting questions at Danny. He yelled and slung his hands around, waiting for silence. "I'll tell you what we're gonna do. We're—"

"Ta hell with what we're gonna do. Who let them take the Wizard in the first damn place! Weren't anybody watchin' the still?" somebody yelled from the back of the crowd.

Danny tried to see who it was. He had been afraid this would happen. "Jim Bob—"

"Kill Jim Bob!" someone screamed.

"He let the Yuppies take the Wizard!" added another.

"Traitor!" shouted yet another.

Jim Bob jumped behind Danny.

"Hold on, jus' one minute. I'll have ya know Jim Bob did all he could ta stop them Yuppies. Why, we're lucky they didn't take Jim Bob, too." Danny was beginning to regret that he told Jim Bob he would protect him. Fact is Danny wouldn't have minded seeing Jim Bob strung up. They needed the Wizard. No one needed Jim Bob.

"What we gonna do 'bout the Wizard?" asked Luke Sizemore, a big, dumb guy who spent too much time asking dumbass questions. Of course, this one seemed right on target.

"Yea," the crowd said as a whole.

"We're gonna get him back."

Everybody started screaming. "Yahoo! All right!" A few started heading for their trailers to arm themselves for battle.

"Wait one minute!" Danny said. "We can't all go north and start a war with the Yuppies."

"How we gonna get the Wizard back then?" Luke asked.

"We gonna sneak up there and take the Wizard back guerilla warfare-like," Danny said. "I needs three volunteers."

Jim Bob whispered into Danny's ear. "You gotta take me. Ifin ya leave me here, they'll kill me."

"I can't do that. One of the Yuppies might recognize ya," Danny answered in a whisper.

Most everyone volunteered. The hardest part was choosing three competent enough to get the job done.

The three volunteers met at Danny's trailer the very next night. They wanted to get the Wizard back as quick as possible. Jim Bob redeemed himself by scouting out the homes of the Yuppies and finding out where the biggest cocktail party would be held that night.

They had determined that two couples would have the best chance of infiltrating the Yuppies' clan. Luke Sizemore and his wife Mary had volunteered. Folks said Mary was so cold to Luke, she must be heartless. Danny had chosen Angela Johnson to come with them as she was the only single woman in the Estates. Angela didn't like sleeping alone, and she wasn't very particular or careful, so of course she had a bunch of kids who didn't know who their daddies were.

Since they knew how the Yuppies dressed, the four of them slipped into a house where the family had died of the virus and found suitable clothing. After donning their disguises, they followed Yellowbrick Road into Emerald City.

The outside of the house was lit with Tekki torches. A few people stood around the pool, talking about trading stocks and their latest computer upgrades. They definitely weren't in the Munchkin Village Estates anymore.

It seemed silly to Danny. Even Luke and Jim Bob knew you needed electric to run a computer. The rumors of electric being restored had made it to the Estates, but Emerald City still had no power.

A tall, balding man wearing a tuxedo walked up to them. He carried a large tray containing pieces of meat stuck on toothpicks. "Would you like an appetizer before the main course?"

"I sure would!" Luke plopped the food into his mouth.

Mary gasped. Danny had to resist the impulse to slap Luke's hand away from the food, and blow the mission then and there.

"Don't you know what Yuppies eat?" Mary whispered to her husband as the butler had walked away. "I swear, ya ain't got a brain in your head!"

Luke started to gag, hoping to force the meat back up his throat.

"Stop it," Danny ordered. "You'll blow our cover."

"I wonder what the main course is," Angela said, making a face.

"That would be virgin breast." All four Wizard-seekers turned to see who had spoken. "Taken from a tender young morsel, of course."

The man smiled, and they could see all of his teeth. His long pointy nose had a wart on the end of it. "I'm W. W. West of Flyingmonkeys.com, the host of this party, and I don't believe I know any of you. Of course, this is the biggest, most glamorous party we've had in town for quite a while."

Angela slipped her hand into the man's and batted her eyelashes. "Yes, it is. Why don't you introduce me to the rest of your guests?" The others were impressed by her easy use of Yuppie talk. It made them wonder who else she had been sleeping with.

Angela and the host moved away from the others.

"What do we do now?" Luke said.

"We separate and mingle," Danny suggested. "Ask some questions, but try not to be too obvious."

"We can do that. I can talk jus' like them."

"I'll do my best to keep 'im outta trouble." Mary grabbed her husband's hand and dragged him inside.

Danny followed them into the house and walked over to a group of well-dressed men holding beer mugs. It appeared that would be his best chance of learning the Wizard's whereabouts.

One of them saw him approaching and turned to face him. "What do you think? Should I put my money into AT&T stock?"

"Well," said Danny. *How do I get outta this without 'em knowin' I'm not one of 'em? I have no idear what they're talkin' 'bout.* Danny shook his head.

"Yeah, you're right," the man said. "Nobody talks on the phone anymore. When was the last time you called anyone or had anyone call you?"

"I don't remember," Danny shrugged.

"That's exactly what I mean. Nobody uses the phone. Much cheaper to E-mail. Though I don't get much of that either."

"That's for sure," one of the other men said.

The conversation drifted to talk about money market accounts and certificates of deposit. Danny nodded his head and pretended he knew what they were talking about.

Eventually a beer found its way into his hand. He took a swallow and recognized it as the Wizard's special stock. *Have the Yuppies already put the Wizard ta work, or is this somethin' they had put away?* Danny wished he knew more about beer making. He couldn't stop himself from belching and almost blew his cover.

All the other men stared at him. "Sorry," he said with a shrug. He swallowed hard and tried to talk their talk. "Where do you get such good beer?"

One of the men put his arm around Danny's shoulders. "All you have to do is follow me. I'm Charles Michael Gray III. Charles to my friends." Charles guided Danny towards the door, and they left the party.

They walked ten blocks over weed-infested streets. They approached a large brick building, and Danny saw the words COUNTY JAIL printed on the side. "You keep your beer maker in the jail?"

"It's the safest place in town. Do you know of a better place to protect him?"

"I can't say that I do," Danny said.

Charles moved up to the building and held the door open.

Danny stepped into the jail. He found that someone had kept the furniture dusted and the floor swept.

Charles walked by him without saying a word. Danny followed him into an elevator that took them up three floors, so apparently they had at least figured out how to get power here—perhaps a generator. When the elevator doors opened, he found himself walking through one of the jail's cell blocks.

Angela, Luke, and Mary sat on the floor of the last cell. They all stood when they saw Charles and Danny approaching. A sheet had been taken off one of the two bunks and taped to the ceiling, hiding the toilet for privacy. The Wizard peeked his small balding head out from behind it. "I see they got you, too."

Charles pointed a gun at Danny. "Well, well, well. I didn't think you fit in, but I couldn't be entirely sure. It's nice of your friend here to point out you're one of them, and not one of us."

"Don't pay any attention to the man behind the curtain," Danny said. "I've never seen 'im before in my life."

Charles ignored him and spoke to the prisoners. "All of you against the back wall with your noses touching bricks. I don't want anybody playing hero." After everybody in the cell did as he had commanded, he reached into his pocket with his free hand and unlocked the door, never taking his gun or his eyes off Danny. He motioned with the gun for Danny to enter the cell.

Danny turned around when he heard the door clang shut. He watched Charles vanish down the corridor before addressing the others. "I know how I ended up here, and I got me a good idear how the Wizard got here, but how 'bout the rest of y'all?"

"I know how they brought me here," said Angela, "but I have no idear how they figgered I weren't no Yuppie."

If she were a'trembling at the party the way she's doing now, no wonder they figgered 'er out, thought Danny.

"It's not my fault," said Luke. "This guy said that some Bark guy was the greatest musician what ever lived, and I had to let him know this guy couldn't be gooder than Elvis."

"I'm sure the guy meant Bach," said the Wizard. It didn't surprise anybody that Wizard knew who the Yuppie meant; everybody knew the Wizard was a genius.

"I don't care what the fella's name is. Bark or Bach. He can't be gooder than Elvis."

"I tried keepin' 'im out of trouble," said Mary with a sigh.

"Does anybody have any idear how we're gonna get outta here?" said Danny.

Nobody had any constructive ideas.

"What do you think they're gonna do wit' us?" Luke asked.

"We're dinner," said Danny. "Well, all but the Wizard. They'll want to keep him alive to keep on makin' his special brew."

"Maybe ifin I refuse, they'll let ya'll go," said the Wizard.

"Maybe, but it's more likely that if ya don't do as they ask they'll eat ya first."

They slept uneasy that night, each one of them wondering how the Yuppies would cook them.

The next morning Charles, W. W. West and another Yuppie arrived at their cell. West pointed at Mary. "You're coming with us, my precious. We have something special planned for you."

Mary grabbed Luke's arm. "Don't let them take me."

Luke stared at West. "Ya'll have to kill me 'fore ya touch my ol' lady."

"We plan to do that," Charles said. West cackled, and the other man smiled.

Danny stepped up to the bars. "Listen, take me. Those two are married. Can't ya let them have a little more time together?"

West nodded in Angela's direction. "What about her? Is she married?"

Danny saw no use in lying. "Um—"

"She's married to me," said the Wizard.

"Since we want you to be happy, I guess she gets to live a little longer," said West.

Charles bent down to unlock the cell door. "You all know the drill. Nose against wall. All of you except this gentleman here."

After the others moved to the back of the cell, Charles pulled the door open, and Danny stepped into the corridor.

Less than a second later there was a burst of gunfire, and Mary screamed.

Danny turned and saw Angela on the floor with her left hand clutching her right shoulder, blood flowing between her fingers.

"I told you I didn't want any of you trying to be heroes," said Charles, though Danny saw that the nameless man had fired a revolver.

Danny tried to make it back into the cell and got elbowed in the stomach for his trouble.

"You're going with us," said Charles.

Danny took one last look at Angela. Things weren't going the way he had planned. He had found the Wizard, but it didn't look like he would be able to find a way home.

The man who had shot Angela forced the gun into the small of Danny's back.

The four men walked out the doors and down the block. Danny decided that there was no way he would be the main course at a Yuppie dinner. When he felt the gun's pressure lessen on his back, he spun around and slammed a fist into his captor's nose. He heard the bone break and saw blood spurt out the man's nostrils.

Danny kicked Charles in the groin, leaving only him and West. He bent down to grab the first man's gun and turned towards the Yuppie.

Both men had firearms pointed at each other. "It looks like we have us a Mexican standoff," said West.

Danny pulled the gun's trigger. He watched West fly backward and onto the ground. "It's only a Mexican standoff 'til one of us shoots," said Danny.

He plugged the other men with bullets before either could stand. He grabbed Charles's keys and ran for the cell.

He had to stop and catch his breath once he reached it. He listened, but didn't hear anyone coming after him.

As he approached the cell the others were contained in, he saw everybody kneeling around Angela. Mary turned and noticed him.

"Is she dead?" Danny asked with a gulp.

"I'm fine," Angela said, trying tried to get up, but Mary and Luke gently pushed her to the floor.

"You better let her see if she can stand," said Danny. "We needs to get out of here."

Angela staggered to her feet and took two steps forward before stumbling. Luke and Mary caught her before she fell.

Danny unlocked the cell door. Mary and the Wizard moved out first while Luke helped Angela out the door.

"We needs to get back to the Estates as fast as we can," said Danny.

"Then ya better leave me here," said Angela. "I'll slow ya down."

"I ain't leavin' nobody behind."

With that being said, everybody followed Danny down to the main floor of the jail. West blocked the exit.

"You should have made sure I was dead," West said. "And you definitely should have taken my gun with you."

The man took a shot at the group. His aim being wide, he missed all of them.

Everybody dove for cover.

"I'm going to kill all of you," West shouted.

Danny popped up from behind a desk and took a shot at him.

"Fuck," West said. "That hurt. I'm going to make you pay for that."

A bucket of mop water had been shoved under the desk. Danny grabbed it and started to peek over the desktop. He saw the Yuppie peering down at him and threw the water into the Yuppie's face.

"What did you expect that to do? Melt me?" West laughed.

"Nope. Jus' wanted a 'straction." Danny hit him with the bucket; he didn't want to shoot anybody at point blank range, getting blood and guts all over himself. He figured brain bits would be one hell of a thing to wash out of his new clothes.

He didn't kill the Yuppie this time either. He couldn't take the chance of any Yuppies hearing the shot, but he did remember to take West's gun.

After searching through the jail's supplies, they handcuffed West to a desk and taped his mouth shut. He could move some, but the desk slowed him down, and he couldn't yell for help.

The five Estates members left the jail. They had to make it home before nightfall, before the Yuppies got off work and headed to their parties. Fortunately they had plenty of daylight left.

"Are we gonna move when we get back to the Estates?" Luke asked.

"Why'd we do that?" said Danny. "Now that we've got the Wizard back, we can offer them Yuppies alky-hol so they won't eat us. I don't think they'll be bragging at their hoedowns 'bout how easily we rescued the ol' man. Besides there's no place like home."

Mark Fewell has been writing for over ten years, and has had sixty stories and ninety poems published. His work has been published in *Marion Zimmer Bradley's Fantasy Magazine*, *Bizarre Bazaar*, and *After Hours*.

When not writing, he works as a machine operator in an artificial Christmas tree factory, where he has studied Bubbas in their native habitat—the cafeteria.

DOG

Ajax

Dog's tail thumped the ground as he laid in the yard,
He jerked, then twisted, and bit his fleas hard.
Dog stood, shook, then yawned as he stretched,
He sniffed at the ground where his master had retched.

Dog walked to his doghouse beneath a large tree,
He lapped at his water, then took a long pee.
Dog walked to the deck and there in the back
Was a bag of Ol' Roy in a shiny new sack.

He ran up the stairs and pawed at the bag,
Dog chewed as he clawed and then a wet rag,
Flew at him through a large rip in the screen,
"YOU GIT OUTTA HERE!" yelled the woman Erlene.

Dog jumped backward as the door opened wide,
He ran towards the woods as Erlene ran outside,
He stopped at the tree line, his getaway clean,
Dog winced when Erlene hit the washing machine.

The "BOOM" was gawd-awful and over she pitched,
with a "SMACK!" hit the lawn, where she moaned and
she bitched,
The look on Dog's face was "What the hell was she
thinking?"
Then the smell wafted in—that Erlene had been
drinking.

His face split in a smile as Dog trotted past,
He knew in this race, Erlene had placed last.
Dog ascended the stairs wriggling with joy,
Good dog? Bad dog? Who cares? Ol' Roy!

Ajax lives in the Midwest amidst an ever-changing group of friends and acquaintances. Often he ponders the great questions of life, but then gets bored and has a sandwich. Look for an anthology of his work thus far coming soon from Yard Dog Press.

QUEST FOR THE HOLY GRILL
Everette Bell

A latticework of branches separated the forest floor from a bleak autumn sky like a petrified spider web. Limbs cracked and leaves crunched under foot as a behemoth of a man, pressing against the stitches of his tattered overalls and faded flannel shirt, charged into a clearing, bow in hand. A quiver of arrows bounced on his back. Exhausted from the exertion the man's breath pounded from his gaping mouth. With very little grace he knelt beside a fresh deer carcass. An arrow sprang from the buck's muscular neck, tip buried deep in a crimson splotch.

Guthrie stroked the deer's massive rack with his meaty hand. "Sorry, fella, but I been sippin' old Artimis' home brew. I can't help but shoot something when I get that fire water in me."

The man had difficulty controlling his wheezing as he fumbled for the flask in the front of his overalls. He puckered his grimy lips around the mouth of the flask and drank deeply. Fire in liquid form raced down his throat scorching a trail to the pit of his stomach causing his face to flush.

"Yeee! Haaaah!" Guthrie bellowed like a barbarian on the battlefield. When his two cousins broke through the wall of dead branches at his back, Guthrie was still swinging his bow overhead. "Jake, Kyle, over here! I got the sum bitch!"

"Will ya shut your damn mouth," Kyle barked. "We're right behind ya, and the way you carry on I'm gonna have a damn head ache." He was a tall gangly man wearing army fatigues—suited for a man about two inches shorter and twenty pounds lighter than he was—with wild hair and an unshaven face. A John Deer hat sat loosely atop his head like a wine cork not pushed tightly back into the bottle. His mouth gave rise to a disgusting smacking sound as he pulled his parched tongue away from the roof of his mouth and chewed to moisten his pallet. Pressing a finger against the side of his nose, the man forced air out his clear nostril sending a tendril of snot blasting to the ground. In the aftermath, a booger rested on his upper lip, but he took no notice.

"Hey, Guthrie, why don't we make camp here and start carving that bad boy up?" As he spoke he unsheathed the hunting knife on his belt and unslung the axe from his back.

"Cuz we're going to find a grill at the temple, that's why. I want to taste that outdoor flavor Artimis talked about." Guthrie smiled showing off the half dozen yellow teeth in his mouth.

"You ever eaten meat grilled over a charcoal blaze? Huh, what about a gas grill? You honestly tellin' me that you want me to waste this buck on a campfire when we are only a couple of hours from the temple ruins?"

Kyle dug his finger up his nose and flicked a booger onto a nearby tree trunk. "My daddy said it was about twenty year ago, right after the plague hit, when he last ate grilled meat. Guess I was a kid, and we were out four-wheelin' when the riots started."   A dreamy look crossed his features. "He said that meat was the sweetest thing he ever ate in his whole life."

"See what I mean?" Guthrie nodded. He looked over at the third man who had remained silent through all the talk. "You think we oughtta hold out for the temple don't ya, Jake?"

His head was oddly shaped like a long narrow melon, and sprouts of hair came off the top of his head. Tremendous buck teeth stabbed outward from a tiny mouth below a pug nose, and his ears looked too small for his head. He also wore overalls like Guthrie's, but they were decorated with flower patches and trimmed in pink. Careful observation revealed that his left arm was about two inches longer than his right. His bug eyes weren't quite even either.

"I don't know." He replied filling the air with spit. "Them folk that was affected by that there yuppie virus, y'all know as well as I do, they hide out in the ruins." Scratching his head like a perplexed monkey, Jake went on, "I don't think we oughtta try it. With the weather getting' colder, them yuppies'll be looking for food and stuff to burn."

Kyle reached over and slapped his deformed cousin in the back of the head. "Hang on ya damn potato-headed baboon. Are you telling me you are afraid of them fuckin' stinky-assed cannibals?" Jake didn't answer. Kyle slapped him twice more. Each blow to the large head was like someone thumping fruit to test its ripeness. "I said are you scared of 'em?"

"I ain't never killed one," Jake mumbled, obviously ashamed. "Every time I see them horrible things I piss myself and run off."

Both Kyle and Guthrie looked away, embarrassed of their kin. "Jesus Christ, done heard it all, now. Ain't you, Guth?"

Guthrie fought against his own weight to lift his enormous body—knees cracking. "How did you get to be so stupid, Jake?"

"I don't know. I asked my mom, but she couldn't remember nothing. Hell, she said she was drunk the whole time she was carrying me in her belly."

Kyle shook his head and grumbled under his breath. "Piss your Goddamn pants, what a disgrace."

Tugging at the straps of his overalls, Jake pleaded for his cousins' understanding. "Y'all don't be mad. I swear I can kill one without pissin' myself."

"No cousin of mine is going to be a dman coward," Kyle said forcefully. He grabbed Jake by the ear and started pulling the man along. "We're going to find you a yuppie, so you can bash his head in."

Jake kept quiet as the tears rolled down his cheeks. He knew Kyle was only doing it for his own good. After all, his cousins had always taken care of him. He trusted them completely.

Guthrie slung the deer over his shoulders and started walking. "Go easy on him, Kyle. He can't help it."

Jake limped with an awkward gait trying to keep up with Kyle. The weight of his own head tipped him forward, and he barely supported himself on his bowed legs. If his cousins wanted to find what Artimis had told them about, he was going to do everything he could to be good and help.

"I'll help you find a grill." He winced.

Kyle yanked him along. "You'll shut up and do what I say."

After two and a half hours of walking down one of the old roads—according to Artimis it had been a busy one before the plague struck—the men arrived at the ruins, directly across from what had once been a field. As if some long dormant urge suddenly awakened, Kyle ran over to the rusted tractor husk next to the road and leapt on it like a cowboy would have done a horse.

"Let's go for a ride, boys!" The man yelled between his pretend engine sounds. "I bet this baby raced like the wind back in her day!"

None of the men had ever seen a tractor—any vehicle for that matter—operate. After the plague had left the world in chaos, those who were unaffected started having massive smash-up-derby rallies. The deadly mixture of free alcohol and lawless highways resulted in destroyed, abandoned vehicles scattered around the landscape.

Guthrie adjusted the deer on his shoulders to relieve some of the pressure. "Will you knock it off, Kyle? We're on holy ground. The almighty Rush Limbaugh may be watchin'."

Jake kept quiet. He was filled with a strange combination of fear and awe. The huge building across the road from them stood solid even after nearly a quarter century of neglect. It had survived the riots and somehow been spared from the rampage of random bazooka violence. Before they left their small settlement of "Ford Dealership", the village elder, Old Artimis, had told the cousins a tale. Many years ago the people quit drinking beer by the glow of the full moon and stopped singing the Willy Nelson hymns that the almighty Rush loved so dearly. In his anger the god allowed the simple-minded Hacket brothers to find two bazookas and a stockpile of ammo that resulted in the the total destruction of the "Jiffy Lube" and "Dairy Queen" villages. That single incident had reinstated the tradition of drinking—only now it was home brew—while singing "On The Road Again".

Painted in letters that covered the entire front of the building was the phrase that the post-plague world was founded on, "Rush Limbaugh Rules". Jake trembled before the house of the lord.

SUPER WAL-MART. The sign was in near perfect condition—proving undeniably that this was once the temple of the mighty Rush.

"What's it mean," Jake asked with the wonderment of a child. "I never did learn my letters."

"Idiot," Kyle insulted the deformed man as he jumped off the old tractor. "It's heaven." The man wearing the tight-fitting fatigues spoke thoughtfully. "In there we will find all the treasures of the world, cheeze whiz, spam, guns and bullets, plastic lawn birds, and..." The man was carried away by the beauty of the building.

Guthrie picked up where his cousin left off. "Charcoal Grills, Gas Grills, Inflatable yard pools, Chia Pets, and Jesus t-shirts."

"Who is Jesus?" Jake asked. "I ain't never heard of him."

Kyle shook his head. "You have got to be the biggest ignorant bastard I ever did know. Jesus was the badest monster truck driver ever before the plague ruined the sport."

"After he lost his leg he took up wrestling."

"Damn, he sounds tougher than a coffin nail." Jake's big eyes widened even more.

Gradually there conversation faded into silence. Beneath the gray sky the pilgrims walked across the barren parking lot, past the demolished cars and blowing trash. A frosty breeze chilled them.

Guthrie looked at Kyle. "Watch him in case any of them yuppies show up. He's your responsibility while I deal with the deer, got it."

His cousin nodded his understanding.

"I hope they do," Kyle said, "this boy is gonna kill one without pissing his pants if I have anything to say about it."

They walked through the entrance into the dark building.

"Won't Rush be unhappy that we invaded his temple?"

Kyle smacked Jake in the back of the head producing that deep hollow note. "Didn't you listen to a damn thing we said?"

"Will you two shut up!' Guthrie was very serious. He knew this maze of high aisles was a perfect place for those demented yuppies to hide. "I'm going to lay the deer here and start cleaning it. First thing I want you guys to do is go see if you can find some weapons, and we gotta have some light or those yuppies will be chowin' on us before morning."

As he laid his load down on a clear spot on the ground, a resonating fart ripped from the denim overalls pulled tight across his bulbous ass. In the distance of the gigantic store the sound of scurrying was very evident.

"Hehehehehe," Jake laughed. "Guthrie pootted."

Kyle punched his companion in the arm. "Come on you monkey ass we got work to do." He gave the deformed man the hunting knife from his belt, and he took the ax off his back. "We'll be back with the torches in a few minutes."

Guthrie nodded and knocked an arrow in his bow. He watched as the two men walked deeper into the darkness of the store. The only entrance for light was the front doors, so it didn't take long before they were swallowed by blackness.

Guthrie shook his head at the stupidity of those knuckleheads. Long after he could no longer see them, he could hear them banging into things and arguing who had the smelliest farts. Twice he heard it come to blows.

Suddenly the dark lost its grip on the building and was pushed away by a tiny flame that quickly spread to a small blaze, a mallet head wrapped in cloth. Kyle tucked his lighter back in his pocket while talking to himself, "Just about out. I'm going to need to find another one."

The glow of the flame illuminated a torn box on the floor. Strewn around it were other mallets and large colored balls. One of the flaps of the box had the word "Croquet" written on it.

"What we got here is a fancy game." Jake said. "Its foreign, so actually you call it Crotch hit. They call it that because you hit the looser in the balls with one of these hammers."

"I know that, stupid ass." Kyle snarled.

Countless items littered the floor all around them. Most of the things were completely alien to Kyle and Jake. They had no words to describe the strange hats with face guards, the shoes with spikes on the bottoms, the strange clubs, the countless sizes of balls—solid and inflatable—and the innumerable other things.

Jake nodded, his deformed face sweet and innocent. He trusted Kyle and Guthrie completely. They were much smarter than him and had always taken care of him. "What do you want me to do?"

Kyle handed the flaming mallet to Jake and made another one for himself. "If you see any yuppies you've got the knife and the Crotch hit mallet. Remember what arrows and bows look like? And guns and bullets? That's what we want."

Jake nodded. "Look, Kyle, we can put them in this." Mashed up against an empty shelf was a cart.

By the glow of his own flaming mallet, Kyle cracked a snaggle-toothed smile. "You ain't always as stupid as I think. I'll take the cart. We're gonna split up, but if you need help yell."

Each of them headed out in a different direction. Kyle quickly found the wall of hunting equipment and started filling the cart with guns and ammo. The next yuppie he ran into was going to regret it. It was strange how just touching the firearms made Kyle crave alcohol. He couldn't shake the feeling. It took everything he had to keep from loading the guns and shooting at random.

Jake carefully waded through the debris and falling shelves of the silent temple in search of the treasured items. Even though he had the blazing mallet to banish some of the darkness, the man was still afraid. At his back was a support column and before him blackness filled with racks of clothes. He heard something. It moved in the darkness before him, closer.

On the edge of the glow from his torch, Jake could see a dark figure skulking around a rack of clothes. A low heavy breathing came from it, and whatever it was moved with its arms dragging the ground.

"Who's there?"

There was no answer to Jake's call. He called again. Still no answer.

That same heavy breathing came again—only this time it was behind him. Jake spun around lifting his torch high. He began to tremble and his thin lips closed around his crooked teeth, but he could not form his terror into sound.

Slinking towards him were three of the dreaded yuppies. Still clad in the rags of their designer suits and casual wear made to resemble the attire of those living in third world nations, the emaciated creatures bared mutated fangs at their victim. Dark holes where eyes had been leaked bloody fluid, but it was their sense of smell that brought the ravenous creatures to the living.

The sound came from behind again. Jake screamed and turned. Two more of the beasts were climbing out of the clothes racks. One was wearing a chicken suit, carrying a golf club.

The front of Jake's feminine overalls darkened as his warm urine ran down his leg. He managed a scream.

"What has he done, now?" Kyle said in disgust as he heard the simpleton yell for help. From his cart he picked up a shotgun and box of shells. Fitting the ammo into the chamber he heard the man's screams become more intense.

"Jesus, you damn retard. Give me a minute."

With blazing mallet in one hand and shotgun in the other, Kyle set out in the direction of Jake's voice. He figured Jake was just being a baby again—poor bastard had probably already wet himself. Kyle knew he was doing Jake a favor—he was making him a man.

A draft caused the flame of his mallet to flicker, and all around him it darkened briefly. Peeking around the corner of an aisle, he inhaled sharply when he saw Jake backed up against a pillar swinging his torch in front of him. Just out of reach of the fire were five writhing yuppies. As the mallet passed they tried to advance on Jake, but soon the blazing hammer drove them away on its return arc.

"Great, Rush, you gotta help me!" Jake called out. "Don't let these bastard yuppies take me!" Jake's pleas along with more yuppies than he expected to see frightened Kyle. Seeing that Jake had been distracted for the moment he started to back away. If he could get the guns to where Guthrie was they might have a chance, otherwise they were all dead—worse than that they were yuppy food.

Kyle turned and ran with all the speed he could muster to get back to his cartload of guns. Behind him Jake's screams of agony rose into an incomprehensible gurgle followed by the slurping of flesh and cracking of bone. The poor bastard had probably pissed himself before he died—served him right for being a coward.

Nearly tripping over some piece of unseen debris, Kyle bolted into the darkness pushing the cart with one hand and holding his torch in the other. The clatter of his cart intensified as he picked up speed. The last thing he wanted was to get caught by those damn yuppies. Jake might have been too stupid to save himself, but he sure as hell wasn't.

Thundering down an aisle, Kyle glanced back over his shoulder with panic painted across his face. He could hear their foul hisses, distorted cackling coming after him.

"Guthrie!" He screamed. "I've got the guns, but the yuppies are on my ass! Get ready!"

The closer he got to the light at the front doors the less he heard his pursuers. They were creatures of the dark, and unless in dire need of food they would not leave the shadows of the lair.

He came to a clamoring halt three feet from his cousin. Kyle was unable to speak for a long moment as he gathered his breath.

"They...got...Jake." He gasped. Slowly he pulled himself together and stood up. "I tried to stop those bastards, but there were too many."

Guthrie nodded slowly but said nothing.

The tremendous man reached into the cart and pulled out a gun. He looked through the boxes of shells until he found the one he was looking for. Carefully he loaded the rifle.

"Well, that's just the way it goes." He looked over at Kyle. "Did he piss his pants before they got him?"

"No, Guth, he went out like a man."

"What happened?"

Kyle wiped sweet off his brow as he planned his lie. "I told him to stay close, but when I found the guns, he wasn't anywhere around. He screamed, and when I got there, they were all around him."

The larger man cocked the rifle as he listened.

"I tried to get closer to help him, but there were too many of them." He did everything he could to energize his words with passion. "I fired a shotgun at one of the bastards—killed him too—but another one knocked the gun outta my hand."

He brought crocodile tears to his gaunt features to finish his tale. "I watched him fight for his life before they got him... The sons of bitches."

While wiping his eyes Kyle saw the dressed deer hanging from a piece of metal protruding from the ceiling. Large sections of meat were spread out on a counter top under a sign reading "Information Desk".

"Get a gun, Kyle, and let's go get a grill."

He picked up a shotgun and a box of shells. "Now, you're talking. My mouth is watering." He also picked up the torch he had dropped during his rapid arrival and relit the head with a flick of his lighter.

179

Side by side the two men walked down the deserted rows of the store. They stepped over empty boxes, broken glass, various scattered items, and on two occasions old skeletons—one with the head removed. Guthrie was cool and even tempered even when the hissing seemed to be all around them. Kyle was as jumpy as a cat in a dogpound.

"This is it," Guthrie said, looking at a dangling sign, "the outdoor center."

A sudden war cry from ahead of them caused both men to bring the stocks of their guns to their shoulders. Wild and demented, two yuppies with scarred faces and seething boils covering their bare chest ran straight for the men.

The explosions of two gunshots vaulted them against empty shelves. The yuppies were perfectly still except for the lakes of blood expanding from holes in their shattered torsos.

"You gotta make ever shot count," Guthrie warned. "There's more of them out there, and they're waiting for the chance to get us just like they did Jake."

Kyle didn't say anything. He was busy watching his own ass.

Moving past a row of bicycles, Kyle bumped into a piece of a hanging sign. Startled, he was wide-eyed and dropped jawed. The man looked like he had just seen a ghost, and in no time he fired two quick shotgun blasts, annihilating a mannequin sitting in a folding chair.

"Jesus, calm down." Guthrie's voice was filled with anger. "We need those shots."

Saying nothing else he led Kyle around a corner, past more rows of bicycles and already assembled hammocks. He stopped dead in his tracks.

"Come on Guthrie we gotta move. I hear more coming our way." Kyle sounded as scared as his cousin had ever heard him. Sputtering breaths rolled from his tight throat, and he clutched his gun like a life preserver.

"There it is."

Straight across from them was an unusual black pot on legs with a cover. The picture next to it showed people cooking hamburgers.

Guthrie stepped forward. "Artimis said we're gonna need charcoal—they're these little bricks—and lighter fluid."

Next to the grill he started rifling through a box filled with items. "Don't stand there, Kyle, you idiot. Help me get this stuff."

He was too afraid to move. "They're coming!" Kyle screamed. Using his torch to light the areas around him, he fired into the darkness at random. "You bastards won't get me!"

Gunshots echoed like thunder, and Guthrie fell to one knee to avoid friendly fire by his out of his mind cousin. His wandering eyes found a bottle with the words "Lighter Fluid" on it. Next to it he saw charcoal written across a white bag. Scooping them up in one hand, he yelled at Kyle.

"We got the stuff." Then the exploding stopped. All that could be heard was the repeated click of Kyle's empty gun. The front of his pants were pee-seoaked.

"They won't get me! Jake was a god damn coward! He got what he deserved, but those yuppie bastards won't get me!"

Guthrie barked at Kyle. "Shut the hell up and come help me with this stuff."

Kyle seemed to come back to his senses for a moment. "Sorry, man, but we got to hurry."

Running over he grabbed hold of the grill and started pulling it along the floor on its small wheels. By the rattle of the metal, the grill didn't sound very sturdy, but neither of them had ever seen one—they didn't know what to expect.

With torch in hand, Kyle followed the armed giant of a man through the dark labyrinth. Two yuppies, wagging their tongues and hissing, came at the men from the side. The first one slashed its long thick fingernails across Kyle's face, blurring the man's vision with an unexpected stream of blood. Kyle lost his grip on the grill and staggered to the side. The flaming brand fell to his feet making him look like a savage dancing around a campfire.

Guthrie fired his rifle bursting the yuppies head like dropped pottery. "Yeeeee! Haaaaaah!" The sudden gun frenzy had come onto the man, and he fired again, ripping the creature's arm off before it toppled to the ground.

The second yuppie hesitated long enough for the man to get off another shot. The bullet slammed into the unholy creature's chest like a freight train. Its exit pushed a volley of guts out the pale blister-covered back.

Kyle clutched his eyes as he rolled on the floor. Trying to come to his feet he howled in pain and clasped his eyes tightly.

"Come on cuz." Guthrie's voice was full of support "Just get the grill back to where the light is and we'll be fine."

The choice was simple. Kyle could try and make it or stay on the floor and become the next snack for the remaining yuppies. Using the grill for support, he pulled himself to his feet and pushed it. Guthrie stepped to his cousin's side and helped guide him along while he himself carried the charcoal and the lighter fluid along with his gun.

Guthrie saw the light up ahead. He knew they would be safe at least until the sun set.

"I know what you did." He said coldly.

In a pained voice, Kyle answered. "What the hell are you talking about."

"You said you fired at a yuppie to try and save Jake." There was a pause filled with anger. "I didn't hear a shot, Kyle. He might have been stupid, but he was family."

Kyle was terrified. He couldn't see anything. The man wavered around like a drunk on a balance beam. "He was a stupid simpleton! If I tried to save him, I probably would have gotten killed along with him!"

Silence.

"Come on, Guthrie, we're first cousins. That retard was just our half cousin! We been through too much to let that little freak show come between us!"

The pleading fell upon deaf ears.

"That ain't how kin treats each other."

He fired. When the echo was gone and the smell of sulfur was thick in the air, Kyle lay still.

Guthrie smirked grimly at the piss stain on the front of his cousin's pants. He lifted the lid of the grill and tossed the charcoal and lighter fluid inside. There were no other yuppies in sight, so he grabbed the handle of the grill and started pulling.

By the time he reached the lit area at the front of the store, Guthrie could hear yuppies gathering in the darkness at his back. Outside, afternoon was starting to turn to night and the dull gray was being replaced by the steely blue of twilight. For a long moment he looked down at the strange item in silence. He tried to remember everything old Artimis had ever told him about how grills worked, but it wasn't coming to him.

Guthrie knew the sun would be setting soon, and then, there would be no defense from the yuppies. They would hunt him like dogs chasing a fox. No chance for survival would exist.

In the cold silence of the ancient temple ruins, Guthrie called out to his god. "Almighty Rush, guide my hand so that in my final hours I will be comforted by the sweet taste of a rare venison steak cooked over a majestic flame."

Guthrie began to move precisely, but he felt as if a power greater than himself was driving his movements. His hands poured the charcoal and squirted the fluid, wasting none. Then from his pocket he pulled out a book of matches and tossed one into the prepared grill bottom.

Hot flames licked upward further illuminating the old temple. Mesmerized by the awesome godly creation before him, Guthrie knew exactly what to do. He placed the choicest of venison cuts on the grill and smiled as the meat sizzled on the iron grate.

The flames caressed the meat, tickling its belly in a way Guthrie had never witnessed. For a long while he watched in astonishment imagining what glorious flavors awaited him. Prodding the meat with a stick from the floor felt natural, like a homecoming of sorts.

Slipping the silver flask containing Artimis' home brew from his overall pocket, he unscrewed the cap. As he drank and watched his meat cook, Guthrie was at peace with the world. The nearing hisses didn't affect him in the slightest.

Everette Bell has lots of things you've probably never read in various publications you've probably never heard of. With any luck that will change one day.

He considers himself an expert on the wild Bubba, having spent over two decades living in the states of Alabama and Kentucky. Despite the rumors he does not appear in this story.

IT IS WHETHER YOU WIN OR LOSE
Rob Gates

It had been a rough few weeks all over Elmerville, even before the murders started. Bobby had gone and accidentally shot himself in the shoulder—again—and a small band of Yuppies had come through town. Some locals, they had sport with 'em before we were finished taking care of 'em. Not me though. I couldn't bring myself to do it quite that way. I'll never enjoy killing, I just know I have to do it sometimes.

See I was a Yuppie once, a bleeding heart liberal do-gooder and computer programmer. I still get those cravings for flesh sometimes too, though I've found that Spam calms them down. See Doc VonTrap, he fixed me up good before his death. Shame that Missy had to go and eat him. No, I know they never reported his death that way, but I was there. Test Subject Number 374962. Don't ask me why the number was so high, there were only a couple hundred of us. And I don't know what happened to the others. Hell, I never met most of them. I did the only thing that seemed reasonable when he died. I went back to my roots. VonTrap, he thought that might have been why I was such a successful test subject. Kinda funny really. I went running like hell away from here and ended up running like hell to get back.

So I settled in back in Elmerville, taking up residence in the old library. I thought folks might not take kindly to my coming back to town, seeing how I'd been absent for so long and how both my folks had died in the meantime. But they surprised me. A few old friends took up my side, and I said a few helpful things to people,

185

and before long I was town teacher, doctor, sheriff, judge, and general advice guy. Over ten years ago now it was.

Anyway, where was I. Oh yeah, the rough week. Being the closest thing to law this town has, I get involved in anything out of the ordinary. But despite my expectations when I first arrived here, this was the first time I was involved with a real life murder. Oh sure, people kill each other all the time, but murder implies a certain amount of mystery, and that's what I had on my hands. Jimmy Duncan, my old high school buddy, lying quietly on his bed completely naked in a trailer locked up tight. Dead. This wasn't going to be easy, especially considering the fact that I had no idea what the hell I was doing. My training in being "the law" consisted of a few years watching reruns of *The Practice*, *Ally McBeal*, *NYPD Blue*, and *Law and Order*. They weren't going to help much with a situation like this. Of course, I had a few hundred mystery novels on the shelves that might do me some good.

So there I was, sitting on a chair in Jimmy's trailer. I'd been through the bedroom twice already with nothing obvious jumping out at me. I hadn't touched the body yet, and was running out of ideas. Like I said, this wasn't going to be easy. That's when it struck me. Something was missing. I went back to the bedroom, knocking the beer I'd snatched from his fridge off the table in the process. Well, Jimmy wasn't going to care, so I picked it up and didn't bother with the floor. I just hurried back to the bedroom. Sure enough, it was gone. The banner from our State Championship football game back in high school. I knew Jimmy had never taken it down from his bedroom wall. Don't ask me how I knew that, suffice it to say that there were reasons I never thought I'd fit in here in Elmerville.

There was a blank space on Jimmy's wall where the banner should have been. There it was. The CLUE. But what the hell did a nearly twenty year old football game banner have to do with a dead body on a bed today?

Alright, alright, so it wasn't exactly a breakthrough. But it was a start. Poor Jimmy though. I didn't exactly want to carry him back to the library, so I was going to have to do the autopsy right here. Maybe on the table outside, since someone might want the trailer or the bed. I won't bore you with the details of the ordeal. I did get an audience for a while, and some helpful advice from a couple of Jimmy's neighbors. But the advice would have been much more useful if I had been planning on deboning him or chopping him for later eating. About halfway through, it almost seemed like a good idea as one of the cravings hit. I probably shouldn't have done it, but I did take a little piece off a leg. So sue me. No one noticed.

When all was said and done, there were no bullet wounds, no knife marks, no bruises around the neck. There were no signs of a heart attack or stroke or anything like that. There was a chance that his death was from natural causes, but some hunch told me that wasn't the case. There was one thing I did notice, but it didn't seem important at the time, and it was a little embarrassing to talk about. So I didn't mention it. Poor Jimmy.

We packed him up, and a few of his neighbors carried him to the cemetery. Someone would arrange for a quick funeral party, and I knew his place would be worked over within days. Jimmy wasn't married and had no kids. His glory days were behind him. That's why the banner had still been on his wall. Living in the past kept him from ever finding that special woman. Well, that and a few other facts about Jimmy I wasn't about to share.

So now I had what I just knew was a murder, and a clue. Not that the clue would do me any good. No one seemed to have seen or heard anything unusual, and I still had no idea what that old banner had to do with anything. I figured something would come to me, and there wasn't much I could do now until either inspiration struck or someone came forward with more information. So I settled in for dinner and a few movies. It turned out to be the last real peace and quiet I'd have for a while.

It must have been about four in the morning when I opened my eyes, awakened by the sound of shattering glass. It was nearby. Really nearby. I threw on some shorts and ran towards the kitchen, a baseball bat in my hand. The threat of bruising is usually enough to defuse situations with the drunken locals, and Yuppies wouldn't be breaking windows. I got to the door and still hadn't heard anything else, so I reached one hand quickly around the corner to turn on the light. Score one for me, my ears had been right. The kitchen window was broken, a rock was on the floor—the likely culprit. The rock came neatly wrapped in a piece of paper tied around it with fishing line. As I got closer, I noted that the paper was newsprint, old newsprint. I quickly cut the fishing line, and unfolded the paper. Perhaps it was the early hour, but my attention was first drawn to a couple of car ads and part of an article on one side of the clip. This wasn't exactly helpful. Thankfully, I managed to think of turning the paper over, and there it was, the next clue. It was the front sports page of a local paper, from the day after that long ago football game.

My hunch had been right. Jimmy's death wasn't an accident. And somehow it was related to a football game nearly twenty years ago. It was time for a stroll down memory lane. I took the article, and started wandering around the library picking up a few other things. High school yearbooks and other newspapers from around the same time might be helpful. I settled in to relive the last great moments of Jimmy Duncan's life.

The year was 2007, the year he and I were both seniors. Jimmy was the star quarterback of the football team. Not that he was pro material or anything, but he'd had a good year. The whole team had played way above expectations. Far enough above that the team made it to the State Championship game. Now, I don't know about anywhere else, but for this area that's *Big*. So Jimmy, the rest of the team, and indeed the whole town, were strutting around like peacocks for the weeks leading up to it. The boys were practically gods for a while. Hell, they could have killed someone and everyone would have looked the other way. But really, they were decent guys, decent for jackass jock boys that is. Nothing more than being a little forward with their girls, who truth be told were rather compliant given the near-god status of the guys, and being a little heavier on the macho-pick-on-the-geek stuff. Yeah, that was me, Jack Whitten the geek. I wasn't exactly the class whipping boy, but I wasn't high on the chain either. I walked a tenuous line of being accepted because of my friendship with Jimmy and a few of the other guys from way back and being laughed at for being a bit too smart.

But this stroll down memory lane wasn't about me, it was about the *Big Game*. So I started there, with the articles about the game itself. Funny thing about that game was, for all the glory days before hand, Elmerville got its ass whipped. No one outside of town was surprised; the team's luck just finally ran out. The team played the mediocre way they had been expected to all season. And they lost, 48-10. There were no injuries to the other team, no mention in any of the articles about cheap hits, nothing. So I was willing to rule out revenge from outside. Which left one obvious thought—someone from Elmerville was the culprit.

Feeling like I'd made progress, and fairly convinced that I wasn't able to pull all-nighters the way I used to, I settled back in for a few more hours sleep with that thought rolling around my head. Someone from Elmerville. But if it *was* someone from Elmerville, who

189

and why? And what about a lost game twenty years ago had led to Jimmy's murder now? Sleep didn't come easy.

I slept later than I wanted to, but woke feeling like I hadn't slept at all. Nothing like a little excitement to remind you that age was catching up with you. After breakfast and coffee, I set in for another long day. I figured if the game was the key, I'd start with the players and work from there. Living in the library had its advantages. I had knocked out the wall into the town hall and its records, and turned the old break room into my kitchen. Heck, I had even managed to get a computer running and had access to electronic stuff. I had all sorts of research material at my fingertips, so I started a list of the team members. Half of them I dug up from my own memory, and the rest I filled in from the team photos. There were twenty-eight guys in all, but I knew a few of them had died and weren't likely to be Jimmy's murderer. There might even be more who had died that I didn't know about, so I'd work at that angle for a while to cut down the list.

I still wasn't completely sure I was on the right track that morning when I started, but mid-afternoon something happened that clinched it. Mike Stearns, the center for the losing football team, was found dead by his wife when she returned from the hairdressers. He was naked, like Jimmy. Like Jimmy, there were no obvious wounds. I didn't even bother with an autopsy, assuming I wouldn't find anything. I did however quickly check on two things and sure enough, it was just like Jimmy. Now I knew that what I had seen on Jimmy wasn't just a side effect of who Jimmy was, it was actually another clue. I didn't say anything to Peggy Stearns, she wouldn't have appreciated the news, especially since the color didn't match what she was wearing. But as soon as I got back to the library, I added the facts to my list of clues. Both Jimmy and Mike had lipstick smears at the base of their manhood. And both had been used from behind very recently.

Now, I hadn't thought the second part was important in Jimmy's case because, truth be told, he had been doing that for years. Heck, I had done it with him on more than one occasion. But as far as I knew, and in a small town that knowledge goes far, Mike was as straight as they come. That meant it was important somehow. But how the heck did lipstick tie in? It was time to step up the investigation, especially if the body count was going to keep piling up at the rate of one a day. I needed to quickly weed through the team list and start talking to people.

So I worked on the list, crossing off the dead guys, and ended up with fifteen people. Still a long list, though maybe some of them would still be dead since records became spotty during the height of the plague years. I wouldn't know for sure until I started to talk to folks, and I knew exactly where to start. Every town has a few know it all gossips, and Elmerville was no different. Fortunately, one of them had decided I was God's gift to women way back in high school when she was a cheerleader and had never stopped. She had never noticed that I still hadn't returned her advances. Normally I steered clear of her, but this time I'd play up the charm and see what I could get. So I washed up, and headed on over to her place.

I won't bore you with the details, let's just say my witty repartee was lost and the double meanings were completely missed, but I got the information I needed. After another shower to wash the stink of her perfume off me...I have no idea how she came up with the conviction that more was better where perfume is concerned...I sat down with my list and crossed off most of the remaining names. Of the fifteen guys left, ten had died flat out either of the plague or during the riots, and two had left town when I had and had never come back.

Heck, even the water boy had left town. That left three guys; Tony Barnes, Danny Anderson, and Paul Grant. Tony had been a starter on the team, and now lived in town with a wife and eight kids. Danny had been the kicker. He lived alone one town over—that one raised an eyebrow unrelated to the case, but I filed it away for later. Finally, Paul Grant had been a bench warmer, backup quarterback who never played in a single game that year. I'll give you three guesses where I started.

Paul Grant lived in, if its possible, the bad part of town. He'd been married either four or five times according to Betty, though wasn't married now. He'd also run through just about every job possible in town. He sounded like a stereotypical loser to me, but did that make him a murderer? That's what I needed to figure out. I knocked on his trailer door about 6:00PM and got no answer. I knocked again, louder, and still got no answer. As I was debating the finer points of law about breaking and entering my hand absent-mindedly turned the door handle. It wasn't locked and the door swung open. Well, it wasn't breaking so what the hell. I started in, quickly grimacing from the smell.

So much for the obvious answer. Paul Grant appeared to have been dead for a couple of days, and there were signs of a slight struggle. Paul was a big man though, and the struggle seemed far too limited. And sure enough, there was the lipstick and the signs of the other bit. Had Paul been the first? It seemed that way, and no one had noticed until now. Poor guy. I looked around, just in case there some other clue, convinced I wouldn't find anything since I hadn't found anything at the other scenes. I don't know why my eyes were drawn to it, but once they were it stuck out like a sore thumb in the filth that was Paul's home. It was one of those cheap stick on ribbons, bright and shiny like new. I just knew, without a doubt, that this ribbon was a clue. Unfortunately my moment of insight ended there, and I had no idea why it was important. How did an old football game, a blow job, lipstick, butt pounding, and a shiny ribbon all fit together?

What I did know was that I was down to two possible suspects. One lived here in Elmerville, and the other not too far away. While my gay bells had gone off hearing about Danny, I had to assume there was a 50% chance he was a killer. But at least I might have an in, a way to get talking, so I started calling in some favors from the guys in town I'd paired off with over the years. It seemed that Danny was indeed family, and wasn't involved with anyone. He also tended to hang out in a few specific places, so I had an idea where to start. Well, if he turned out not to be a killer, he sounded like just my type, but first things first. I took a third shower for the day, remembered to tell someone about Paul, and then hopped in my truck and drove over to Stanton.

Danny wasn't hard to find, if he was the murderer he was sticking to regular routines. He was hanging out in a bar, sitting by himself at a table, so I bought some of the homebrew beer and dropped into the seat across from him. A few eyes turned to watch me sit, but everyone drifted back to their own conversations. He was nice to look at, but there were two things I was keeping in mind to keep me from doing anything foolish. The first was that this wasn't the place, as much as my fellow family members had been open about what they knew about Danny he was probably as quiet about it in town as I was. The second, and significantly more important was that there *was* a 50% chance that he had already killed three men.

"Hey." I said by way of greeting, smiling a little as I sat down. He looked up from studying water circles on the table in front of him and nodded with a vague smile. He lifted the glass I had placed in front of him, took a sip and put it back down, focusing back on the water circles. He shrugged a little, with a slight almost inaudible sigh. In a quiet voice, pitched so it wouldn't go far from the table, he finally spoke "How'd you figure it out?"

Was this the murderer? My mind was reeling as I pondered his question. Was it a confession? Was he acknowledging it? Maybe he was talking about something else, but I couldn't be sure. I had to play my cards carefully. "The clues were there, I just put two and two together."

He sighed again, looking up now, at me. "So what happens next?"

Another answer that could fit with a guilty man. "Well, we finish our beer and then you come quietly back to my truck."

"Ah well, sounds better than sitting here thinking about it." He picked up his beer, gulped down the rest in a single gulp and slapped the glass back down on the table. I quickly followed suit and motioned for him to get up and head for the door as I walked behind him. All eyes watched as we walked out.

"So what are you going to do with me?" He asked as I pointed out the truck and headed him towards it.

I had my hands in my jacket pocket on my gun, this was when it could get messy. "I'm going to ask you a few questions, about Jimmy Duncan and...." As I finished Jimmy's name, Danny sighed heavily and closed the truck door. He looked down and seemed even sadder than he had before. My hand solidified its grip on the gun at this response to Jimmy's name. There was a connection here, and the likelihood that I had my murderer had just increased. I started the truck in silence, and began driving back to Elmerville. Danny didn't protest or make a move.

"So....you knew Jimmy?" I asked, a bit more sharply than I had spoken before. If this was the murderer, I was going to make sure he understood that he killed a friend.

"Yeah, Jimmy and I were buddies. Sounds like you knew him, too. I'm gonna miss him. I just hope they catch the bastard that killed him." He sounded so sincere. Now I was really confused, but I kept the one hand close to the gun in my pocket.

"I'm Jack Whitten, I'm the one trying to figure out who killed Jimmy and at least two others." I watched his face for any reaction, and I got a smile of recognition. "I've narrowed the suspects down to two. You're one of them, and you're going to need to tell me everything you've done for the last few days." I tried to sound rough, like a cop from NYPD Blue.

"You... you actually think *I* killed Jimmy?" Danny laughed. "Is that why you came in and sat down across from me?" He sounded vastly amused. "I thought..." More laughter. "So you're Jack, Jimmy mentioned you a few times". He sat back in his seat after his burst of humored excitement, shaking his head and still chuckling to himself. This wasn't the reaction of a guilty man. I was pretty sure of that, and my hand came out of my pocket. We were just about back to Elmerville, what with the long silences and all, when he added "If you've got a beer or something at your place, I'll tell you everything I've done for the last few days—no problem". He went back to chuckling to himself.

We arrived and went into my place. "This is great", he said, looking around the library. I gave him a quick tour, and then sent him to sit while I grabbed a couple of beers. I came back in, handed him one and told him to spill. So he did, with a story so complete and obviously verifiable that either he was the best actor in the world, or he wasn't the murderer. The only thing that didn't make sense was his reaction when I had first approached him in the bar, so I asked him about it. He laughed, "I, ahhh, thought you were just someone come in to pick me up for sex". He looked away, a little red in the face. "Not that I would mind".

I won't bore you to death with the details of what followed. It's none of your fucking business anyway.

It was about four AM when I again heard the sound of breaking glass. I was a bit groggy as I shushed Danny and went creeping towards the kitchen to find another rock with another newspaper clipping on my floor. I was getting tired of broken glass, but concentrated on the latest clue. It was a team photo picture from the big game. Everyone on it was X'ed out except Danny, even Tony Barnes. I suspected my body count had risen by one, and went to tell Danny to stay put while I went to investigate what happened to Tony. As I was struggling to get dressed, he asked the question that I hadn't come up with yet.

"If Tony's dead, and I'm not the murderer, then who is it"?

That stopped me short. I said the only thing I could as I finished getting dressed. "I don't know".

I left Danny pondering the same question I was pondering, and hopped in the truck to drive out to Tony's. I found exactly what I expected. Tony was dead, with all the same signs. It was almost anticlimactic. I was just turning to head back out from his place when I saw it out of the corner of my eye. The clue that I had missed at the previous locations—though thinking back, I realized it had been there. I cursed under my breath, sure now that Danny wasn't the killer, and armed with a new set of suspects.

As I pulled back into the library parking lot, I noticed a light on and figured Danny was awake. I walked in casually, not expecting trouble. That was a mistake. I came through into the main room calling Danny's name, only to find myself face to face with the killers. That last clue had been right on target, though the fact that there were two of them was a surprise.

"How nice of you to finally join us Jack" said Betty Kent, town gossip and former cheerleader. Her companion, Jill Peyton, just smiled, gun to Danny's head as he sat tied to a chair between them. "You know, it was good of you to bring Danny here for us to save us the trouble of going to Stanton to get him".

I pondered what to do, and nothing came to mind. I'd just have to keep stalling for time and ideas. "You two? You're the killers"?

"Oh yes, all of them, and Danny here will be the last".

I thought about making a dive for Jill, she wasn't exactly spritely and I could probably take her in a drawn out fight. But beer and age had weighed me down, and in the short term she'd be able to pull the trigger before I got to her. So. Betty loved to talk, and I knew my questions would keep the scene playing out. She'd continue on as long as she had an audience. "How did you do it"?

"The same way we used to get the boys up for a game, silly. We just strolled in, all prettied up", at that she beamed, trying to flash a lascivious smile which instead came out somewhat like a retarded monkey trying to see its own nostrils, "and they were like putty in our hands".

As she spoke, I heard something outside, but neither of them reacted so I didn't let on. Still no ideas had come. "Why, Betty"?

"We were both cheerleaders that year, Jill and I, and that was going to be our ticket out of town. We did everything we could to make sure the boys won. We revved them up before the games, we offered ourselves to the competition and slipped stuff in their beer, anything. We were going to be cheerleaders for the state champions, and the Dallas Cowboy Cheerleaders were going to hire us. Then they did the unthinkable. They lost, badly. And no one remembers also rans. And worse, no one remembers cheerleaders for losers".

I was sure now that someone else was in the library, and I did everything I could to not betray that fact with my eyes as I followed the movement mentally. "Why now? The game was nearly twenty fucking years ago".

Betty paused for a moment, and I thought maybe she had heard something, but she was just preparing to speak. "Jill and I were talking on my fortieth. You didn't remember my birthday Jack, no one does. Anyway, we was talking and drinking, and realized that every problem we've had, the fact that our lives went nowhere was the result of one thing—these boys failed us. They *screwed* us, and they never apologized. It was time they paid. So we did to each of them what they did to us, screwed them—with help from a strap-on—and took their lives away. This time we slipped a little rat poison in their beer. I'm sure the other girls would have helped us if they were still alive".

It was at this point that things got dicey, as a book (I later learned it was a copy of the bible) came flying from the second floor overlooking the central area and smacked into the back of Jill's head (now that's what I call bible thumping). Jill went crashing forward with a shout, the gun went scattering across the floor, and both Betty and I turned to look towards the laughter erupting from behind and above. I was the first to realize the situation had changed and turned back to the scene in front of me while Betty still watched stunned as the lithe, short-haired woman who had thrown the book slipped back away from the railing and out of view. I quickly calculated the distances to Betty and the gun, and realized the gun was closer so went for that as Jill seemed to be a non-issue for the moment. By the time I had the gun in hand and began approaching Betty, she had started to turn back around, but she knew she was in trouble.

"Jack, now, you wouldn't use that on me, would you? You wouldn't just kill me like that?" Her voice was starting to tremble as I approached, a cold look in my eyes. "Please Jack, please." I was right in her face now, the barrel of the gun pointed at her head. I smiled darkly and she screamed. As I turned the gun to knock her in the head with the butt she crumpled to the ground unconscious.

Danny let out the breath he had been holding as he watched, and I stooped to untie him.

I looked up, eyes scanning the second floor railings and called out, "Whoever you are, you can come out now".

I needn't have bothered, as she came walking in from the right, already on the first floor. Something about her looked familiar, but I couldn't quite place her. "Th..thank you, whoever you are, you just saved our lives. But, who are you?"

She smiled, and laughed a little. Her voice was a little deeper than I would have expected, and the smile was ringing all sorts of bells, but I still couldn't place her. "You mean you don't recognize me, Jack? We went to school together after all", and she smiled a somewhat mischievous grin, like she knew a secret I didn't. "Come on, how about you, Danny? You knew me better than Jack anyway." Danny looked her up and down carefully, studied her face, but stood there just shaking his head though it was clear he was having the same close-but-not-quite experience of recognition.

She stuck out her hand casually. "Brian Fredericks, though you can call me Brenda now". Danny's jaw dropped first, mine barely a second behind.

"Brian? The waterboy Brian? But you left town ages ago."

"Well, that's true, but I came back once everything was done. No one ever guessed. Not even my old football buddies. I've just been one of the girls here in town since I got back. I picked up on what Ms. Motormouth there might be planning. I just didn't want the spotlight. I've kept a pretty low profile since I got back, and too much attention might make someone recognize me. You two I figure are okay, since you've got your own little secrets." She raised an eyebrow lewdly at that one, and we both knew there was no doubt she was Brian.

"So what do we do now", Danny asked. Suddenly reminding us we had two unconscious murderers at our feet.

"That's easy hon, Jack here arrests them, they get convicted, and then fried. No one's gonna believe either of them over Jack. Let's see, what else, yeah you two will quietly get a little serious nookie going on. And me, I'll go back to my husband". Brian/Brenda smiled again, amused at her own cleverness. "Take care guys", and with that she swept forward, planted a big kiss on each of our lips, and slipped back out the way she'd come.

Danny and I just looked at each other for a few moments, shaking our heads. Danny spoke first, while my gaze moved to the two unconscious women. "What a night, eh? Let me help you get these two locked up."

Still looking at the bodies, I suggested "maybe I'll just eat them instead." There was a pause, a long pause. Danny looked a little shocked, trying to assume I wasn't serious, but not so sure. I looked up at him and started to laugh and Danny finally joined in. He sounded relieved.

We put the girls in a makeshift cell, and slipped upstairs for a few beers. Danny had a few too many, and passed out.

I had to break the bad news to him when he woke up. It seems the girls somehow managed to escape during the night. It's what I told everyone else, too. But they had it coming after killing all those guys and threatening me and Danny. They're off the street now, and I won't be craving flesh for a while. Worked out well all around I think.

Rob Gates is Editor of the online review magazine, Wavelengths Online, focusing on genre works of special interest to gays, lesbians, bisexuals and transgendered people. He also writes freelance reviews for a number of gay and lesbian publications around the country, including the national magazine the Lambda Book Report. After years of criticizing other people's work, this is his first professional fiction sale.

While he occasionally tries to deny his Bubba roots, they often show in his lack of fashion sense and his love of all things cheaply barbecued. He and his partner live in Washington DC, home of the first Bubba President in ages.

DOIN' THE DRIVE-IN

Bradley H. Sinor & Lee Martindale

"This just ain't right! I tell you, Mac, this Just Ain't Right!"

"What ain't right, Billy Ray?"

"This!" Billy Ray Woods picked up one of a dozen eggrolls that lay on the tray he had just set on the counter. He held it with two fingers, like it was a piece of roadkill that had aged on the asphalt for longer than was good for it.

"An eggroll? What's the matter with it? It's perfectly natural," said Mike "Mac" McHenry. "Hell, my folks always used to order extra eggrolls, whenever we went out to eat chink. They're good stuff."

Mac and Billy Ray had been friends since the second grade, and Mac had long ago learned that it made no sense, in the long run, to try to understand what Billy Ray's reasoning on things was. It was easier to just ask a few questions and let him rant on for however long it took.

Billy Ray shook his head and dropped the eggroll down on the tray, alongside the others just like it that they had taken out of the oven. It struck with a dull plop, sending small pieces of crust flying off in a half dozen directions.

"Look, I'm not an idiot. I know Chinese food's good eatin'. Hell, you've had my Aunt May's sweet and sour pork. That's not the point, Mac. The problem is having it *here*, that's what don't seem natural and proper." To emphasize his point, Billy Ray stretched out his arms as if he were trying to embrace, not just the kitchen, but as much of the outdoors as he could include. "This is the Canyon Wall Drive-In Theater & Open Pit *Barbecue*. Not the Canyon Wall Drive-In Theater and Happy Hong Kong Chinese Restaurant. You've seen the menu Mrs. Abernathy posted for this Saturday night."

"What are you talking about?"

"She wants to serve this stuff *instead* of the ribs and pulled pork we *always* serve! You know we got to start cooking that pig sometime today if we're going to have it for Saturday."

"Yeah, I know." Mac picked up the clipboard with the weekend's menu written in neat block letters. Sure enough, there was nothing on it that needed to be barbecued, just baked, stir-fried or tossed. Chinese food and salad. "Maybe she's trying to help us all eat healthy. Maybe she's trying to di-ver-si-fy, keep the folks from getting bored with eating the same thing every week."

"Mac!"

"Tell you what, I think it's time we took our break," Mac said. He knew if he didn't call a halt right now, Billy Ray was going to go right on ranting about the menu for another hour.

So before his friend could say anything else, Mac pulled his apron off and headed for the kitchen door. The building that had been turned into a cook house had once stored the maintenance equipment that was necessary to keep the Drive-In open and running. So it was at the far end of the property, but it still had a full view of the Drive-In.

Mac had always loved this place, ever since his pa had brought him the first time when he was three years old. The theater had apparently been built, according to what folks said, nearly a decade before that, right at the beginning of what his pop, Jackson "Jack" McHenry, had described as "when things got really weird."

"Not that things weren't weird before that," he'd always add. "It's just that that's when the times just got weird enough to merit their own name."

As he fumbled to get a cigarette from the pack he'd rolled and filled that morning, Mac noticed something coming down the center of the theater screen—a person suspended from a rope with what looked like a tool bag over his back.

Since the screen was nearly two hundred feet tall and pushed nearly up against the canyon wall that gave the place its name, that meant whoever it was either had to rappel down from the top of the cliff or climb up the side of the screen and go from there. Working your way along the top of the screen before rappelling down was not the easiest thing to do, so most people who drew screen maintenance duty preferred to work off the cliff face.

Whoever was up there this time hadn't done that. The ropes were strung from the center of the screen. It wasn't that difficult, just a bit unnerving.

Lighting his cigarette, Mac watched the worker for lack of anything better to do just then. The person made his way over to a piece of metal hanging loose on the far left side of the screen. There'd been one hell of a wind storm whipping through the canyon last week, and this was the last of the things that needed to be repaired before the show Saturday. Not to mention how tacky it would look hanging loose like that at Sunday services.

It might have been a gust of wind, or something else entirely, but suddenly the climber started twisting to one side, struggling to maintain balance. This wasn't anything new; wind shears in a canyon were as normal as the sun coming up. It was when the air got too still that people started to worry.

Luckily, the only casualty was the cap the climber was wearing. As it fell away, white-blond hair came tumbling out from underneath.

Mac felt his stomach drop away as well. He knew that hair. The only person in three counties who had that color hair had no business being up there by herself; Mac's sister, Martha Elaine!

Not a month ago his old buddy Steve had been working up on the screen by himself. His rope had gotten tangled and he'd gone head first straight down, a hundred feet into the playground. They'd found him, dead of course, in the middle of the merry-go-round, stretched across a couple of plastic horses named Butterfly and Parsnip.

"We work in two's on the screen, always. A partner can save your life," Mrs. Abernathy had decreed.

"Marty! I'm going to kick your butt if you go and get yourself killed," Mac sputtered. That the only one close enough to actually hear him was Billy Ray didn't matter.

"Look, man," Billy Ray said, still ranting about the eggrolls. "What are we going to do about this stuff? I tell you it's just wrong."

Mac found himself suppressing an urge to belt the other man. "Eat 'em, serve 'em, stuff 'em up a squirrel's ass. I don't care!" Mac was worried about his sister hanging a hundred feet above the canyon floor. He wasn't in the mood to listen to Billy Ray's shit.

"But.." sputtered Billy, his eyes going wide as half dollars.

"Look, if you've got a problem, I suggest you go talk to Widow Abernathy. She owns the place, so she sets the menus!"

"I will, then," Billy Ray said with conviction.

"Well, you better wait till Raven Harkness leaves."

"Raven! Great, that's *all* we need. First we get these damn eggrolls at the Drive-In, and then we get hookers." he moaned "What's this world coming too!?"

"This isn't bad," *said* **Raven** Harkness. "It tastes almost like *real* Dr. Pepper. If you ignore that odd fishy aftertaste." She set the mason jar down on the table, clinking the ice that floated in several inches of dark liquid.

Ellen Abernathy smiled. If there was one thing her dear departed husband had taught her, it was that, in business, you sometimes had to deal with people that you didn't necessarily approve of. Raven Harkness was one of them. Of course, if truth be told, it wasn't the girl herself Ellen didn't approve of; it was the business she was in.

It was, she mulled silently, a Sign of the Times. In the Good Old Days, a woman like that, with whom so many men crawled into bed—for money!—would have found herself on the receiving end of the massed displeasure of every Respectable Woman in the county. And now one of those Respectable Women was crawling into bed with Raven herself—in a manner of speaking.

Ellen's people had been working on the formula, as well as those for Coke and several other soft drinks, for over a year. There were still supplies of the syrup available, but who knew how long they would last? "Most folks around here don't have your educated palate. I'm thinking that we'll try it out on them this weekend, along with the new menu."

Something in the old woman's tone caused Raven to raise one carefully plucked eyebrow. "I suspected, when you invited me over, that it wasn't just to take the Pepsi Challenge. Or in my professional capacity," she added, anticipating a blush. What she got was twinkling eyes and a chuckle that passed quickly and turned again to mild worry.

"Actually it was for 'professional' reasons I called you over," said Ellen quickly adding, "but not *that* profession."

Raven cocked her head at the theater owner. She had a bad feeling right now that the next words out of Ellen's mouth were going to be, *"I know the truth."* But they weren't.

"We've been getting our supplies of barbeque dry rub spices and meat tenderizer from you for six months now. When you said you could get us the spice mix for the Chinese food, it made sense. But we got it in a couple of days ago, and Billy Ray and Mac tell me about half the bags of Chinese spice looks like they've been opened and resealed, and a third of the bags of meat tenderizer are labeled 'MSG: Not For Resale'. I haven't asked any questions about where or how your sources are getting this stuff and I'm not going to." Ellen's demeanor turned from folksy to hard businesswoman as she spoke. "But there is one thing I will not stand for, and that's being sold shoddy goods. You promised me that these things were going to be fresh and restaurant-quality, and I thought we had an understanding. We may just have to dump this batch, use what dry rub we have left over, and put off this 'Chinese Night' until we can find a reputable supplier."

It was a problem, but not the one Raven had expected. "I'm just as upset about this as you are, Miz Abernathy. Not about the meat tenderizer; I'm sure you already know MSG is the same thing, right? But there's no excuse for the spices being opened like that, and I promise you I'll have a word or two with my 'source'. My guess is somebody at the factory got greedy, short-weighted the packages, and is selling it on the side. It won't happen again. Heads are gonna roll over this." After all the legwork Raven had put in on this project, the heads of those who'd nearly put it in jeopardy wouldn't just roll; they'd be stuck on the nearest flag pole. "Tell you what. Go ahead and use the stuff in the shipment Saturday night, and I'll make sure the next order is on the house."

Ellen thought about it for a second or two, then nodded. "That's only good business. I'm sure he'll want to know he's got a thief working for him. We'll consider this as having come to an understanding then."

Raven smiled and said, "Is that all that was bothering you, Miz Abernathy?"

Ellen took a deep breath. "Since you put it that way, no. I know I said this low-fat, low cholesterol idea sounded good when we talked about it, but..well, it's got me a little worried. I mean, eating healthy is a good thing, I guess, but around here, we're kinda traditional. I'm not sure how my customers will take to the whole thing."

"Eating healthy *is* a good thing," Raven replied quickly, glad to have the subject changed. "Especially since there hasn't been a regular doctor around here since..."

"Since Doc Morgan left for that AMA convention in California and never made it back. First place the Plague hit, I hear."

"Yeah, that's how I heard it, too." *And,* thought Raven, *from much better sources than yours.* "And it's not like you're destroying tradition, just giving it a little break. A couple of weeks to get folks used to it, then a Chinese night once or maybe twice a month. Good old-fashioned barbecue the rest of the time, just like before. Think of it as a nice change."

The older woman thought about it for a long while, then shrugged and nodded. "You're probably right. Although if Poor Mr. A isn't lookin' down from heaven this very minute and clacking his dentures like he used to do when he was upset with me, I'd be mightily surprised."

Raven laughed. "Think of it as doing a Public Service, Miz Abernathy. People are going to thank you." *Just not the ones you think.*

Shortly thereafter, Raven politely declined an invitation to stay for supper. "I thought I'd have Cook try out your Moo Gou Gai Pan recipe, along with Sweet and Sour Venison and eggrolls" with the excuse that she had a "date" that night with one of her "regulars". Ellen carefully schooled her features against a look of disapproval and walked her guest to the front door.

"If it's not pryin'," the old woman said as they stood on the front porch, "you seem like too bright a woman to be doing what you do for a livin'. You ever done anything else?"

Raven laughed. "Yeah. Before the Plague. I was a Personal Fitness Trainer."

Raven did, indeed, have a "date", and it *was* for the purpose of conducting business. At dusk, an 18-wheeler pulled off the two-lane that ran in front of Raven's modest house. Anyone who cared to be watching - and three of her neighbors always cared on a regular basis - would recognize it as the same patriotically-painted cab, with "Pennymann Transport, Proud and Independent Since 1986" painted on the doors, that pulled up this time every week and stayed until the next morning.

Anyone who cared to keep watch—and those same three neighbors always kept watching—saw the same almost-middle-aged, almost bald, almost-good-looking man slide down and envelop That Woman in a bone-cracking hug, which almost always ended with him grabbing a double handful of butt that was almost-covered by a short flowered skirt. Anyone still watching—and getting those three neighbors away from their windows would have required intervention by the National Guard—would see him lift Raven over his shoulder and carry her, her squealing and him laughing, into the house. "He seems like a good ole boy," each of the watchful neighbors would mutter to themselves. "He could do a whole lot better than that whore."

Raven walked to the window of her bedroom, her blouse hanging open to display the cobweb black bra. She pulled the curtains closed, with a smile and a wink aimed at her neighbors. A moment later, her "date" dropped a CD into the player next to Raven's bed. Music began - "Bolero" - playing background to noises of feminine giggles, male moans, the sound of bedsprings settling into a more-or-less steady rhythm, and an assortment of other sounds that her neighbors would be expecting to hear.

The click of the CD player was like the click of a TV remote control, so quickly did Raven and her "date" change channels. From blatant sexuality to cool professionalism in three nanoseconds or less. But then Raven Harkness, investigative agent for United Pharmaceuticals, Inc., and her partner on this particular assignment, Penn Mulroney - formerly attached to the U.S. Treasury - were nothing if not professional. To the point of being downright stuffy.

"I still don't understand why we're going to so much trouble on this particular test," Penn commented as he pulled a high-tech note pad from his overnighter. "Why can't we do the same thing we did in Harlan, Kentucky and Gun Barrel City, Texas? Grab a significant representative sample of the population, split it up into a control group and a test group. It's far more efficient, and we get better test data that way."

"It's easier, I'll grant you," Raven replied, "but it's also extremely wasteful. When The Company finally develops a vaccine, those are potential customers being eliminated after those tests. And besides," she continued in response to Penn's derisive snort, "there comes a time when science has to come out of the lab and go into the field."

"Well, it's in the field this time in spades. That trailer out there is stuffed to the roof with enough equipment to record separate telemetry on every man, woman and child who shows up Saturday night," Penn said.

"Good. The sooner we wrap this one up, the better I'll feel. We came too close to blowing it tonight, and I might not be able to pull it out next time." Raven described her visit with Mrs. Aberthany, concluding with the *"understanding"*.

"Good work, Harkness. If this whole diet theory is right, that MSG is key to proving it."

"I read the reports just like you do. Why do you think I've been pushing the stuff to Abernathy for the last few months? MSG breaks down the enzymes that form in the presence of meat, heat, and barbeque sauce. If the enzymes are what's conveying immunity, the absence of them should result in verifiable data."

"That plus the healthy dose of plague germs we slipped into the Chinese spices. But I agree, the sooner we get our data and get out, the better. So I suggest we get a few hours' sleep, then go out to the site and get the containment field generators and data pick-ups placed before dawn."

"Good idea," Raven answered, lying down on the very edge of her king-size bed and arranging her limbs in a pose reminiscent of Sleeping Beauty.

Penn stretched out on the very edge of the other side, placing a machine pistol on the cover between them like a sword. "Wait until you see what the techs worked out in the way of individual transmitter/antenna units," he said, as the music, and the accompanying sound effects reached their climax.

"Oh?" Raven prompted as she counted to ten, reached across Penn and turned off the strobe lights and mirror ball.

"Chopsticks."

Saturday night began like any other at the Canyon Wall Drive-In Theater, Open Pit BBQ and Full Gospel

Evangelical Church of the Fully Redeemed. Just before six o'clock Mac came riding up on his ATV to the main gate to find over thirty cars waiting to buy tickets. It wouldn't be dark for two, maybe three hours, but that didn't matter. Like every other Saturday night, people were here to enjoy themselves, eat, and party!

First order of business, as always, was turning on the marquee. It could actually be done from the projection booth, but Mrs. Abernathy preferred having it turned on at the secondary switch near the entrance. It was how Mr. A had always done it, and she saw no reason to change.

Mac scanned the line of waiting vehicles: cars, trucks, a couple of dirt bikes, a farm tractor pulling a wagon full of people and even (God forbid) a mini-van. Okay, the mini-van happened to be painted in camo colors and sported a Confederate battle flag on the window, but it still looked strange - or so Mac thought.

"Hey, that you, Mac?" A one-eyed man about Mac's age leaned out of the window of a blue Bronco. Even without looking, Mac would have known Joe Partridge's voice.

Partridge had been sitting in front of the marquee long enough to finish a beer and a couple of cigarettes; the remains were lying on the ground next to his car. Tonight he was wearing an eyepatch with a big cat's eye painted on it, one of several dozen he owned, most with even more bizarre designs. The man had lost his eye two years before in, depending on which story you believed, either a hunting accident or a run-in with a rake while working in his mother's garden. Mac favored the latter explanation.

"Yo, Joe. How's it going?"

"Fair to middlin'." Partridge reached down to the floor of the cab and pulled out a can of beer that he held out for Mac. "Want one?"

"Pass. Maybe later."

"More for me," laughed the one-eyed man. "So what kind of candy-assed movies are you guys showing tonight?"

Mac sighed. It wasn't as if this was the first time that someone had asked that question while sitting in front of the marquee, and it wouldn't be the last.

"Double feature tonight, Joe. *Die Hard XIV* and *Revenge of the Underwater Nazi Cheerleading Ninjas.*"

"Any good?" asked Partridge. As if he hadn't seen both a half-dozen times before. The Canyon Wall Drive-In might not have the widest selection of movies to choose from, but their customers seemed to approve of what did make it to the screen.

"Finest kind!" Mac told him.

The distinctive sound of a semi's air brakes caught Mac's attention. He watched a big Kenworth tractor-trailer combination come slowly rolling up the road. The driver expertly guided it off to one side, parking in an area fifty yards from the box-office. From this distance Mac could read the words "Pennymann Transport" painted on the door. A man in a blue baseball cap slid out of the cab and walked toward him.

"Howdy," said Mac.

"How do," said the driver. "Okay to leave my rig out here and walk in?"

"Not a problem. Got ourselves a nice picnic area next to the concession stand. Plenty of places to sit and watch the show," Mac replied. "I'll have the box office open in just a few minutes."

"Sounds good to me," the man nodded. "You guys just keep an eye on my rig."

"Will do." And they would, thought Mac. There were guards up along the canyon walls with nightscopes and deer rifles, as well as security on the lot armed with shotguns, who kept an eye on things. Just because Mac hadn't heard any reports of zombie attacks in several months didn't mean there hadn't been any. But, more likely, the worst they'd have to deal with would be a few drunken fights.

Half an hour later, a yellow Barracuda came rolling up to the box office. Sitting behind the wheel was Raven Harkness, dressed in cut-off jean shorts that most definitely showed off her legs, a tee shirt that ended just below her boobs and tight enough to cut off circulation to them, and lizard-skin cowboy boots. "Looks like it's going to be a good night, Mac," she purred.

"It always is at the Drive-In, Miss Harkness," nodded Mac as he took her money. "You enjoy yourself."

"The name's Raven, and I definitely intend to do just that."

"Hey, sugar." Penn slid into the Barracuda next to Raven, one arm sliding around her shoulders.

"I was wondering when you'd show up." She snuggled into the crook of his arm and nuzzled his ear for the benefit of occupants in neighboring cars.

"Well, I've been busy, sugar, busy. Just wandering around here and talking to some of the folks. Real friendly people in this town." Penn returned the ear nuzzle and murmured, "Of course, if they knew about the mikes and telemetry transmitters we planted earlier, plus the back-ups I've been palming onto speaker poles for the last hour or so, I'm not sure how friendly they'd stay."

"Doesn't matter, does it?"

Penn's lack of answer was answer enough. He leaned past the woman as if adjusting the volume control on the speaker hung in the window. "I just got back from 'makin' sure the rig was okay'. Signal input five by five on all channels and recording. We'll not only get all the data the techheads want, we're getting every bad joke, fart, and moan that goes on here tonight. By the way, where're the guns?"

One of the rules Ellen Abernathy enforced with a vengeance was "no guns at the Drive-In". Getting caught with one meant getting banned from the theater for up to six months at a time. Patrons checked their firearms at the box-office, where there was a nice, big, solid-bolt steel locker and an armed guard, and reclaimed them only when they left. The arrangement didn't set too well with a lot of folks, but when it came to the Drive-In, what Widow Abernathy wanted, she got.

"In the false bottom of my trick bag. Back seat next to the cooler. Your .45, my 9MM and a couple of Uzis in case the party gets a little rougher than expected."

Penn reached into the bag and began to forage around for the trip mechanism. He pulled out a couple of items, each one causing his eyebrows to creep toward his non-existent hairline a bit more. Raven wasn't sure, in the fast dimming light, but she thought he blushed a time or two.

"Your cover includes an 18-wheeler. Mine includes these."

Penn stuffed the items back into the bag as if he suddenly remembered he wasn't wearing rubber gloves. "Your expense reports must make interesting reading."

*"**What do you mean you** ain't got no ribs!"* roared Calvin Howard. He was standing across the counter at the concession stand , not two feet from Billy Ray, yelling loud enough to be heard all the way up the rim of the canyon.

"That's what I said, Calvin. No ribs, no sloppy joes, no nothing like that. You got a choice of egg rolls, sweet and sour venison, or moo gu gi pan," Billy Ray told him again. "Combination dinner gets you a choice of two of the three, and the Deee-lux Combination gets you all three."

"You want me to eat chink? I've been dreaming about good old-fashioned Drive-In barbecued ribs all week! And you want me to eat *chi-ya-nee-zzz!*"

"I don't care what you eat, Calvin, or if you eat at all. Order something or get out of the way. We got other people who want to get their food 'fore the movie starts."

"This is downright un-American. It Just Ain't Right," Calvin grumbled.

"Don't I know it." The sight of Sarah Marie Cunningham, next in line and decked out in very tight-fitting jeans, only momentarily took Billy Ray's mind off the miseries, or the thought that this was going to be a very long night.

The first indication of trouble at the Drive-In came precisely one hour, seven minutes and twenty-two seconds into the first feature film, and was announced not by data streams, bouncing gauges, or the blinding white light of film breaking. The signal was a high-pitched male scream from the far south end of the very back row.

It erupted from the cab of a 1972 GMC pick-up belonging to and occupied by one Jimmy Dean Haskell. The young man, after several months and considerable effort, had finally convinced one Carla Jean Bevins to perform an *unnatural* act upon his person. He'd looked down, inhaling in preparation of telling the young woman, "Hey, easy... not so hard with the teeth," to find the aforementioned young woman—eyes oddly glazed, skin oddly pale, and blood gushing from her happy grin—swallowing a mouthful of meat.

Over thirty years in the movie theater business, first with her late husband, then on her own, had accustomed Ellen Abernathy to every sound that should or shouldn't be heard around an operating Drive-In theater. That odd banging noise she heard coming from the projection booth as she made her regular route down the hall to her office wasn't one of them. Thumping wasn't one, either. And it was not a noise that inspired a lot of good feeling.

"Hey, D.A., is there something wrong?" She pushed the heavy door to the booth open.

David Allen "Call me D.A." Morris had been the projectionist at the Canyon Wall Drive-In Theater for five years. When she'd hired him, Ellen had figured he'd be gone in a few weeks with just enough money in his jeans, an itch in his feet, and a step or two ahead of an irate husband or father or two with shotguns. But D.A. had surprised her; he kept his nose clean, worked hard and seemed right at home in the projection booth,

From the doorway Ellen could see him standing, with his back to her, next to one of the projectors. His head, at an odd angle, was moving up and down, hitting the side of the big metal casing.

"D.A.?" she said again.

The projectionist didn't seem to hear her at first. Then he turned slowly around to face her. In the crook of his arm was the big yellow tiger-striped cat that hung around the place. But it was D.A.'s face that held Ellen's attention. There was a large wound on the side of his forehead, from which blood dripped down across pale gray skin. His eyes seemed unfocussed and drifted from side to side.

"Damn, D.A., not you!" Ellen backed out of the room quickly, slamming the door hard behind her. As she sprinted down the hallway, she couldn't shake the image of the cat, sitting quietly in D.A.'s arms and purring as gray-skinned fingers moved gently through its fur.

Mac was taking his first opportunity to relax all evening. There hadn't been a car in a half-hour and it didn't look like there would be. Most of the regulars were inside. But Mrs. Abernathy insisted, as had her husband before her, that the box office stay open until half an hour into the second feature. It was almost a sure thing that somebody was going to come roaring up the road in a cloud of dust and total confusion as to why the movie had already started.

He pulled a paper bag out from under the main counter of the box office. Inside were two eggrolls, a container of sweet and sour venison, a can of beer and a Butterfinger. "Nothin' like a balanced diet," he said to himself, "something from each of the four basic food groups."

Two bites into his meal, Mac heard *something*. He wasn't all that sure just what it was that he had heard. It *could* have been shouting - or screaming - coming from inside the theater grounds. Or it could just as easily have been from the movie. He could see, on the screen, the guy who'd taken over the DIE HARD series from Bruce Willis beating up one of the second-banana villains.

Eggroll in one hand, Mac picked up the walkie talkie and thumbed the transmit button. "This is the box-office. Anything going on back there that I should know about?"

"I'm not.." **Penn never finished** that sentence. His pistol came flying up from the car seat, centered on a target outside the car window behind Raven's back, and fired twice in quick succession. Raven grimaced from the pain of the shot going off so fast and close to her head. She went deadpan when, a split-second later, brains and blood rained over the Barracuda's yellow skin. Then she was moving, her own gun in hand as she opened the car door and rolled out. She nearly landed on top of what had been 70-year-old Nettie Thomas.

At least a dozen figures moved in different directions in the darkness beyond the car. From the shambling gait, it was fairly obvious that they had "gone over".

"Geez, I was hoping for one or two, a short sample for data purposes, but this is what I'd call an embarrassment of riches." Before Penn could answer, Raven leveled the muzzle at his head and sent three rapid shots into the skull of the former Harry Dennis, local mechanic.

Less a matter of a half hour than of hundreds of images that blended into each other. Less a matter of thinking than of reacting. It was quickly obvious that she and Penn were not the only ones who'd ignored the "no guns" rule as, here and there, she saw flashes from gun barrels and heard the discharge of any of a half dozen different types of weapons, from pistols to shotguns.

At one point Raven noticed a young woman, white-blond hair spilling over a black duster, moving among the cars like a battle goddess. A gun in each hand, Martha Elaine McHenry was quickly and efficiently taking out one infected zombie after another. Not far from her, Ellen Abernathy was doing a fair imitation of The Crone, working a slow and methodical pattern across the parking lot with a pump-action short-barreled shotgun.

"You go, girls," muttered Raven as she thumbed the clip release on her pistol and slid a fresh magazine in before the spent one had hit the ground.

"Is there anything left, Penn?" asked Raven.

Her partner shook his head and let his shoulders slump a little. "Just a big bunch of burning rubber and ripped up metal," he said. "I did manage to salvage a couple of things." Penn held up a pair of blue and white fuzzy dice.

"Oh, good grief, not those ugly things," she laughed.

At some point during the outbreak, a pickup and a couple of cars made a dash for the exit. The problem was they all three tried to go through an opening that had been built to allow two cars at a time to pass.

The results had been as good as any Demolition Derby. The cars rammed into each other, then catapulted forward and crashed into the pickup. The whole tangled mess went skidding against the wall of the canyon and rolled straight into Penn's Kenworth. To say the explosion was loud enough to wake the dead might have been an understatement, and besides, the dead seemed to be awake already. Six hours later, it was still burning and people were only beginning to get close to it.

A dozen men with fire extinguishers were standing watch around it to keep the flames from spreading. A CB call had brought the volunteer fire department out, who'd hooked into the drive-in's water system for something to pour into the wreckage.

"This is going to make some real interesting reading back at the home office," commented Raven as she watched the flames. "They're expecting data for the diet hypothesis."

"Well, they ain't going to get none, not this trip anyway," answered Penn. "What say we send them a take-out order of egg rolls."

Bradley H. Sinor Growing up in Southwestern Oklahoma Brad spent many years at the Drive-In theatre studying bubbas in their natural habitat, along with their reactions to various stimuli; food (usually BBQ), liquid (soda or beer) and visual (movies that normally featured car chases, serial killers, Ninjas, explosions, and beautiful women usually wearing very little).

Brad's short fiction has appeared in the *Merovingen Nights* series, *Time Of The Vampires*, *On Crusade: More Tales Of The Knights Templar*, *Lord Of The Fantastic: Stories In Tribute To Roger Zelazny*, *Horrors: 365 Scary*

Stories, Merlin, Such A Pretty Face, Warrior Fantastic, Single White Vampire, and other places. He will have stories appearing in *Dracula In London*, and *Personal Demons* this year, and *Dark and Stormy Nights*, a chapbook featuring all three of his Merovingen stories as well as a never before published story will be coming this year from Yard Dog Press.

Lee Martindale's fantasy fiction has appeared in *Marion Zimmer Bradley's Fantasy Magazine,* three MZB-edited anthologies, the recently-released anthology *Outside The Box* edited by Lou Anders, and assorted small-press and electronic venues. She is also the editor of the groundbreaking anthology *Such A Pretty Face: Tales of Power & Abundance*, published by Meisha Merlin Publishing.

Lee was born and raised in one hotbed of Bubbadom (Kentucky), and has lived for over twenty years in another (Texas). She and her husband George currently live in Plano, TX.

DADDY WAS A BIG QUEER BUBBA

Selina Rosen

As I sit watchin' my sister Jewel knock squirrels out of a tree with her wrist rocket an' a fist full of marbles, I am once again awed by her resourcefulness an' beauty. Unfortunately I had ta marry ma fat, ugly cousin Arlene 'cause Jewel turned out ta be just as gay as Daddy was.

That's right! I said ma dad was gay. An' ya know what else? I'm real proud of that big queer fucker.

That weren't always the case though. As a kid growin' up in *The Confederate Flag Must Fly* trailer park just outside of OKC, havin' a queer fer a daddy had made my adolescence a livin' tormentuous hell. It didn' help none that Daddy had named me Elton after his favorite queer singer. An' there was nowhere ta hide, cause everyone in the whole damn country knew.

I don' rightly remember as I was jus 'bout five when it happened, but the story went somethin' like this ...

It was the last year of the Jerry Springer Show. Jus a few months afterwards Jerry retired 'cause ah he broke his hip tryin' ta get out of the way of a angry transvestite on a show called "I may be a big ole girl, but I'm a humpin' yer man". Anywho, my mama drags Daddy on the show ta tell him that she's been sleepin' with her cousin Roy Don. Well, Dad got really mad, an' before he could stop himself he's a chokin' Roy Don right there on the stage. Daddy always was a big, strong man, an' Steve—you know, Jerry's bouncer—had gotten too feeble ta really stop much of anyone. I'm thinkin' that's how ole Jerry got hurt by that there cross dresser.

But I durggreses ... The crowd was a yellin' "Jerry! Jerry!" so loud that it takes them awhile to realize that my daddy ain't mad at my mama, he's mad at Roy Don. Seems he was a sleepin' with Roy, too. It was a big ole hoopla right there in Technicolor, an' it was all the people in the trailer park talked about fer years.

When they got home Mama filed fer divorce. Daddy moved into a apartment in OKC, an' took up with a young pretty boy named Brian. Roy Don moved ta New York ta follow his dream of becomin' a show girl.

Mama never did have a nice word ta say bout Daddy, an' after the divorce she couldn' stop bad-mouthin' him. I guess I was too young then ta know what people were sayin'. I jus knew I missed ma daddy. I missed watchin' him drive into the trailer park an' block all the roads with his big rig. I missed helpin' him mow the trailer house yard (one pass down the left side, an' one down the right) an' I missed the grill filled three or four times a week with some sort of delectable bar-be-qued meat. Daddy just loves ta grill outside, hell I've even known him ta grill Spam!

The sheets hadn't been changed yet when Mama got rid of the grill. She never could stand bar-be-que, an' she said the smell of it made her think of Daddy an' how he really liked meat.

Daddy would come an' get us an' take us to his apartment. He would play games with us, an' sometimes he'd take us huntin' an' fishin'. Always he would fire up the grill on the balcony an' grill us up a whole batch of barbequed somethin'. Jewel an' me we'd chow down till we was full as ticks, an' then go ta sleep listenin' ta Daddy tellin' us 'bout the good ole days when you could own yer very own assault rifle, an' about rock an' roll fore the censers ruined it. He'd tell us stories about somethin' called rock-a-billy music an' a man called Elvis who he said was the king.

Those were good times. But when I turned nine I suddenly learned just what people was sayin' bout Daddy. I realized why Brian was always there, an' why Daddy kept pattin' him on the ass all the time, an' it had nothin' at all ta do with some football thing. I felt so stupid I began to believe all the hateful things Mama was always sayin' bout Daddy.

It finally dawned on me (I always has been a little slow) what the kids in the trailer park was teasin' me 'bout, an' I started gittin' in fist fights almost daily. I was a little scrawny kid, so I was always gittin' ma ass kicked, an' somehow this became Daddy's fault, too. By the time I was ten I wouldn' visit Daddy no more.

Mama was at least in part to blame for the way I felt bout Daddy, but she still got all powerful mad when I refused to go. Seems Mama had big plans for the weekends. No doubt layin' round on the couch screwin' some low life an' watchin' the TV. Mama considered that ta be like yuppies goin' ta the spa; it was her work out, an' she didn' want it interrupted by no smart-assed kid who wouldn' stay in his room.

She started sending me ta stay with my Uncle Jimmy on the weekends, so as I could be round a 'real man'. Jimmy weren't much of anything an' never had been. He'd hurt his back while working as a night watchman in a mattress factory—never did know how he managed that one—but it got him on the dole, an' there he'd stayed ever since. Some folks said that getting a government check had been a life-long goal of his.

All the week ends I spent with him I never saw him do nothin' more strenuous than sit on his ass, drinkin' beer, eatin' pork rinds, an' fartin' an' belchin'. But at least he grilled every weekend jus' like Daddy. Lookin' back I guess I shouldn' put ole Jimmy down. After all, I owe my life to his bar-be-qued bacon an' weenies, an' they weren' half bad eaten', neither.

I missed out on a lot the next two years. While ma sister kept goin' ta Daddy's an' gittin' ta hunt an' fish an' hear all his great stories, I was stuck in Jimmy's pig waller of a trailer watchin' him sweat, occasionally turn some meat on the grill, an' tell me how ta be a man.

"Yeah, son," he'd say. "Ain' nothin' in this world like a hot, wet, tight pussy. Ya sure don' wanna end up no sissy like yer Paw. Ya'd surely miss out on all the good stuff. Jus' don' get how a man looks at another guy's hairy butt an' finds love. Somethin' sick an' twisted 'bout a world where people are tellin' ya ta jus accept one guy stickin' his dick up another guy's ass. Why ya'd think there weren't enough pussy in the world! Hell, ya can throw a rock an' find a willin' female, an' ifin she ain' willin' a little rope'll fix that."

Yeah, it was real clear why the community as a whole felt better when I was with Jimmy instead ah my perverted Daddy.

I was twelve when the flue first started, an' had just found the pleasure of pullin' on my pecker so I had everythin' ta live fer. We started hearin' on the TV 'bout people gettin' sick, most were dyin', but some was goin' plum crazy. No one we knew was even sick. That was till Mama started actin' real funny.

Now Mama had spent her entire life in front of a TV. Whether she was cookin' (poppin' burritos, or ramen soup in the microwave), cleanin' (makin' a path so you could walk from the front to the back of the trailer without trippin'), workin' (as a at-home phone solicitor), takin' a bath (once a week whether she needed it or not), or screwin' (usually done while we were at school, or gone on the weekends an' on the couch in the livin' room so that she wouldn' miss her soaps, an' sometimes while she was "working"). No matter what she was doin' she was never more than a few feet away from one of the three TV's in our trailer house.

Well as you know all them yuppies got zombified from not eaten bar-be-que an' from workin' their whole lives in front of them there computer screens. Somethin' bout the radiation them screens put out, an' I guess the TV screen had done the same thing ta ma mama 'cause she went plum crazy, too.

One minute she was layin' on the couch eatin' her second box ah twinkies an' watchin' *Days of Our World Turning Light* jus' like normal, an' the next she was throwin' the Twinkies down an' screamin',"What the hell is this shit! Nothin' but fat an' calories. I need a good healthy salad with bean sprouts an' a fat-free dressin'." Then she turned the TV off; the silence was terrifyin'.

Jewel was two years older than me an' has always been a good deal smarter, so she knew this meant somethin' was terrible wrong. She grabbed me by the arm an' started pullin' me out of the trailer jus as Mama started screamin' hysterically an' runnin' after us sayin', "But first maybe a little human brains."

We ran all the way ta Jimmy's house with Mama right on our heels carryin' a big ole carvin' knife that Daddy had once used ta dress deer. When we got there Uncle Jimmy was layin' outside his trailer door blockin' it like so that we couldn' get in. We thought he was dead, but it turned out he was jus passed out drunk. We knew this because as we ran to the next trailer house we could hear him screamin' as Mama started slicin' an' dicin' on his ass.

I was sure Mama was gonna kill us next fer sure, an' then I heard the familiar sound ah Daddy's air horn. We turned an' saw Daddy skidding his big rig ta a stop sideway right at the gates ta the trailer park, then he ran around the truck an' headed fer us, shot gun in hand.

"Come on kids," he yelled, an' it was then that I realized that Mama had finished killin' her brother an' was done after us again. We ran towards Dad, an' I saw the shot gun kick before I heard the blast.

Daddy always had been a good shot. He kilt Mama with one shell.

We fell into our daddy's arms as Brian walked up beside him with a pearl handled 44 in his delicate hand, an' the whole trailer park seemed to descend on us at once.

"What they hell's goin' on?" Willie asked.

"That damn queer done went an' kilt Fanny Mae!" John Thomas screamed.

"Ain't like that, I saw the whole damn thing," Erlene Johnson screamed back. "Fanny Mae went plum ape shit crazy, kilt her brother an' was after her own kids. She mustah had that there Yuppie Flue shit."

"We ain't got time fer this shit people!" Daddy screamed. "We just came from OKC, an' there is a whole bunch ah them yuppies headin' this way, jus' as crazy as ole Fanny Mea was."

"Then we gottah get outah here!" John Thomas screamed.

"Ain't time, they ain't far behind us, an' there ain't no back way out," Daddy said. "Earl, Harry, you guys get Jimmy an' Fanny an' take them about a mile up the road. That oughtah slow them yuppies down some. You women go get the pickup trucks an' circle the park. You men go get your guns, rifles, crossbows an' knives, an' all the ammo ya can find. We're gonna have ta make a stand right here."

They all started to move, an' then John Thomas screamed, "Stop wait a minute! Are we all taken orders from this queer butt fucker now?"

Every one stopped an' looked at each other, an' then Harry said, "Come on, any of ya got any better ideas? Ya know how smart them queers always is on TV."

When the zombies hit us that afternoon they weren't expecting to meet a armed an' ready camp. They were crazy with the sickness an' easy ta kill. I even killed me a couple with my 22. In three hours we had killed every damn one of them. Damned yuppies never did know nothin' 'bout firearms an' huntin'. We got us a shit load of them fancy SUVs an' mini vans, too.

After that no one made fun ah me or ma daddy any more. In fact they made Daddy president of the trailer park, an' he leads us whenever we go into what's left of the city to forage for the essentials of life—ya know, stuff like Twinkies, beer an' soda pop.

Daddy an' I have a really good relationship now. I sort of like this new world of ours, ain't no laws. Ya can more or less take whatever ya find, an' ain't no one ta look down on anyone else.

I jus' wish ma sister weren't queer.

Selina Rosen is the kind of asshole who edits an anthology and includes not one, but *two* of her stupid-assed stories, while rejecting better pieces.

What ah bitch!

THE FIGHTING 77TH

Keith Berdak
~ TO MY MOTHER, JEANETTE BERDAK,
AND MY LATE FATHER, USAF MSGT. SY BERDAK ~

My men and I had been chasin' the Talibaptists for over an hour. The enemy squadron numbered a dozen or so, strung out in a snaky line through the tick-infested woods just outside of Annapolis, Missouri. We and the townsfolk had tolerated the fanatics for a few years now, but this time they had gone too far! The dumbasses had just kidnapped three of our women: Loose Bruce's wife, sister and cousin, along with my wife and lefty's niece. We weren't no zombies, but we was fer damn sure itchin' to taste blood!

"Nail him, Bruce!" I shouted, as the hooded, white-robed figure of a rearguard straggler came into view. Loose Bruce bounded forward with his huge huntin' knife, took a mighty swing, and split the T.B.'s mushy head right down to his chin. A loud growl, followed by a semi-human, snivelly whine and a wet crunch told me that my best dog, BeeToo, had took the throat out of another.

We were soldiers of the 77th Missouri Militia, a survivalist group of men, women, brats, cats and dogs living in a fenced compound of seven ratty trailers on the banks of the Black River, a few miles outside of Annapolis, MO. Annapolis is a town of 300 farmers, hunters and housewives, along with a few private landowners who mostly keep to themselves. We often trade with folks in town, and most of our boys was there right now, helpin' the townspeople set up defenses on

231

this hot spring mornin' of the year 55 A.K.1 , (or 2032 A.D., on the Jesus H. Christian calendar). Summer tourist season was comin' soon, and that meant the arrival of flesh-eatin' zombies. They would come a float-trippin' down the Black, lookin' to "do lunch" on whomsowhatthehellever they could run down.

At first we weren't sure what had caused the businessmen and other city folk to turn cannibal and even more of them to just up and die. An occasional broadcast on the short-wave would say it was a plague, Satan's work, or any of a shitload of other things. A bio-illogical weapon seemed most likely to me; another damn conspiracy by our Commie-infiltrated government! It ended up bein' some sort of virus.

Loose Bruce, however, had his own theory.

A few years back he had lost a farm that had been in his family for over a hundred years, all due to a piece of paper signed by some burro-crat in St. Louie who was too chickenshit to meet Bruce face-ta-face. As far as Bruce was concerned, the step from blood-suckin' banker to flesh-eatin' zombie was a little tippy-toe. But we'd deal with Zombunists in due time; right now there was other butts what needed kickin'!

With most of our boys in town being led by "Big" Dick Cholomax, there was only five of us to deal with this mornin's crisis. "Loose" Bruce Wilkins was the guy takin' point. He was my right-hand man, a tall, muscular ex-con with a taste for beer, weapons, mayhem and female relatives. Up there with him was Lester "Lefty" Schmidt, the short feller who had earned his nickname the hard way, by takin' a dump right on top of a spring steel trap he had set and forgotten about. When the shit hit the pan, the trap snapped shut and bit his right ball off! I reckon you could say that trappin' and crappin' don't always mix! Lester's 16-year old son Jimmie Joe Bob was a clumsy pile of zits and grease, but he was tryin' hard to do good. Jim's 11-year-old brother, Billie Bob

Joe was a small, useless turd. What the boy lacked in smarts he made up for by being an asshole, always grabbin' at the girls and playin' stupid impractical jokes. We all hated him, and even his daddy couldn't stand the little fartknocker. No one woulda been sorry if the boy got shot by a Talibap or ate by a zombie.

My name is Eustace McKracken, known to my people as "U-Mac". I'd been chosen to be our commander, mostly due to my eight years of high school and my brief experience as an Army motor pool sergeant over at Fort Leonard Wood. A handsome and charismatical feller, I was six-foot tall, 45 years old, with huge sideburns and thick black hair, just like The King. I was equipped with a big-ass beer gut (they say that it's a wise man who builds a shed over his "tool", but I had me a 3-car garage!).

But I was also a natural leader, mean as a pissed-off gator, and well-learnt in the use of all kinds of weapons. My constant companion was my dog, a big black German Shepherd I called "BeeToo". I named him after those Stealth Bombers that the Air Force used to fly out of Whiteman A.F.B., up near Sedalia. He was fast, sneaky and fearsome, and damn near smart enough to hike his leg and spell his name on the side of a methane tank! But his name was mostly due to his skill at saturating a target area with dog-doo cluster bombs.

Like many militias in this state, we had started out as a white supremacist group, armed to the teeth and filled with hate. Back then, I didn't have much love for folks of color. After all, it had been a Black army major who had brung me up for a court martial; somethin' to do with missin' weapons, ammo, grub, solar batteries and a few cases of the new Mo-lecular Duk-Tape. I had hightailed it down to Annapolis with some army buddies and a few truck-loads of supplies where, with some like-minded folks, we formed the 77th, a bastion of Whiteness in a world turned dark by the disease that we just called "the Curse". To tell the truth, though, we was more interested in drinkin', shootin' guns, and holdin' fart contests. We was too lazy for any race wars.

I admit that we hadn't always been the nicest folks around. We had done our best to avoid inbreedin' (Loose Bruce aside, but he didn't have no kids) by grabbin' the occasional women that floated the Black River in summers past. They resisted us at first, until the Curse struck and they noticed that the folks around these parts seemed to be immunitized against it. Then, they was glad enough to stay on. I even married one, a partial blonde of French descent by the name of Cindy Sue Blanche Gravoise. We was well-stocked with essentials: Cheap-Ass Beer and Barbecue Sauce, pork rinds, beans and Twinkies, along with plenty of good huntin' and fishin'.

Still, we was a rough bunch, usually filthy and drunk. Hell, I was one of the few who could halfways read and write! Yep, my boys was rude, crude, and dumb as dungheaps. But they was family, and my late mama had taught me not to speak badly of family; leastways, not when they could hear ya, and 'specially not if they was drunk and packin'.

Some folks in town was religious types, mostly Pantycostals. Any of 'em would tell ya to yer face that ya was goin' to Hell if ya didn't follow their particular version of Jesus H. Christ, but at least they sometimes did it with smiles on their faces! We, however, had our own faith.

Just a few years back a wanderin' preacher named Missouri Smith had tought us a new faith, *The Way of The King*. Smith had told us that Jesus H. had come back in 1935 A.D. as a young boy in Tupelo, Mississippi. He didn't return as Jesus H., because He recollected what the Romans did a couple thousand years ago; He also knew that comin' back in His True Form would be bad for the money-makin' racket that religion had become. Those who was now His most faithful believers would be the first ones to grab a hammer and some nails! He was in no mind to go through that again! And I'll be double-dipped in dog-doo if Rev. Smith's beliefs didn't make sense!

I had been raised as a Baptist, but I do remember the shrine to The King that my mama had put up in the trailer, with posters, records, candles, and a buncha other worshipful stuff. I knew that He was a great singer, but I hadn't realized that He was the One True Savior, who had been ressurrectummed to bring about the blessed time known as AHUNKA-HUNKA-BURNIN'-LOVE.

"But The King had seen that the world was headed down the outhouse fast", Missouri Smith preached, "So after 42 years of His Ministry on Earth, He called upon His Alien-gels to take Him back home. I was an actual witness when the little gray fellers came in their space ship and levitationalized Him up, having left a dead clone in His place to fake His death. They Ass-ended into the Heavens, but not before The King had telepathetically sent His Word into my noggin, to spread around in these evil times."

And Smith had told us that we should give up our racist ways, and shared with us a story of one of The King's wonders. The Miracle of the Multiplication of the Cadillacs. Then, in a voice that carried a tune like a bucket of catfish stinkbait, he sang us one of The King's hymns, which sounded vaguely like one of the songs my mama used to play on the eight-track...

"Love Me faithful, love Me sweet, I thought I was dead;
Fell right off the toilet seat, landed on my head.
Woke up on a space-ship, replaced by a clone.
But My Words should be held dear
In every Bubba's Home.
Love Me Faithful, love Me true, though for now I'm gone,

Off with small Gray Aliens, snatched right off the john.
Though I'm far from Earth now, someday I'll return;
least I'm not 'six underground',
Getting' ate by worms!"

And with tears in our eyes, we realized that carryin' hatred in your heart was like luggin' a bag of wet manure; at the end of the day, the only one who stunk was you! Besides, all it took was a look at the Talibaptists to see that "pure" white folks was anything but superior!

The Talibaptists was a whole 'nuther case o' the crabs. They wasn't really Baptists. They was mostly a mangy lot of Koo Kluks, a few Christian Coagulationists, some survivin' Branched Davidiots and some of them crazy snake-handlin' folks from Tennessee. They called themselves "The Neo-Branchin' Davidian Church of the White Jesus Hitler Koo-rash Christ." We just called them "Talibaptists' after the Taliban, those moronical fundamentalists who took over Afgannystan a few decades back; you remember, the guys who was spared the plague by virtue of having blowed themselves up with a home-made nuke-yuler bomb! Our Talibaps had the same narrow minds, the same way of treatin' their women like dogs, and a deep hatred of anything that might bring joy and happiness. The T.B.s were led by a fat 55 year old feller who called himself "Dave Bob Hitler Koo-rash the 5th," after the original, pencil-dicked Nazi asshole hisself, along with that fool Dave Koo-rash from back in Wacky, Texas, who convinced a bunch of Davidiots that he was Jesus H. Christ returned, only this time with bad eyesight, along with a taste for guns, drugs and under-age girls. That turd had rewarded his flock by setting himself and most of them on fire back in 16 A.K.

Dave Bob the 5th claimed to be a great-great-great-grandson of the original Dave Koo-Rash (by one of his ten-year-old brides who had escaped *The Big Weenie Roast*, as we called it). Dave Bob 5 prevailed upon his flock to keep the white race "pure" by marryin' only within the 'family'. Back when he was just an annoying loudmouth preacher up in town, he would rattle on about how "fine" and "pure" his group's kids were, and always had a bunch of the little snots with him in their filthy white sheets and pointy hoods. We had wondered if he kept them covered just for being ugly! He had even sponsored "Mein Summer Buybull Kampf," as he called it, but it was shut down when too many kids started to come up missing, particularly young girls.

His second-in-command was his son, Dave Bob the 6th, only 11 years younger than his daddy and "Aunt Mama." This scrawny turd was usually covered in sheet and hood; he was said to be ugly enough to haunt a new double-wide on a sunny day, and it was he who instipated the policy of keeping' all their girls on ankle chains, only able to reach the stoves, the outhouses and the beds. In their eyes, women was only good for cookin', feedin' and breedin'. His reputation for cruelty towards women and kids, all done in the Lord Jesus Hitler's name, was unmatched. As far as I was concerned, he and his folk had lived their final day, and would be meetin' their Heavenly Führer soon.

"Good boy, Bee!" I hollered to my dog as he dragged back the mangled carcass of the Talibap he had just killed. We pulled off the remains of the critter's bloody white hood, and stared in shock.

"Damned if he ain't even uglier than you, Boy!" said Lefty to his eldest son. "I guess what they say 'bout inbreedin' is true, after all!" His younger brother Billie Bob Joe snickered at this, and Bruce thumped the little shit upside the head, earning a squeaky yelp.

"Sheeit, this fool looks like one o' them walkin' catfish, crossed with a baboon!" I exclaimed, as I inspected the stiff up close. He had long, ape-like arms, pale, almost blue greasy skin, and looked more fit for tree-climbin' than walkin' upright. His eyes was about two inches farther apart than was normal; that's probably why they carried the machine pistols. They couldn't see straight forward, and relied on putting a bunch of lead in the air, hopin' to get lucky. This boy's fingers looked long and wormy, and his thumbs was short and close to the wrist, makin' him look even more like a big, ugly-ass monkey.

"I reckon that's why they's called *Branchin' Davidiots*, snickered Loose Bruce. "They oughta still be climbin' around in the branches!" We all had a brief laugh, then headed up the trail that the bunch had been draggin' our girls along.

The whole brouhaha had started early that morning. Our women had been out in the shallows of the river, gigging some fish and frogs. As was typical in the spring, they was wearin' little bikini tops and cut-off shorts. And, as usually, Jimmie Joe Bob Schmidt was hidin' in the weeds watchin', with hand in britches and eyes on the girls. Suddenly, he had told us, the gang of T.B.'s had come a lurchin' out of the woods, quickly surrounding the women.

"Dave Bob 6 hisself was leadin' the bunch," Jimmie Joe had said in his crackin' voice. "And he accused them of witchcraft, since they was half nekkid and carryin' little pitchforks. They grabbed Cindy Sue and the rest, and said that they was to be burned at the stake at midnight! I runned back as quick as I could!"

"Ya done good for a change, boy!" I had told him. "Mount up, men! We're goin' hunting'!" I had grabbed my favorite gun, an old AR-10 assault rifle, along with my Colt .45 Auto and a few grenades. The rest of the boys had loaded up, and off we marched through the moldy-smellin' woods in pursuit of the Talibaps.

238

Which had brung us to where we was now.

A few hundred yards up the path we stopped at an 8-foot chain link fence, topped with razor wire. We was treadin' dangerous ground now, 'cause we was on the edge of Copperhead Springs.

The owner was a crazy old coot named Kev Bird, who was rumored to be a witchy-wizard by the locals. He and his woman, an old Black gal named Nettie, had owned the place for 40 years or more. They both had fearsome reputations for bein' real smart, well-stocked with a shitload of exotical weapons, and a taste for practical jokes of a lethal nature. The folks in town still chuckle about the night Kev Bird snuck over to the Snake-Handler's trailer in the Talibaptist camp and replaced their tame rattlers and pythons with some snakes he got from Australia. At the next prayer meetin', eight of the fools put their faith to the test, got bit by critters that make our cottonmouths look like earthworms, and died real quick and painful. What a hoot! That gag put Kev and Nettie at the top of the TB hit list, but the Dave Bobs had enough sense to know that retaliation would get a real shitstorm dropped on their pointy heads.

We'd seen the pair in town on occasion; Kev was tall and lean, with long hair pulled into a ponytail. Nettie was more petite, and they both looked a lot younger than the 90 or so that everyone said they was. They always carried these long, slender black canes, wrapped up in Mo-lecular DukTape (You could strap a deer or your kids to the hood of your truck with no fear of them gettin' blowed off; it would only come loose with a de-bonding spray). We knew that they had spent some time in South America, and had brung back some strange shit.

The property had once been called the Silver Springs Resort, which was more of a last resort until Kev had bought it and fixed it up. On the property were two stone cabins and a large clubhouse, in addition to a fresh coldwater spring and a big cave, the Many-Cat Cave, which overlooked the Black River. From where we stood we could see a big greenhouse (I reckoned he was growin' pot), a few satellite dishes and a tall wachtower that stood on the bluff. We had heard that he renamed the place Copperhead Springs, in honor of his having been snakebit many years back (the snake died). Supposedly, they'd since been bit by so many kinds of snakes and spiders that they was pretty much immune to damn near any poison Ma Nature had created!

The Talibaptists had cut a hole through the fence, and had took themselves a shortcut; brave move on their part! There was only four of them in sight, and we watched them approch Nettie, who was stooped down in her garden. They loped on over and tried to grab her, yellin' the whole while about gettin' bonus points for burnin' a woman who was both Black and a witch. She started cussin' the gang, and kept smackin' 'em with her cane, all to no avail. We was ready to rush forward and help the lady, and maybe gain some allies...

Suddenly one of the TBs grabbed at his ass like he was stung by a hornet, which do get mighty big in these parts. Ten seconds later, another of 'em slapped at his neck. They started swaying as if drunk, and within a few minutes, they dropped to the ground, twitchin' and foamin' at the mouth. Kev Bird strode down the steps from one of the cabins, carryin' the black cane, what we now figured to be a blowgun. He walked over and kicked at the two freaks, who was both turning blue.

With slack-jawed wonderment, we came out from cover and went over to say howdy-do. BeeToo, who don't often take to strangers, ran up waggin' his tail and nuzzlin' at Nettie. Then he hiked his leg on the dying Talibaps, posting a "pee-mail" note for all other dogs to read.

Kev Bird saw that we all had our weapons put away, and took his hand off of the pistol that was on his hip.

The two surviving Talibaps stood there shaking, and a big yeller stain was spreading across the white robe of one of 'em.

"Well, I guess the ouabain-batrachotoxin mix works pretty well," said Bird to Nettie. And he smiled at us and said:

"Howdy, boys! Seems like we have a common problem," just as the two remaining Talibaptists turned to run. "We'd better fetch those two back here. I'm sure we can persuade 'em to tell us what the hell they're up to!"

"See if you can wing 'em, Jimmie Joe!" I ordered. The gawky teen anxiously leapt forward with his M-16, aimed, and tripped over a rock, firing up into the air. His sqirrely-assed little brother giggled again, and I just shook my head, 'cause I knew in my heart that young Jim could be a fine man and soldier, if he'd ever get his shit together.

"That boy couldn't pick his own nose without pokin' his eye out," I whispered to the others. I'd have to pull him aside later on; Jim Joe could use a little talkin' to, man-to-man, to boost his self-confidence.

The two Talibaptists was runnin' fast. Nettie picked a metal dart with a little red cone at the back and a thin bit of tubing filled with some green shit at the front, popped it into the back of her blowgun, and blew softly. The dart sailed through the air and hit one of the runners in the ass; he passed out in a few seconds. Loose Bruce picked up the rock that Jimmie Joe had fell over, gave it a toss, and hit the other fool in the back of the head, knocking him out. Lefty and an embarrassed Jimmie Joe dragged the two back.

Introductions was made, and Nettie invited us on back to have some tea. As she was brewing, Kev Bird took us for a tour, and we was impressed by all the shit he had gathered. In the clubhouse he had an old Toyoter Land Cruiser which not only had wheels and tires, but was set up to run on either propane or methane. He also had some military-type computers, some old desktop PCs and a bunch of odd lab equipment. He told us:

"Most of the satellites for communication, global positioning, as well as some of the Keyhole spy birds are still up there, though the orbits are getting out of whack, with so few around to control 'em. In our travels, we 'acquired' some late-model satellite phones, and we can tap into the SpySats to keep an eyeball out for zombies and those idiots up the road." He then pointed to a computer screen that showed our own camp, which looked kinda like a trash heap from outer space. He punched a few buttons, and we all got a King's Eye View of the Talibaptists's compound, which was overlaid by a topo-pornographical map of the area.

The SpySat was passing fast, but Kev had it shootin' pictures and video the whole time. You could make out people on the ground in the camp, and one of the last things we saw as the "bird" flew out of range was the blubbery form of Dave Bob 5, comin' out of a real nice big double-wide with a huge swasticker on the roof, draggin' a small, dark haired female with him. He chained her hands to a pole, and tore the shirt off her back. Then the picture turned to static.

Everyone in the room got a truly evil look on his face; we was ready to open up a big ole crate of Whupass and charge the few miles to the TB camp! Kev Bird calmed us down enough to start puttin' a plan together. He said that the computers would have a good photo-map of the Neo-Davidiot camp in about ten minutes; then we could figure out what to do. Nettie came back with some real nice tea, and she and Kev led us and the two TB captives, who was just comin' back to their senses, over to have a look-see at the greenhouse.

The first thing I noticed was that the greenhouse roof was covered in the super-efficient clear solar batteries that had been developed fifteen years ago. The roofs of the other buildings had them as well. We went inside, and Kev told us to watch our steps. The whole inside was surrounded by a moat about twelve foot deep and twelve foot wide, with a concrete bridge crossin' over to where the plants was growin'. The smooth-sided moat had lots'a branches and rocks in it, and was divided into four-foot sections. We could see the slithery movements of snakes in the underbrush. I told my dog to wait outside, and he was happy to do so.

"That's the critters Nettie and I brought back from South America, along with a few sent by friends in Africa and Australia," said Kev. "We milk 'em for venom, and we lent a few of those long, slender fellows," he pointed out a pale brown one, about seven-foot long, "to the snake-handlin' boys awhile back. It's called a taipan, and it's the third deadliest snake in the world. What a ripper! I wish I could have seen those fools trying to sing and dance with these fellas! They don't take much to being Buybull-thumped!"

We walked very carefully over to where the plants was. Loose Bruce and Jimmie Joe Bob was both disappointed to see that there was no pot plants growing. As a matter of fact, most of the things there looked pretty damn strange. Some were big vines with white flowers, and others looked sorta like some of the shit that growed around here, like Queen Ann's Lace. I tried reading the neatly-wrote labels on each of 'em, but I wasn't much good with scientifical names. *Strophanthus gratus, Strychnos toxifera, Colchicum autumnale;* the names didn't mean shit to me, but Kev Bird assured me that they were part of his arsenal. He picked some leaves off of one of the Colchi-coo-whatevers, and handed them to Nettie, with a glance toward the two Talibaptists captives. She nodded.

"I'll make you two boys some tea," she said to them. We had took their hoods off earlier, and they didn't look as strange as the others we had seen. Then, we asked 'em what the hell was goin' on, after reminding 'em about the snakepit. They got scared, and started yapping. We found out that they had thirty-eight men and boys of fightin' age, armed mostly with Mac-10 machine pistols, some semi-auto handguns, and a few deer rifles. Their women knew their place, and would all be hiding. They didn't have dogs; dogs didn't much like the "pure" ones, which probably meant the strange monkey/fishboys. We learnt all about their traps, and what little strategy their pointy heads could devise.

"And who was the dark-haired gal gettin' chained to the pole?" asked Jimmie Joe, who was gettin' really pissed off about a fine young thing bein' in the hands of these creeps.

Our prisoners turned even whiter than they was to start with. I reckon they didn't know about Kev's satellite, because they started babblin' on about us using Satanic Powers of Sight, and how their Savior, Dave Bob Hitler Koo-rash the 5th, would smite us all down.

Jimmie Joe repeated his question, emphasizin' his point by punchin' one of 'em in the mouth, knocking out half of the boy's teeth, leavin' him with two. And the whimperin' Talibap spit out blood and mumbled:

"We snatched her off the river with her family, and told her she was to become a bride to the Most Holy Rev. Dave Bob 5. She wouldn't 'graciously submit' like she was supposed to, so we killed her Ma, Pa, and little brother. I'm sure she's a'gettin' the same lesson all the girls get. She's gonna burn along with your she-demons tonight!" He finished with a bloody, gap-toothed smirk.

They musta been grabbin' girls off the river, like we used to, but for their own evil purposes. Rednecks though we was, we didn't put up with anyone mistreatin' women that way; although that's how we got our women in the first place, we'd always been nice to 'em since. We knew that our girls would castripate us in our sleep if we even looked like we was gonna pull any shit like that! Besides, our Lord King would most surely get royally pissed! Jimmie Joe and Bruce was about to throw both of the dipshits to the snakes, when Nettie returned, carryin' a tray with two glasses of tea, complete with ice cubes and little lemon wedgies. She smiled as though everythin' was fine and dandy, and said:

"You boys look a little like you done had the shit scared out you! Here's a couple glasses of nice herbal tea to steady your nerves!"

"We ain't drinkin' nuthin' from a Ni..." one of 'em started to say, but thought better of it. "Why, thankee, ma'am, that'd be real kind of you." They made pinched-up faces, but they drank it on down. They bitched about its bitter taste.

"You boys go on home now," she shooed them out. They looked around mistrustfully, as if somethin' was gonna eat 'em, but we just stared with poker faces. The two then ran out, and scuttled off through the woods. And, of course, little Billie Bob had to start spoutin' off, before anyone could kick him.

"Why in the hell did you do that, you crazy old broad?" he screeched in his ratty-assed voice. Nettie just smiled, and asked us all to have a closer look at the plants in the greenhouse. As we did, I noticed a bunch of bright colors moving in the trees. At first I thought they was Christmas lights, like the ones my late mama'd had a'glowin' on the old trailer all year 'round. Then I could see they was a shitload of little toady-frogs, in all the colors of the rainbow! They was about the size of the spring peepers that lived around these parts, singin' every warm evenin'.

And Kev pointed us to a huge glass contraption, about the size of the broke-down refrigerator on our front porch. I'll be damned if it wasn't the biggest ant farm I'd ever seen! It was filled with a buncha scurryin' little piss-ants, which would march out the single opening and cut off bits of leaves. They'd drag the bits on back to the nest, but the toady-frogs would always manage to gobble a bunch of 'em down. Kev said that the piss-ants, toady-frogs and most of the plants was from South America. He told us:

"In addition to the various alkaloids that the plants produce, they also contain bacteria indigenous to the Amazonian rain forest. When the frogs eat the ants, all of these chemicals are metabolized into potent batrachotixins, which are secreted through the frogs' skin. We just rub the darts on the frogs' backs. Doesn't hurt 'em a bit!"

"U-Mac," asked Bruce, "what the hell did he just say? Sounds like Rooskie!" He was usually puzzled by big-ass words.

"He's sayin' that they're poisonous. So don't touch 'em none, and fer damn sure don't put none of 'em in your mouth!" I replied, as the little fart Billie Bob grabbed a tiny yeller frog and did just that -- prob'ly thought it was candy. I was gonna smack the boy in the head, but his dad Lefty whispered:

"Hold on, Boss! Let's just see how well this shit works," as the little prick made a face and spit the toady-frog out. The tiny frog hopped back into the trees. We just watched and waited as billie Bob started sweatin' and swayin' on his feet. Within about two minutes, he was on the floor, twitchin' like a beached garfish. Kev took one look, figured out what had happened, and, I swear, his face turned whiter than a Klukker's butt! The rest of us stood around as Billie Bob Joe Schmidt, well, "croaked." We was still standin' around, lookin' grim, and Kev looked like he thought we was gonna start shootin' any second! He was reachin' for his pistol, and Nettie grabbed her blowgun. Things was lookin' pretty tense...

Finally, we of the 77th Missouri just wasn't able to contain ourselves no longer... and busted out laughin' our butts off!

"We all hated that little turd anyways!" shouted his older brother. Kev Bird let out a sigh and shrugged. He and Nettie dragged the stiffening Little Billie out to the compost pit, where she had already dumped the two dead Talibaps. Kev mentioned that he had devised a way to process and liquify the methane gas that was comin' off all the rottin' stuff in the compost; he ran his truck on it. Nettie used the compost in her garden, and said somthin' about having good tomaters later in the summer.

We asked Kev about weapons, and he said that, in addition to the Taurus 9 mm pistol he had a Chinese SKS Assault Rifle. We knew the gun well; it was a cheap knockoff of the good old Rooskie AK-47, but the barrels were usually so crooked you'd just as likely hit yourself as your target. He preferred to use the natural products that he growed and raised, and he kept notes on which did what to who. I got to feelin' he enjoyed bringin' mysterious and interesting death to his enemies, just in an environmental-friendly sorta way. Which reminded him:

"Nettie, how long has it been?" And she looked at her watch and replied:

"About forty minutes. They should've reached the edge of their camp by now. I'm sure the other Talibaps are shittin' their britches now!"

"What are you two jabberin' on about? I asked, in a polite sort of way.

She smiled and said, "It's just after noon, so that means those two fools are probably dropping dead right about now. The idea was for them to reach the edge of their camp, and to fall over twitching and choking. The tea I gave them contained colchicine, which takes a while to work. Their kidneys are failing, too, and with any luck they are puttin' on a good final show for their pals right about now."

"I get it!" said Jimmie Joe Bob, "psychopathical warfare! Those dummies will think it's Devil's Magic!" We of the 77th nodded at the cleverness of Kev and Nettie's plan, but we also looked at our tea glasses a bit cockeyed, and didn't ask for *no* refills.

We was headed back to the clubhouse to plan our attack when Loose Bruce had himself a brain-fart:

"Say, U-Mac! Couldn't' we mount the Minigun on top of Kev's truck? We could go in a'blazin' away, and extermulate the whole lot!" This was not a bad idea, seein' as how all five or our own trucks was up on blocks. We had this old M-134 rotatin' gun that could cut down big-ass trees with a shitload of 7.62 rounds. Normally, you'd mount it in a copter or C-130 Spectre gunship, but a truck would do just fine. It was a hard weapon to handle, though; it tended to kick a lot and spit lead all over everywhere! Jimmie Joe about crapped his pants upon hearing this.

"Wait a minute, Sir!" the boy shouted. "What about our women? And them kids that the TBs have been grabbin? We can't risk usin' the Minigun! Couldn't we be heroical and save 'em all without killin' 'em?"

I reckon Jimmie Joe had gone sweet on the dark-haired girl that we saw on the satellite picture. I figured that some of the kids that had gone missin' from Koo-rash's Buybul Kampf might still be alive, mabe for the sick romancin' pleasures of Dave Bobs 5 and 6, but Kev Bird suddenly said:

"I've got it! The Dave Bobs have realized that their breeding for racial purity is turning out nothing but those monkeyfishboys! They're trying to bring in some fresh blood, because their gene pool is becoming a cesspool! I guess their dream of a White Reich isn't working out!"

Well, this did constipate things somewhat. In the old days we woulda saved our girls, looted the place, and blasted the crap out o' the enemy camp, since anyone who wasn't one of us musta been against us; that old, hate group militia mentality again! But now, as Followers of The King, we was obligated to do some good, and we had a shitload of bad to make up for!

"Jimmie Joe Bob is right," I said. "Along with our gals, there's some innocents what need rescuing! Besides, if we end up saving some of the missin' kids from Annapolis, we oughta at least get a few rounds of free drinks at the tavern! Kev Bird, do you got a CB or short wave radio? We need to get hold of Big Dick Cholomax right away. And let's see if your computers have made us that map yet!"

Kev nodded, and we headed over to the computers to see what kinda map they had spit out. We had ended up with a table-size photo, which was overlaid by a topo map and what Kev said was precise global-position points. It was still early afternoon, so we had some time to make us a decent plan for attackin' the Talibaptists after it got dark. Kev Bird started pointin out features.

"Well, they've cut down most of the trees within the camp area, but they have some big ones just around the perimeter." He then pointed out eighteen shallow foxholes, which was dug close to the tree trunks in a half-assed fashion.

"It looks like the whole camp is a rough square, about two hundred yards across," I said. "And looky over there! There's a pretty big area that's been dug up and covered, and not too long ago." Truth to tell, it looked kinda like old aerial shots of the mass graves over in Bosnier, from back when a meglo-moraniac fatass similar to our Koorash boys also had him a plan for "ethical purity".

"Well, we know the big double-wide is where Dave Bob 5 lives in luxury," Lefty said. "I reckon the nice single trailer next to it is where his lumpshit son lives.

Our gals will most likely be tied up in the center clearing. Their girls'll be hidin' in the other trailers." I thought a minute, and then said, "I'm a'guessin' that they'll put the monkeyfishboys in the foxholes, to soak up some lead. When we start shootin', the others will try to spot our muzzle flashes. Sheeit, this could be a rough one, boys!"

Kev Bird gave us all a long stare. "You know, these blowguns are pretty easy to use. You don't really 'aim' them. You just sort of 'point and shoot'. I could make a fair shot out of any of you with a couple hour's practice. We could take out their perimeter troops real quick and quiet!"

"How in the hell are we gonna know exactly where they's at?" asked a confused Bruce. "They could move around a lot, and there ain't no moon out tonight, so even them white sheets'll be hard to spot!"

Nettie dug around in a big plastic storage tub and pulled out some small, flat boxes and some sorta oddball-lookin' headgear.

"These," she said, holdin' up one of the little boxes, "are global positioning units, accurate to within a few inches. I can program the map into them, and you'll always know where everything, including yourselves, is at!" Then she grabbed one of the weird-lookin' devices, and added, "These gadgets here are night vision goggles. You can switch between 'light amplification' or 'thermal imaging'. Either way, those bastards will be lit up like it was daytime!"

Lefty, who had gone over to fiddle with the radio, came back with a disgustipated look on his face. "Well, I got hold of Big Dick in town, and he and the rest of the boys was drunker than skunks!" he told us. "They're gonna hitch up the wagon and head back to our compound after another round at the tavern. I'd say they ain't gonna be much help tonight!"

"I guess 'we' is all we got," I said to the others. "Wait a minute, Lefty! Have Dick let the townsfolk know that we may have found thier missin' kids, and see if he can get 'em to show up with weapons at the Talibap camp about, oh, 12:45 tonight! We could use their help moppin' up." I turned to Kev Bird, "Kev, why don'cha take us out to practice with these blowguns?"

We all went outside, and Kev Bird gave us each a blowgun and some little metal darts. He set up a few small paper targets against some tree trunks about seventy-five feet away, and told us, "You don't have to blow too hard. Like I said, just 'point and shoot', and you'll be surprised!"

Jimmie Joe Bob tried first, and hit within an inch of his target's center. We all took our shots, with various degrees of success. Jim and his dad, Lefty, were the best shots. Those darts really hit hard; we needed pliers to pull 'em out of the tree trunks, which was oak! It would put a nice hole in someone's skull, I'm sure! The Black River looked real purty, and it seemed a shame that a buncha ugly-ass stiffs would be floatin' down it soon. Kev led us to the cave's entrance, and unlocked the huge welded gate.

About thirty feet into the cave you could hardly see your hand in front of your face. First we turned on the little boxes, which gave off enough glow to read the maps on 'em, and to see the small red dots that showed each of our positions. Kev told us to put on the gogglers, which we had hung round our necks. We flipped 'em on, and about shit our britches! It truly was bright as day, only with a green glow to it.

The cave was long and wide. Kev Bird set some targets halfways up towards the far end, and we all tried shootin' the blowguns again, this time with the goggles on. Jimmie Joe Bob was a natural, and his old man was purty good, too. It was decided that those two would go with Kev in the first wave, and silently kill whoever they could. The rest of us would follow with guns, blades and grenades. We'd be able to use the thermal vision to see where the Dave Bob Koo-rashes were, as well as to be sure where Cindy Sue and our girls, Jim Joe's "lady love" and any other captives was stashed.

As we left the cave, BeeToo came up to get his butt scratched, and that gave me another idea, which I shared with the others. "We need as much help as we can get! We got a shitload of dogs back home, and BeeToo ain't 'fraid o' nuthin'. The other dogs will follow him; might at least add to the Talibaps' confusion, and maybe chew up a few of 'em, too!" The day was startin' to grow old, and we had to get our butts in gear.

The plan we came up with weren't no great work of genius. All of us would hide in the woods outside the enemy camp, and let the dogs run in first, snarlin', shittin', and hopefully bitin'. With that distractipation, Lefty, Jimmie Joe Bob and Kev Bird would take out the guards. The thermal vision of the gogglers would let us pick out the blubbery shape of Dave Bob Koo-rash the 5th, the tall, scrawny-assed form of his son, and the deformed bodies of the latest few litters of Talibaps. Some of the older ones looked kinda normal, so we had to be damned careful about who we was killin'.

Kev provided us with tiny radio headsets so's we could stay in touch. He also gave us these pullover vests that looked kinda like double-thick woven pot-holders. He said they was synthetic Spider Web Vests, which would stop a bullet better than Kevlar. I looked at mine doubtfully, but put it on; they was better than the "nuthin'" we currently had! Nettie and Kev rehearsed with Lefty and Jim till they was absolutely sure which darts was for knockin' out, killin' fast or killin' slow. Nettie would tag along to help out anyone we rescued; she had her potion bag, which contained herbal medicines and a few of her special "just in case" items. I noticed that the sack was wrigglin' around a bit, so I asked her about it. She mumbled somethin' like "Freddy Lands". A strange name; it must've been one of her pets.

We all got into the Land Cruiser with Kev and BeeToo. It started up with the sound and smell or a huge, malignorant fart; he was runnin' it on methane for sure! We was goin' back to the 77th's camp to pick up some dark clothing and extra stuff, and to get the dogs movin'. It was six miles between the TB camp and ours, a distance which Bee and the other dogs could cover pretty quick, once we got 'em motorvated. He'd already piss-marked the trail up to Copperhead Springs; hot damn, that dog could hold some liquid! We'd hopefully be in position to attack about 10:30 p.m., which should leave plenty of time to save the day.

We pulled up into the camp, which looked purty poor after seeing Kev and Nettie's place. The remaining women, rugrats, and men too old to fight had made us some sandwiches of leftover bar-be-cued deer meat, and filled our canteens with the good water from our spring. They was real scared, thinkin' we'd get killed along with the kidnapped women, and then a larger Talibaptist force would sweep in, killin' and pillagin'. I had to think up somethin' to say, to give them hope in this desperate hour. I wasn't no great public speaker, but I took to the podium; that is, I got up on the old warshin' machine out in the middle of the yard, and thought to myself;

I look upon these rotten-toothed faces and I see fear, anticipation, and an almost visible cloud of stupidity. But I see more in the bloodshot and drunken eyes of my people; I see hope, hope for survival, and hope for a better future. Dreams of nice, shiny double-wides, trucks with wheels and tires instead of cinder blocks, a virtual pornucopia of Twinkies, spray-on cheese, and a shitload of porkrinds, bar-be-que and beer!

I belched to clear my voice, and began to speak, hopin' The King Hisself would inspire me.

"Well, troops, it sure as hell looks like we got us a bit of a tussle up ahead! The numbers are again' us," this caused a bit of whimperin' in the crowd, "but we got us a couple badass allies!" I indicated Nettie, who looked like a voodoo witch, and Kev Bird, who had dressed in black jeans and sweatshirt over his spider-web vest, with blowgun slung over his shoulder on a strap. Damned if that codger didn't look like a Ninjer from an old Kung Fooey movie! The crowd looked at the two nervously.

"We're a'goin' up against some evil assholes, and the odds ain't great, but with The King's Blessing, we'll come back victorious!" I did figure that we could take the Talibaps, but my people still looked doubtful and chickenshit. My own faith was startin' to get all shook up. I guess fear is contaminagious, and a little moral support woulda cheered me and my few troops a bunch! I finished up lamely with, "Don' worry none! The King is watchin' over us all!" This got applause from Loose Bruce, Lefty and Jimmie Joe Bob, but the rest looked like they knowed they was doomed. Then my dog, BeeToo, came over and took a piss on the rusty front of the warsher I was standin' on, and I got real depressed.

Suddenly, the entire buncha folks gasped! Each face took on the look of the truly dumbfoundered, and a few was even droolin'! Jim Joe jumped up and pointed with a shaking hand.

"Look!" he hollered. "It's a Goldang Miracle!"

I jumped down to see what all the fuss was about.

Maybe it was a trick of the lantern light, or maybe my dog was one talented sumbitch! But maybe it *was* a *true* miracle, because, as the dog whizz dribbled down the warsher, it cut through the rust in such a way that the image of a face took form ... the Face of The King, complete with a halo and some kick-ass jewelry!

"Looky here, folks!" I yelled, so excited I was about to piss *myself.* "The King had blessed our cause!" And everyone came up to see the miraculous sight.

Loose Bruce let out a whoop and shouted, "Damn! This old piece of crap is now a piece of Holy Crap! We got ourselves a 'Shroud o' Urin!'"

Now the whole camp was jumpin' and squealin' their praise of The King, and I decided that we should leave on a high note.

"Come on, team," I said to my rag-tag commandos, "it's time to hitch up the wagons!" And then I remembered a bit of somethin' I'd read in high school, by Billie Shakespeare or one of those other fellows. I jumped up onto the now-Sacred Warsher and shouted:

CRY HAVOC, AND LET SLIP THE DOGS FROM UNDER THE PORCH!" BeeToo took the lead, and a dozen mutts followed, yelpin' their fool heads off. I swear that my German Shepherd gave me a wink as he ran past!

Kev Bird drove with lights out, using them night vision gogglers. On the way we painted our faces black, and checked our weapons. We parked about a half-mile from the Talibaptist compound, and plotted our present and intended positions for the attack. No time for B.S. now; we was ready to go to war!

Kev, Lefty and Jim Joe snuck off into the night; we had decided to go in seventy-five yards behind them in case they needed backup. We could hear the dogs comin' in, and ran through the woods to see how things was brewin'. After the outer guards was killed, we figured the alarm would go up fast.

With the gogglers I could see Kev and Jim Joe take blowgun shots at two glowin' blobs that was stickin' their heads out 'o holes about fifty foot apart. They dropped without a peep. It's a damn good thing we had night vision to assist us, or none of us woulda seen four of the monkeyfishboys in dark clothin' hidin' in trees, ready to pounce! Our radios was all on, and I heard Lefty quietly warn Jim and Kev. Within about twenty seconds, four bodies fell out of the trees and hit the ground like so many bags o' horseshit! Then we could see and hear the dogs runnin' in.

At the approach of the dogs, a bunch of fishboys freaked, jumped up and started runnin' around like headless chickens. At first the dogs all cocked their heads as they stared at their foes, who was mostly on the ground, lookin' like chimps. The dogs wasn't sure whether to go up and sniff butts or to attack, but they soon rushed in for the kill. There was some gurgled screamin', and the poppin' sound of the machine pistols, but our mutts did their job fast! So far we had killed twelve of the enemy. Why didn't the racket bring on a Talibaptist response?

We had spread out about twenty-five feet apart, movin' toward the main camp in a half-circle. Suddenly, Nettie called over the radio to warn us of a gruesome discovery.

Right in front of us, stuck up on branches planted in the ground, were skulls. Little bitty ones. Most of 'em appeared to be from the dead inbreds, but some of 'em looked to be from normal kids, likely those missin' from town. I guess this was supposed to frighten away interlopers, but it got us even crankier than we was to start with! We was for damn sure gonna make certain that no Talibap would see another day!

As we moved in closer, we could see the central area, and we could hear Dave Bob Koo-rash the 5th givin' his sermon of hatred through a loudspeaker. Lucky for us that he loved to hear hisself jabber, 'cause it drowned out our approach. He was wearin' a silky purple robe like the Klukkers. I think it meant he was the Grand Drag Queen, or somethin' like that. Most of his flock was gathered in a circle, listenin'.

"Brethren and Sistren, we have a sacred task to do tonight!" he said in his annoyin', whiny voice. "We have witches to burn! And how do we know they's witches? Because they was carryin' these! He brandished the frog gigs. He went on, "And they have the ee-vill power to turn decent men into stone!" And some of the boys, no doubt the kidnappers of our girls, nodded and grabbed at their own crotches.

"I myself have felt this ee-vill power, as I ran my hands over the smooth, silky bodies of these fine lookin'..." then he caught himself, and in the lantern light we could see a small bulge growin' in the front of his robe. "Anyways, bring out them witches!"

And down the steps of the big double-wide, being pushed by tall, normal-lookin' men in Nazi-type Brownshirt uniforms, was Cindy Sue, Lefty's fourteen-year-old niece, Sheila Mae, and Loose Bruce's wife, cousin and sister, Betsy Lou. They was nekkid as jaybirds, and their bodies was covered in welts and bruises. Behind them, in a red silky robe like his daddy's, was the lanky, hooded figure of Dave Bob the 6th, who was no doubt the cause of the injuries. These boys really seemed to take that "Old-Time Religion" to heart, because they loved to inflict pain! He was draggin' a strugglin' young girl about sixteen years old; she was the dark-haired gal from the satellite photo, and though she was beat up the same as our gals, I could see that she was a pretty young thing. I was pissed as hell and ready to charge in, and I'm sure Jimmie Joe Bob was rarin' to tear 'em all new buttholes! Kev was nowhere in sight, but he called me on the radio.

"U-Mac, I see what's going on," he said as the women were dragged to these two big old TV antenners and chained by their wrists to the cross-beams. There was a lot of firewood and flammable stuff underneath. "I'm going to try to hit one or both of the Dave Bobs with reserpine knock-out darts! We can use them as hostages, or save 'em for a proper sendoff." He whispered frantically, "You gotta keep Jim from..."

But Jim couldn't hold back. He musta picked out two of the fast-killin' darts, which Kev had marked with little smiley-face stickers, because two of the Brownshirts that was holdin' "his" girl dropped to the ground, with the darts stickin' out of their foreheads. More of the Brownshirts jumped up in front of the two Dave Bobs, trying to spot where the threat was comin' from, as well as to protect their leaders.

Then Jimmie Joe Bob got brave and *stupid!* He jumped up from cover, firing a three-round burst from his M-16 into another Talibap soldier, cuttin' a bloody hole through the fool's gut, all the while yellin' shit like, "Ya bass-turds! I'm 'a gonna send the whole shitload of ya straight ta hell!" Along with other manly, battle-cry stuff. The four girls stopped cussin' their captors for just a sec, and the little brunette looked at Jim with a small bit of hope in her eyes. He gave her a quick smile, then a rifle shot rang out. I could see that he had taken one in the chest as he fell to the ground. I followed the muzzle flash and saw four guys comin' out of the Snake Handler's trailer, all armed with deer rifles. I fired and dropped one. One of the Brownshirts saw me, and was about to blast me with an old Luger (for that full-stylish Nazi look, I guess!). I couldn't get my assault rifle up in time ...

Suddenly, BeeToo lunged out of the bushes, and with a bigass snarl, took the fool's gun hand off, right up to the elbow! Then my dog staggered, stumbled a few feet, and fell next to me with a bloody bullet wound in his side. He whimpered a bit, then was still. My eyes filled with tears; he was a damn fine dog, better than a brother to me! No time for grief now; poorly-aimed lead was whizzin' through the air all around. We had to end this quick!

I was really pissed now, and lookin' for fresh targets. I saw old Nettie sneak up behind the approachin' snake-handlers, and she tossed her sack right into the middle of the trio. Out of the sack came four snakes, which looked somethin' like young cottonmouths, but with pointier, spear-shaped heads and dark, triangle markin's on their backs. They were each about three foot long, and didn't look happy. Nettie quickly danced away into the darkness.

Well, I guess religious conditionin', along with a few generations of inbreedin', had made these boys damed strong in their faith or damn stupid! Years of getting' snakebit by copperheads, rattlers and the like durin' prayer meetin's gives these folks some immunity to the venom. They automatically dropped their guns and took to singin', prayin' and dancin' around the snakes. Musta thought they was boas, 'cause they picked 'em all right up, and started puttin' 'em on their heads, in their mouths, and even in their pants!

I heard a rustle in the bushes and turned quick, and there was Kev Bird with a big grin on his face. It disappeared when he saw BeeToo's carcass, but he ignored Jim Joe. I guess he must be a dog lover like me.

Kev snickered and whispered, "I can see that Nettie left some pets with the snake-handlers! In about five minutes, they'll be out of the game!" The guy who'd put the snake in his pants was presently screamin' real loud. I guess that his snake had found itself a little pink "mouse" to bite! The faces and arms of the others was swellin' up and turnin' nasty colors. "Most folkes in Latin America that died from snake bites were bit by the Fer-de-Lance," Kev added.

"Hardy, har, har!" I replied sarcasmically. "I heard o' them Lance-heads! Nasty buggers. I ain't seen nor heard from Bruce nor Lefty in awhile; we'd best give 'em a call." I was also wonderin' where the rest of the enemy was. We hadn't took out more than twenty. I didn't credit them for havin' much smarts, but they had already given a fair display of rat-like cunning! We'd at least managed to draw the fightin' away from the clearin' where our girls was shackled.

Suddenly there was a loud explosion, which sent little Talibaptist meatballs and mangled portions of a trailer into the air about a hundred feet away.

Lefty called in. "Hey, boss! Some of these bastards were hidin' in holes dug under the trailers, and shootin' out from the gaps in the skirtin'. I think I got four or five of 'em with that grenade!"

That was dandy, but now I had to give him some rough news. I told him straight up, "Lester, your son took a bad hit in the chest." I could hear his gasp over the radio; he loved *that* boy for sure. "But he went bravely, and took three or five of the turds with him!" I was damn near ready to cry myself!

Lester composed himself and said, "Well, sheeit! At least he died heroical! I gotta go! These gogglers show some movement in that back trailer! Looked small; might be them missin' kids!" I heard him greet Bruce, who was goin' along to provide some cover. They musta been charged by some more Talibaps, 'cause I heard another grenade, and saw some crap flying in the distance. I reckoned the Dave Bobs musta snuck off to save their own skins, 'cause we'd all lost track of them in the confusion. Kev Bird'd lit out runnin' to free the girls, when a loud rifle shot rang out. He took it in the back, and nose-dived into the ground about ten yards from the center of the clearing.

Dave Bob 6 came strollin' out from behind the big double-wide with a smokin' deer rifle, followed by his old man. Dave Bob Koo-rash the 5th was holdin' a can of Cheap-Ass Grill-Lightin' Fluid, along with two liquid-filled bottles that had rags stuck in 'em. He smirked and strode over to where the girls was chained up, and shouted out:

"Okay, you Sons of Satan! Come on out with your hands on your heads! I know you're here to save these devil-women!" He poured lighter fluid in the girls and the kindlin' underneath, then snapped open a lighter and lit the rags in the bottles. "Only I can 'save' their sinful souls with fire! But they's gonna burn right this second if you all don't give it up!" Our girls started screamin', strugglin, and swearin, and the young brunette started cryin'.

I looked around me to see if we had even a slight chance. They must've got the drop on Nettie, Bruce, and Lefty, because those three was either dead or unconscious, being dragged by a group of armed Brownshirts and snarly monkey/fishboys. Kev was face-down in the dirt, not far from where Jimmie Joe Bob was layin' on his back, M-16 still gripped in his stiff arms. It sure woulda been nice if Big Dick and the boys from town were to come chargin' in! Instead, the survivin' members of the Talibaptist bunch started movin' into the clearin'. Some of the Brownshirts were badly wounded and limpin', and the few remainin' monkey/fishboys approached, movin' like chimps. One even started jumpin' up and down on Bruce's still body. Some of their women came out, at least as far as their ankle chains allowed. They were a sad-lookin' lot, dressed in dirty rags.

I knew I could take one or two TBs with my rifle, but that would just get me killed, and our girls would still burn. I looked around, hopin' for a miracle, when I saw a little twitch in Jimmie Joe Bob's face. The bloodthirsty crowd didn't see him look right at me, signalling with his eyes to get on up; he'd cover me. Great! Our only hope was also our worst shot! He was good with the blowgun, but he couldn't hit the barn-side of a broad with his rifle! But I also saw Kev moving a little. Maybe that spiderweb vest worked after all! We might just could pull this off, with The King's Blessing, and a huge pile of luck! I was nervous, but I got to my feet and walked to the edge of the clearing.

"Well, it's about damn time you got here, Useless Eustace!" shouted Cindy Sue when she spotted me.

Damn! I hated when she called me that! My girl, all right! Never one to let impending, painful death get in the way of some pinpoint strategic bitching! While she ranted and raved, Dave Bob the 5th came over to give me a hard look.

"So, you's the leader of this sorry bunch of hairytics, eh?" he asked smugly. He was ten feet from me, and about thirty feet from the girls now. "My son over there," he indicated the hooded Dave Bob 6, "will put a bullet in your gut, but not before you see these whores of Babby-lon get purified of their sins!" And he turned and raised the flaming bottles, ready to throw...

... When the report of an M-16 rang out, loud enough even to drown out Cindy Sue's squawkin'! Jimmie Joe Bob, lyin' on his back, had made the shot of his life! The single round busted one of the bottles of lighter fluid, spillin' the burnin' liquid all over the Rev. Dave Bob Hitler Koo-rash the 5th! He lit up like a huge fireball, with his purple robe meltin' to his skin.

Cindy Sue, still chained up, but at a safe distance, yelled, "That's what ya get for wearin' cheap polyester, you fat lumpa' crap!" She appeared to have forgot that most of her wardrobe of stretch pants and tube tops was made of the same shit.

Then to me she hollered, "Eustace! Dave Bob 6 has the keys in his robe! Git off your fat ass and get us the hell outta here!"

At that moment, the fishboy who was jumpin' on Loose Bruce stopped, no doubt because Bruce's muscular arm had shot up like lightnin' and popped the bastard's scrawny neck! I saw Kev Bird get up, lookin' like his back was hurtin' bad. He helped Nettie up, and she pulled up his shirt and web vest. He had a bruise about six inches across, but the vest had stopped the bullet. Other than a bullet-shaped dent, it wasn't damaged at all!

Dave Bob the 6th started runnin' for his life, with me, Bruce and a limpin' Kev Bird hot on his tail. He threw away the keys to the chains, hopin' to distractipate us enough to get away. Jimmie Joe quickly found 'em anyways. As I passed, Jimmie Joe was over by the women with Nettie, undoin' the chains. Jimmie Joe went to the shiverin' young brunette with a blanket, and gently wrapped it around her shoulders. As we ran past, I heard her tell him what a great hero he was, and I'm sure his face got as red as my neck!

The last thing I heard him say was, "Don't worry, Miss! You're O.K. now! My name is Jimmie Joe... James! Let me give you a hand!" Damned if that boy had not only just saved all our lives, but it appeared he'd got him the girl, too, just like in those cheap romantical books that my own honey reads! The young woman fell into Jim's arms, sobbing away.

Dave Bob 6 was movin' fast, with his Klukker robe held upover his legs like a skirt. But me, Bruce, and the limpin' Kev Bird was fueled by anger, and we caught up to his scrawny ass right at the edge of the area we suspected was mass graves. Loose Bruce tackled the sumbitch, then yanked him to his feet. While Kev was lookin' through his toxic inventory for somethin' especially nasty, we pulled off Dave Bob 6's hood.

Well, to say that this fool was ugly enough to make a train jump track and take a dirt road was an understatement. He had the wide-spaced eyes of his young'uns, and the splotchy pockmarks on his face made him look like he had spent a lot of time with his head up his old man's fat butt! He was shakin' like a nervous virgin at the prison prom, and his eyes had the insane, glazed look of the truly apeshit! Bruce, who had been holdin' Dave Bob 6, dropped him to the ground, and pointed towards the battle scene, which was well-lit by spreading fire. We could see a crowd of people headed our way, and we wearily reached for our weapons.

The approaching group was led by two of our girls, Betsy Lou and Sheila Mae, who had replaced their clothing with some of the over-sized brown Nazi shirts from inside the double-wide. With them were some of the captives they had freed from their ankle chains. In the group, walkin' together, was Lefty, Jim Joe, and the dark-haired girl, who gripped Jim tightly. Bringin' up the rear was a larger group, could it be survivin' Talibaptists, out for revenge?

I'll be damned if it wasn't Big Dick himself, with thirty of so of the men and women from Annapolis. They was armed with shovels, pitchforks, and a shotgun or two, and they was pushin' four bedraggled Brownshirts with 'em.

"Lefty told us about the possible gravesites," whispered Dick, who looked kinda like a big, round, bearded Sasquatch. "We convinced some of these Naziboys to come along to do some diggin'!" He then strolled over to Dave Bob 6, who was just standin' up. Back in the old days, Big Dick had practiced Karate, and he now put his skills to use. Dave Bob 6 received such a kick in the balls that he would need to reach down his own throat if he wanted to scratch his crotch cookies!

As Dave crumpled back to the ground, I asked, "What about the rest of the Talibaps? We could still have a big brawl a'comin!" But Lefty and Dick started laughing!

Lefty said, "Well, U-Mac, I guess the Branchin' Davidiots was true to their faith after all, because exceptin' for these dumbshits we brung along," he nodded at our Brownshirt captives, "all those that was still there jumped into the fire with their messiah! With all that blubber on him, I guess he's gonna burn for a spell!"

I figured that with a name like Dave Koo-rash, it was traditional to set your own ass on fire; we was just there to provide some assistance, should he have had second thoughts.

We then forced Dave Bob 6 and his boys to strip down to their boxers; they had some exhumation work to do. I couldn't help but laugh about their undershorts, which was all covered in little swastickers, along with various ugly stains of brown and yeller.

Big Dick took a look at Dave Bob 6, standin' in his underwear, and busted out with a huge guffaw, tellin' the crowd, "Damned if he don't bring to mind an anal-rexic version of that critter from that old movie, "Eee-Tee, the Extraterrestcle!"

We laughed. But when the people from town, those who had lost their children at the Buybull Kampf, stepped forward, we shut the hell up. Dave Bob 6 looked like he was about to faint. He knowed what would be found, and there was nobody left to protect his ass. I had Kev use the thermal vision to pick out possible gravesites (he had said that the ground temperature would show up different if the body wasn't too old). Jimmie Joe ... "James", gently collected some shovels from the grim-faced townsfolk, and handed them to me.

I threw shovels at Dave and each of his boys, and told 'em, "You sick assholes brung this on yourselves!" I pointed to the spots Kev Bird had indicated, and ordered them to dig.

Lefty then came up to me and whispered, "Boss, I almost lost me a good son today." I noticed that he didn't mention the younger one, whom nobody gave a shit about anyways! "We know what these folks from town are gonna find. Maybe we oughta give 'em Dave Bob and his boys, to deal with as they please! It might give 'em some small bit of comfort and some much-needed payback!"

When Dave Bob 6 uncovered what was left of a small, headless corpse, still in the rotted remains of a Sunday dress, I just couldn't take no more. I put Dick in charge of the situation. I figured that the grievin' and sorely pissed-off parents would finish off Dave Bob 6 and his boys, but they might could use a little help. I was sick of this haunted place of death, so I joined Kev Bird, Bruce, Lefty, "James Joseph" and his newly-rescued girlfriend, introduced as Mary Louise Jensen, and trudged back to the main camp. Twenty minutes later we started hearin' mushy thumps in the distance, followed by gut-wrenchin' screams and the loud blasts of shotguns.

We approached the oily, burnin' remains of Dave Bob Hitler Koo-rash the 5th, where we found Nettie and Cindy Sue seated, starin' at the flamin' pile of stinky goo. Cindy Sue got up and walked towards me, with a blank look in her eyes. I almost winced, expecting a big-ass hissy fit for leavin' her behind. Instead, she fell into my arms, and took to cryin' so hard that her bright blue eye makeup and black mascara ran down her face, lookin' a lot like an old-time tanker truck leak. For once I didn't say nuthin' stupid. I just hugged her tight.

Nettie and Kev Bird came up, carryin' a makeshift litter. Damned if it wasn't BeeToo hisself, bandaged up tight! It would be awhile before he was out waterin' trees again, but he was alive, thanks to a poultice that Nettie had made from snake venom extract, no less!

As we walked away, Nettie started singin'. "A-Hunka-Hunka Burnin' Flab," and we all joined in with a downright terrible-soundin' chorus.

We met up with Dick and the rest of our boys and went on over to Copperhead Springs to unwind. Kev Bird put the soo-prise on us when he winched a huge cargo net out of the cold spring, filled with a shitload of canned beer! We'd deal with the remains of the Talibaptist camp tomorrow; now it was time to party!

I'm sure that The King was smilin' down on us from up in that U.F.O. with his alien buddies; we had done what needed doin', no more, no less! We had joined up with new and powerful allies, killed off some dangerous assholes that really needed killin', and had brung Jimmie … "James" that is, together with Mary Louise.

There ain't nuthin' more inspirational than new romance, and besides, that boy badly needed to get laid! I think it's improved his aim.

We looted and burned the remains of the Talibaptist camp the next morning; the property woulda been nice to occupy, expecially that fancy double-wide. But the whole damned compound reeked of misery and death. We just steered clear of it from then on.

Then, of course, it was back to the old routine. We had old weapons to clean and fix, and with Kev Bird's help, new ones to devise. We had to stock up on grub and ammo, and join with the townsfolk to upgrade walls, traps and other defenses. After all, summer tourist season was a'comin' soon.

Keith Berdak was born at a very young age at Scott Air Force Base, Illinois in 1955, the son of an Air Force rocket scientist who really was a "rocket scientist". Growing up as an Air Force brat on various Strategic Air Command ICBM bases across the U.S. instilled in him an interest in all things scientific, particularly prehistoric plants and animals. He was also artistically inclined from the earliest age. Berdak dedicated four years to the production of Abstract Expressionist art, but gave it up after entering kindergarten. Some years later he attempted to study fine art at Lindenwood College (now a university, so they say) in St. Charles, MO, but was instead pushed toward Abstract Expressionism. He left college and pursued dual careers as both an illustrator and professional musician. Inspired by the people that he met at science fiction conventions, he retired from the rather dull St. Louis music scene in 1983 and focused on doing artwork.

Berdak's artwork is best known in the areas of Science Fiction and Fantasy illustration, with paperback and magazine cover work published in the U.S., Japan and throughout Europe. His most recognizable work is the series of cover paintings for Glen Cook's *Chronicles Of The Black Company*, published by Tor Books. He has done a program cover painting for the U.S. Navy Blue Angels, and numerous pieces of commercial work.

Berdak spent a few years in Austin, Texas doing illustrations and computer graphics for Origin Systems, Inc., and did a lot of the artwork for the popular *Ultima* adventure game series. Upon returning to Missouri he started working on various projects with Paleontologist Guy Darrough, including the preparation and restoration of a Triceratops skull and a fossil bone bed at the St. Louis Science Center. He is currently working as project illustrator (and digger) with Darrough and a group of scientists and engineers on the Missouri Ozark Dinosaur Project, a unique dinosaur excavation currently under way in Southeastern Missouri.

In the real world, Berdak works as a graphic designer/illustrator for R.K. Stratman, Inc., where he produced custom art for silkscreen print garments for the Harley-Davidson Motor Company and its dealers. When time permits, he likes to do presentations and "Draw-along" sessions at area libraries and children's hospitals.

NOTE: Keith is not only the author of this tale, but also the cover artist.

YARD DOG PRESS TITLES AS OF THIS PRINT DATE

A Bubba in Time Saves None, Edited by Selina Rosen
A Man, A Plan, (yet lacking) A Canal, Panama, Linda Donahue
Adventures of the Irish Ninja, Selina Rosen
The Alamo and Zombies, Jean Stuntz
All the Marbles, Dusty Rainbolt
Almost Human, Gary Moreau
Ancient Enemy, Lee Killough
Angels of Mercy, Laura J. Underwood
Another Breath, Gary Moreau
The Anthology From Hell: Humorous Tales From WAY Down Under,
    Edited by Julia S. Mandala
Ard Magister, Laura J. Underwood
Assassins Inc., Phillip Drayer Duncan
Assassins Incorporated: Rehired, Phillip Drayer Duncan
Bad City, Selina Rosen & Laura J. Underwood
Bad Lands, Selina Rosen & Laura J. Underwood
Black Rage, Selina Rosen
Blackrose Avenue, Mark Shepherd
The Boat Man, Selina Rosen
Bobby's Troll, John Lance
Bride of Tranquility, Tracy S. Morris
Bruce and Roxanne from Start to Finnish, Rie Sheridan Rose
The Bubba Chronicles, Selina Rosen
Bubba Fables, Sue P. Sinor
Bubbas Of the Apocalypse, Edited by Selina Rosen
The Burden of the Crown, Selina Rosen
Chains of Redemption, Selina Rosen
Checking On Culture, Lee Killough
Chronicles of the Last War, Laura J. Underwood
Dadgum Martians Invade the Lucky Nickel Saloon, Ken Rand
Dark and Stormy Nights, Bradley H. Sinor
Deja Doo, Edited by Selina Rosen
Dracula's Lawyer, Julia S. Mandala
Dragon's Tongue, Laura J. Underwood
The Essence of Stone, Beverly A. Hale
Fairy BrewHaHa at the Lucky Nickel Saloon, Ken Rand
The Fantastikon: Tales of Wonder, Robin Wayne Bailey
Fire & Ice, Selina Rosen
Flush Fiction, Volume I: Stories To Be Read In One Sitting, Edited by
    Selina Rosen
Flush Fiction, Volume II: Twenty Years of Letting it Go!, Edited by
    Selina Rosen
The Four Bubbas of the Apocalypse: Flatulence, Halitosis, Incest,

Shadows In Green, Richard Dansky
Stories That Won't Make Your Parents Hurl, Edited by Selina Rosen
Strange Robby, Selina Rosen
Tales from Keltora, Laura J. Underwood
*Tales of the Lucky Nickel Saloon, Second Ave., Laramie, Wyoming, U
    S of A,* Ken Rand
Tarbox Station, Rhonda Eudaly
Texistani: Indo-Pak Food from a Texas Kitchen, Beverly A. Hale
That's All Folks, J. F. Gonzalez
Through Wyoming Eyes, Ken Rand
Tranquility, Tracy Morris
Turn Left to Tomorrow, Robin Wayne Bailey
The Twins, Selina Rosen
The Undead At My Head, Ethan Nahté
Villains in Training, Julia S. Mandala and Linda L. Donahue
Wandering Lark, Laura J. Underwood
Weirdough, Inc., Selina Rosen and Sherri Dean
Wings of Morning, Katharine Eliska Kimbriel
Zombies in Oz and Other Undead Musings, Robin Wayne Bailey

Fantasy Writers Asylum (A YDP Imprint):

Blood Songs, Julia Mandala
Chaos Heir: Beholden A. D. Guzman
Death's Paladin Christopher Donahue
Gateway to Corimar, Julia Mandala & Linda L. Donahue
Spirit Poles, Julia Mandala & Linda L. Donahue
Tale of the Black Heart, Linda L. Donahue
Traitor's Gate, Linda L. Donahue & Julia Mandala

Double Dog (A YDP Imprint):

#1:
Of Stars & Shadows, Mark W. Tiedemann
This Instance Of Me, Jeffrey Turner

#2: *Out of print*
Gods and Other Children, Bill D. Allen
Tranquility, Tracy Morris

#3:
Home Is the Hunter, James K. Burk
Farstep Station, Lazette Gifford

#4:
Sabre Dance, Melanie Fletcher
The Lunari Mask, Laura J. Underwood

#5:
House of Doors, Julia Mandala
Jaguar Moon, Linda A. Donahue

Just Cause (A YDP Imprint):

The Bitter End, Selina Rosen
Death Under the Crescent Moon, Dusty Rainbolt
Duckrt: Mystery at the Museum, Zeb Rosenzweig
Duckrt Escapes from Jail, Zeb Rosenzweig
Duckrt The Lost Story, Zeb Rosenzweig
Getting It Real, Selina Rosen
The Ghost Writer, Selina Rosen
It's Not Rocket Science: Spirituality for the Working-Class Soul, Selina
    Rosen
Meditations of a Hoarder, Melinda LaFevers
Not My Life, Selina Rosen
Permanent Solution to a Temporary Problem, Selina Rosen
The Pit, Selina Rosen
Plots and Protagonists: A Reference Guide for Writers, Mel. White
Vanishing Fame, Selina Rosen
*Why I Blame Trump on Jesus and Other Things I Don't Dare Say Out
    Loud* Selina Rosen
Yard Dog Color the Covers Coloring Book Brad Foster